I0695139

THE
WEIGHMASTER

A WOLF AMONG SHEEP

THE WEIGHMASTER

A WOLF AMONG SHEEP

A Novel

By

BART AMBROSE

© 2023, Bart Ambrose All Rights Reserved

This is a work of fiction. Names, characters, businesses, places, events, and incidents are either the product of the author's imagination or are used as fiction. Any resemblance to actual persons, living or dead, except as referenced in the author's notes, or actual events is purely coincidental.

All rights reserved. No part of this publication may be reproduced, distributed, or transmitted in any form or by any means, including photocopying, recording, or other electronic or mechanical methods, without the prior written permission of the publisher, except in the case of brief quotations embodied in critical reviews and certain other noncommercial uses permitted by copyright law. For permission requests, write to the publisher, addressed, "Attention Permissions Coordinator," at the address below.

Reach For The Top Publishing, LLC
4940 E. Calle Guebabi
Tucson, AZ 85718
Publisher's Catalog-in-Publication Data
Names: Ambrose, Bart, 1946 -
Title: The Weighmaster / by Bart Ambrose
Description: Reach For The Top Publishing, LLC, 2023. |
Summary: A deputy Sheriff in Arizona unearths a human trafficking ring in 1945. His efforts break up the crime ring and result in a pursuit of a character known as the Weighmaster into Mexico and a titanic revenge-fueled battle to the death between the deputy and the weighmaster.
Identifiers:

Library of Congress Control Number:
ISBN 979-8-9883107-0-9 (Mass Market Paperback
Subjects: Organized crime – Fiction. | Human trafficking – Fiction. | Historic Fiction. | Action – Adventure| Arizona
First Printing: June 2023

This book is dedicated to the hard-working people who came to Arizona looking for a better life after the Great Depression and had the perseverance to carve out a place for themselves and their families.

My own family is among them.

THE WEIGHMASTER

A NOVEL

PROLOGUE

January 1944

Abigail and her family waited for the sun to burn off the chill of the Arizona winter morning. The cotton field they were camped beside was brilliant white in the morning light with frost sparkling like tiny jewels on the tops of the plants. They gathered around a small fire and had a meager breakfast of stale biscuits and coffee. When it warmed up a little, the family gathered their nine-foot-long sacks made of woven cotton and headed for the area where other cotton pickers were working. Abigail, her younger brother, and both her parents would work until dusk stuffing the cotton they picked into the bags, dragging them up to the scales beside a wooden-sided trailer, and getting them weighed. Then they climbed a wooden ladder up the side of the trailer, dragging the heavy bags with them, and emptied the contents of their bags. They repeated the process monotonously throughout the day, hoping a few more days of work here would earn them enough money to move on to California and what they hoped would be a better life than what they left as sharecroppers in Texas.

On Friday, late in the afternoon, Abigail dragged her heavily weighted bag to the scales to be weighed by the Weighmaster. Her family would follow a few minutes later.

"Let me help you with that," the Weighmaster said. He grabbed the bag by its strap and hefted it onto the hook attached to the scale dangling from a wooden tripod.

Abigail was a little embarrassed and said, "Thank you, sir. You're very kind."

"Your name is Abigail if I remember right."

"Yes, sir. But most folks just call me Abby."

"It's nice to know you, Abby. My name is Jim Kiefer."

Abby blushed and stammered, "It…it's nice to know you, too, Mr. Kiefer."

He studied her for a moment. She appeared to be maybe fourteen or fifteen years old, with stringy blonde hair, and bright blue eyes. Her figure just starting to show in her baggy calico dress, but she had a youthful beauty. *Another diamond in the rough.* he thought. *She would do very nicely.*

He lifted her bag off the scale and handed her the strap, then he made a notation in his ledger beside her name. She and her fellow pickers would be paid based on their tallies at the end of the day. Abby dragged the fifty pounds of cotton in her bag to the trailer's ladder just as her father and brother brought their bags up to be weighed.

The Weighmaster went through the motions of weighing their bags, but he kept his eyes on Abby as she climbed the ladder. He smiled to himself as the girl's hips swayed under the dress's fabric as she mounted each step.

He had seen the girl a couple of times at the nearby Perryville market. She usually bought a few pieces of candy after a day's work in the field and then walked back the eighth of a mile or so to her family's roadside camp. He would make his move if she was there this evening.

His instincts were right—the girl showed up a little after dusk. He was watching from his car, parked in deep shadow on the side of the market's building. He got out of the car and moved to stand near the store's entrance. He only had a couple of minutes to wait until the girl came out of the building. He pretended to have just arrived as he walked in front of her.

"Well, hello, Abby! It's nice to see you again."

The girl blushed. "It's nice to see you, too, sir."

"I'm glad to run into you. I've been thinking about something for you, Abby. You are about the same size as my daughter who died last year. I still have a closet full of her clothes that should fit you. My house is nearby, and I can show them to you if you would like some of them."

"I'm sorry 'bout your daughter, Mr. Kiefer, but I ought to be gettin' back. Ma will be fixin' dinner."

"It would only take a few minutes. I can drop you back at your camp and you can show your mom some nice new clothes."

The girl was plainly interested.

"I bet those clothes will fit you perfectly," he continued, "and most of them are pretty new."

"Well…okay. But I gotta get back soon, or my folks'll worry."

"Won't take more than fifteen minutes. I promise. My car's right over here."

He led her over to his Pontiac and opened the passenger door for her. The Weighmaster pulled a syringe from his coat pocket as she slid onto the seat. He pulled the cap off the needle, reached a hand around the side of her head to hold her, and plunged the needle into the side of her neck. Her eyes registered shock in the dim light of the car's dome light before the drug hit her. She was out in a few seconds, and he laid her onto the seat. Then he got in on the driver's side and drove a half-mile from the store to his house.

CHAPTER 1

Sean leaped out the door of the C-46 transport into the early dawn light, and the ground rushed up to meet him from a thousand feet below. It was always a relief when the familiar jerk of his parachute broke his freefall— no matter how many jumps he made. He was part of an eight-member team of the US Army's 101st Airborne "Screaming Eagles". They were the tip of the spear in the Allies' push against Germany, assigned to attack the enemy's central communications headquarters in the small Normandy town below. It was June 6, 1944: D-Day. Sean was in his second year of fighting in World War II.

Impact with the ground jarred his feet and knees, but he stayed upright, disengaged the parachute, and joined up with his teammates. He was caught up in the rush of the jump and impending action against the enemy; it was what he signed up for. They cautiously moved the quarter mile from their drop zone to the outskirts of the town, where they immediately encountered a German patrol. Sean's team leader gave the signal to form his men into a tactical offensive position they had practiced and used many times before. German bullets whistled around them as each man selected his target, and they laid down a withering barrage of fire. The enemy was no match for the team of highly trained commandos—the fight was over in less than a minute and left ten German soldiers dead or dying. The team moved on toward its objective.

Local Allied supporters had supplied the information for the target building; it was now clearly marked on each man's map. The team's assignment was to collect any information they could, and then destroy the communications equipment. Other units of Eagles were engaging the German positions, and Sean's team focused on reaching their assigned target. They only encountered light resistance which they easily dispatched—most of the enemy were engaged with the larger force closing in on the town.

Sean held an expert marksman rating with both a pistol and a rifle, and he was skilled in several forms of hand-to-hand combat. His abilities had saved his or his fellow soldiers' lives several times in earlier assignments—he was frequently assigned some of the most dangerous roles in his team's operations. His assignment on this mission was to quietly take out any sentries or other lookouts before the team breached the target building.

He moved stealthily along the deserted streets, slipping in and out between the old houses. There was a slight chill in the morning shadows, even though it was June. The houses' shutters and curtains were closed, and there was no movement—the villagers huddled in their homes when the battle started. A dog barked in one of them, but there were no other sounds from the buildings. Sean could hear distant sounds of battle, but it seemed eerily still and quiet among the silent old houses. He moved into the deep early morning shadow of a house with a good view of the target building across the cobblestone street. He watched carefully and determined two men were guarding the front entrance.

One of them was smoking a cigarette, and the pungent smell of tobacco smoke drifted across the street to Sean; it made him crave a smoke, too. The guard was staring off toward the sounds of heavy fighting. There was a loud explosion nearby, and Sean used the distraction to move quickly across the street and come up behind the sentry. He grabbed the man's head, covered his mouth, and, in a fluid motion, shoved his K-bar Marine combat knife under the base of his skull. The sentry's spinal cord was severed; he died almost instantly. The man made no sound as Sean lowered him silently onto the pavement. Sean's adrenaline had him on a razor's edge; there was no time to linger, no time for thought of how easily the man had died. The other guard was just inside the doorway, preoccupied with the nearing sounds of heavy combat. Sean turned the corner of the doorframe, and the man turned toward movement he caught out of the corner of his eye. Sean quickly plunged his knife under the guard's sternum and into his heart. He twisted the blade, effectively shredding the heart. The guard dropped his rifle and struggled briefly against the blade in his chest. Sean's right hand was instantly covered in surging blood as he held the knife in place and covered the man's mouth with his left hand to stifle a yell. The coppery smell of blood was strong as Sean quietly lowered him onto the step. He looked into the man's surprised eyes until the light of life left them, then removed his knife and wiped it on the guard's tunic. All his senses were on high alert as he crouched in the doorway, listening and watching for any other movement nearby. He was satisfied there were no other sentries nearby and gave the signal for the team to move in.

They rushed through the doorway and up a flight of stairs
to the crowded communications room. Two tables in the
center of the room were covered in maps, charts, and
printed messages. A half-dozen operators sat at radio units.
Their earphones masked the sound of the team's entry.
They were caught completely by surprise and quickly
dispatched along with four men huddled around the map
table. The gunfire in the enclosed space was deafening and
the acrid smell of gun smoke filled the room. A shouted
alarm from downstairs brought loud footsteps and yells
coming toward the team from another part of the building.
Half the group took up rear guard defensive positions while
the others quickly gathered all the papers and maps they
could find and shoved them into leather valises brought for
the purpose. Then they rigged explosives on the equipment,
set timers, and joined the others to fight their way out of the
building. The exchange of gunfire was deafening in the
enclosed space. Sean lost count of how many German
soldiers they dispatched; he thought there must have been
at least a dozen. His team was highly effective at close-
quarters combat, and a German bullet slightly grazed only
one of them.

The situation in the street had changed dramatically while
they were in the building. The Allied troops' onslaught had
pushed the German defenders into that part of the town. A
German officer spotted Sean's team and directed his troops
to engage them—then the team's charges detonated. A
tremendous explosion ripped the second floor of the
communications building, and it erupted in smoke and
flames. The smoke burned the men's eyes but provided a

brief screen for the team to race toward a nearby burned-out truck for shelter. The Germans had been momentarily confused by the explosion but soon recovered. Sean's team was caught in the crossfire from two converging streets, and two of the team were wounded and down, including the team leader. Another was dropped as he rounded the truck.

Sean ran zigzagging through the intersection to help his downed teammates. A German grenade exploded nearby, momentarily stunning him, and he was peppered by shrapnel. He barely noticed the pain through the surge of adrenaline in his body. He kept going toward the closest injured soldier—the team's leader. He slung him over his shoulder and raced back to the cover of the truck as bullets whistled around him. His ears were still ringing as he went for the second man, oblivious to the enemy's fire. He miraculously got him to safety. That was the last thing Sean remembered before an enemy's bullet pierced his thin steel helmet, grazed his skull, and knocked him unconscious. He lay beside his wounded teammates, bleeding profusely from deep shrapnel wounds.

More Allied troops arrived and drove the Germans back. Sean and the other wounded were carried away by medics. He was in a coma and knew nothing until he woke up disoriented and confused in a British hospital in Leeds, England. It took several weeks of painful therapy to recover from his injuries before he was well enough to be discharged.

He received word that his parents had been in a car accident while he was hospitalized. His father had been killed, and his mother critically injured. It was devastating news; he could only lie in a hospital bed and grieve the loss. He pushed the hospital doctors to release him so he could get home to care for his mother— he was his parents' only child. They reluctantly agreed, admonishing him to restrict his physical activity to allow his injuries to heal fully. He was awarded the Purple Heart for his bravery in the D-Day action and was honorably discharged from the Army.

Sean was still weak when he boarded a troop ship for passage to New York. He had lost weight in the hospital and now lost even more on his ship's journey, plagued by seasickness in the rough Atlantic seas. It was several more days by train from New York to Phoenix; at least he was able to keep some food down.

He was crushed to learn his mother had passed away only two days before he got home. He barely arrived in time to arrange her services— she was buried next to his father.

CHAPTER 2

"Is this a walking stick, Sean?" Annaleigh ran her hand over the bumpy surface of a long black stick with highly polished wood she found leaning in the corner of the living room. It was about four feet long with a well-worn knob on one end. They were sitting in the little two-bedroom house west of Phoenix in Goodyear that Sean inherited after his parents' death.

Sean chuckled. "It's made of native Irish blackthorn. My grandfather called it a *shillelagh*. He brought it with him when he and my grandmother emigrated from Ireland. I loved listening to him tell stories about giving someone a good shellacking with it. He would go on for hours about how he used it to win disagreements if Grandma Caitlin didn't interrupt him. Despite the stories he told, she would laugh and say he mostly used it for a walking stick. Grandpa would glare and go off in a huff."

She put it back in the corner behind a small table. "Are you going to keep it?"

He gave her a sly look and said, "Well, it was handed down to my father. Now that it's mine, I think I'll hang on to it and pass it on to my future son."

She smiled and blushed slightly. "Is that an announcement?"

"Take it however you want," Sean said with a chuckle.

It was one of the few times she had seen his smile since his return from the war. It was nice to see at least a brief change from the stress and worry lines on his face.

They were a steady couple their last two years at Buckeye High School. Sean had been anxious to do his part in the war, and their growing relationship was put on hold after they graduated. She wrote him weekly, but his replies were sporadic after his basic training. The news that he had been wounded and hospitalized in England was devastating to her.

His parents had moved from Buckeye to Goodyear when Sean's father had been promoted to district commander of the Maricopa County Sheriff's Department office in the adjoining town of Avondale. Their home was now Sean's. It was a small bungalow, but comfortable. It had a modest, well-equipped kitchen, a living room with a couch, coffee table, two chairs, two well-furnished bedrooms, and a small but efficient bathroom. Sean's mother's hand-crocheted doilies still graced two end tables and the backs of the chairs. A tall wood cabinet housing a Philco radio stood on the floor in one corner. The single-day calendar on the wall in the kitchen still showed July 14, 1944. It was a stark reminder of the day of Sean's father's death and his mother's critical injuries. He couldn't bring himself to change it.

He had asked Annaleigh to help him sort through all his parents' belongings and decide what to keep. She loved Sean, although she had never told him so, and was happy he asked for her help. She had stayed close to his parents while he was away and now shared his grief. Helping him deal with the loss of his parents would help them both.

"I can't seem to ever finish all the stuff I have to take care of," Sean told Annaleigh. "Seems like I get one thing done, and two more pop up in its place."

"I'll help you organize it, Sean. We'll get it done."

He had spent his first days back in Arizona taking care of the myriad things the sudden death of his parents required: death certificates, insurance documents, house payments, mortgage, power bills, and notifications to relatives in other states. It seemed the list was never-ending. But none of that was as daunting as dealing with all the physical reminders of his parents' lives in the house.

A photo album on the coffee table caught Annaleigh's eye, and she began leafing through it. "These are mostly photographs of you, Sean."

"Yeah, my mom was a real camera bug. She was always taking pictures of me. It was embarrassing. Still is."

Annaleigh laughed. "Look at this one— you were all dressed up in new clothes to start first grade. You were so cute!"

Sean's face turned bright red. He sat down beside her as she turned the pages. There he was: playing catch in the front yard with his father, proudly holding the first little perch he caught from a local pond, his grade school and high school graduations, and showing off his dress uniform when he came home on leave after basic training. He stopped her on a page and put his finger on a photo of him arm-wrestling his father at the kitchen table.

"I loved to arm wrestle with Dad whenever we had a difference of opinion. He always made it look like an effort to beat me." He paused, smiling and remembering his father, before continuing, "I remember the first time I actually won. Dad acted a little embarrassed by it, but I know he really let me win. It made me feel good at the time—I walked around the house sort of puffed up for a couple of days afterward."

Annaleigh stayed quiet, letting him enjoy the fond memory of his father. She was glad to see him smiling again. Then he stood and took down several photos of himself in a grouping with his parents on the wall. "I'll put these away, but I want to keep the pictures of my parents. You have a good eye for decorating—help me rearrange them on the wall."

Annaleigh began moving them around in an attractive arrangement, removing and reusing their hangers. Sean watched her as she stood back, studied the wall, carefully hammered in nails for the hangers, and placed each photograph in a new spot. She had grown into a stunningly beautiful woman and was dressed, as she almost always was, in denim jeans, a western-cut shirt, cowboy boots, and a tooled leather belt with a big shiny belt buckle—a born cowgirl, tall, athletic, and full of energy. Horses, cattle, and rodeo were her greatest loves, after Sean. She would only wear a dress or skirt when she had to, which was seldom. Her figure caught men's eyes regardless of what she wore, and Sean couldn't help admiring the view as she worked. A blonde ponytail and fair complexion made her look younger than her twenty years, and her violet eyes held a mischievous sparkle when she looked back at him and smiled.

They spent two days sorting and cleaning. Sean kept the furniture. The bed of his father's 1942 Ford pickup truck was loaded with most of the clothing and other belongings he would donate to local charities. The couple sat in the cab, preparing to make a trip to deliver the items to a Salvation Army center. Sean said, "You know, sometimes it feels like Dad is sitting here with me. This truck was his baby, and he took great care of it. It's still like new. I'll keep it until it's worn out."

"What about the car in the accident?" Annleigh asked.

"I'm waiting for the insurance company to issue the payment. It was a practically new Chevy coupe."

They finally finished cleaning and rearranging the house, and Sean felt he could make it his home again. "I don't think I could have done this without your help," he told Annaleigh. "I can't thank you enough."

They sat on the couch that evening, and Sean took out his old Martin guitar. His father passed it on to him when he started high school. It had been his bedroom closet since he left for the Army. The instrument felt like an old friend when he strummed it, even though it was woefully out of tune. He took his pitch pipe from the guitar's case to tune it, then sang You Are My Sunshine to Annaleigh. They both laughed when the first string broke with a snap as he strummed the last chord.

"Guess that's the end of my performance tonight!" Sean said.

They laughed again and felt the old spark between them return.

***

A month after Sean's return from England, he got a call from the Maricopa County Sheriff's office asking if he would come in to meet with the Sheriff at the headquarters office in Phoenix. He was puzzled over why the Sheriff would want to talk to him. He hoped it wasn't some new problem he would have to deal with regarding his father's death. The Sheriff's secretary smiled and introduced herself, then ushered him into the Sheriff's private office. The Sheriff sat behind a large, well-polished walnut desk with a few papers in orderly stacks; a man in a deputy's uniform stood beside it. She smiled and stood to shake Sean's hand. "I'm Sheriff Jordan, and this is Chief Deputy Foster. Thank you for coming in today." She was the department's first female Sheriff and also its first female officer. Her husband had been an extremely popular elected Sheriff. He died unexpectedly and she was appointed to continue in his place.

Sean said, "Sheriff, it's a pleasure to meet you. I appreciate all the help from your department with arrangements for my father's services while I was in Europe. I heard that many of the department's people had donated to help with the costs, which was a tremendous relief. I'm told there was a huge turnout by the deputies and your staff at the service. The same generosity and care were shown to my mother as well. I can't tell you how much that meant to me. Thank you, and please convey my sincere thanks to the entire department."

Sheriff Jordan said, "Sean, you have our deepest condolences. We were glad to do what we could in their honor and to help you through difficult circumstances. Your father was a fine deputy and is sorely missed. I knew your mother too. She was a wonderful woman." She beckoned Sean to a seat, and the three sat around the sheriff's desk. She continued, "I know you've been through a lot. I am familiar with your military service, and your country owes you a great debt for what you did." She paused and took a sip of coffee from a mug with her name and the sheriff's star on it. "Hopefully, the war will end soon," she said, "and we expect many changes when all our soldiers come home. This county is larger than several eastern states put together, and our population will grow rapidly after the war. We will need good men like you to help us keep up with it."

Sean studied the woman and waited for her to continue. She wore a conservative-styled black and white striped dress which set off her subdued red lipstick, painted nails, and neck-length hair combed in a stylish wave. She had piercing eyes and a commanding presence which was now offset with a pleasant smile. "I want to offer you a job as a deputy in our department," she said. "We've just established a law enforcement training academy, and the timing is perfect for you to go through that training. Your military background would be invaluable in a career with us." She waited while Sean considered it.

He said, "Ma'am, I am deeply humbled by your offer. I've thought about a career in law enforcement since I was a kid. Before I left for the Army, my father told me that he hoped I would join your department when the war ended." He paused and continued, "I would be honored to work for you."

They shook hands and agreed on a date two weeks away for Sean to enter the training academy. It was the first time Sean had been back in downtown Phoenix since he returned home. He walked around looking at the familiar buildings and stores. It hadn't changed. The familiar radio broadcast tower that topped the Hotel Westward Ho still loomed over Central Avenue. The ornate marquee of the Fox Theatre was advertising the new movie "Double Indemnity" with Fred MacMurray, Barbara Stanwyck, and Edward G. Robinson. All the familiar stores were still there: Korricks, Lerner's, Goldwater's, Kresge's. But the thing that beckoned most to Sean was the Woolworth Five and Dime store. He went in and took a seat on a round, red stool at the lunch counter. His mouth was watering as he ordered a grilled cheese sandwich with fries and a chocolate milkshake. A flood of memories washed over him; it was the same lunch his mother always bought him as a child when she brought him shopping.

He took his time with the meal, enjoying seeing all the shoppers wandering around on the black and white, diamond-patterned floor tiles. A bright red scarf caught his eye before he left. It would make a nice gift for Annaleigh.

 On his way home, he stopped at a market to stock up on groceries. He needed to regain the weight he had lost and start working out to prepare himself for the training program he would start soon. It was the first real bright spot in his life since he had been home.

 That was three months ago, and he was now an official Maricopa County Sheriff's deputy. His first big investigation was about to change his life.

CHAPTER 3

December 1944

Leona slowly drifted into consciousness. Her head felt like a sledgehammer was pounding her skull, the blows pulsing through her eyes. It took her a while to get her eyes open; at first, she wasn't sure she had. She was in total darkness, disoriented, and couldn't understand where she was. She vaguely remembered being in a man's car and something pricking the side of her neck. She knew nothing after that.

She gradually pushed herself into a sitting position and leaned against a rough wooden wall. Her vision seemed to clear, but she still couldn't make out anything in the total darkness. She stood up, braced herself against the wall, and felt her way around the space. Eventually, she gained a rough idea of being in a small room. A metal bucket rattled away when her foot hit it, startling her with the sound. She felt along the wall until she wound up back where she had started. Her foot tripped over something on the floor; she felt around and determined it was a mattress with a couple of blankets on it. It was where she was lying when she regained consciousness.

She started shivering in the cold of the dark room; there didn't seem to be any heat. A wave of nausea overcame her, and she dropped down on the mattress and wrapped herself in the scratchy wool blankets. She couldn't tell how long she stayed there—it might have been minutes or hours. The sound of tires crunching on gravel brought her to full wakefulness. A sudden flash of light outlined what looked like a large door, blinding her with the brightness coming through the cracks between the door and frame. She rose unsteadily to her feet, waiting.

The click of a lock being opened, and a chain rattling caused her to take a step back. Someone flung the door open, and she was again blinded by brilliant light. She squinted through the glare at a pair of high-beam headlights on a car pointing into the room. Rough hands grabbed her and pulled a bag over her head, smothering her again in darkness. Other hands pulled her arms behind her back and tied her hands together.

The unseen hands pushed her stumbling out the door, and then shoved her into the back seat of the waiting car. A deep male voice said, "You be still now and stay quiet. We don't wanna rough you up. We're goin' for a short ride."

The ride over rough dirt roads felt like maybe twenty minutes to Leona. "Where are you taking me?" she yelled through the bag.

A hand came out of the darkness and swatted her on the side of her head. The male voice growled, "You deaf? I said to keep quiet. You'll find out soon enough." Leona said nothing else, and the two men were silent the rest of the ride.

Her head cleared a little more, and she began to remember a better picture of what happened to her. The weighmaster from the field where she and her family were picking cotton had approached her at the nearby market. He said something about his daughter dying and leaving some nice clothes that she could have. He offered to take her to see them, and she got in his car. Then the sharp prick of a needle in her neck, everything went fuzzy, and the world turned black. She knew nothing further until she came to in the shed.

The car slowed and traveled a short way further before stopping. She heard both front doors slam as the men got out, then one of the back doors opened, and she was dragged out of the car and onto her feet. The bag stayed on her head as they guided her up a few short steps. She heard a door open, and she was shoved unceremoniously into a room.

"Welcome to the Orange Palace," a woman's raspy voice said. The hood was lifted, and Leona blinked in the light. When her eyes focused, she saw a woman standing in front of her with flaming red hair done up in sweeping victory rolls. Her lipstick matched her hair, and she had on heavy rouge. Layers of makeup made her skin look like porcelain. Leona couldn't guess her age; she could have been thirty or fifty. She was tall with a voluptuous figure and wore a sheer, orange-colored satin peignoir hanging loosely, leaving little to the imagination.

The woman took a long drag from a cigarette in a silver holder and said, "Relax, dear. You're going to be with us a good long while. How old are you?"

"I'm fifteen, ma'am. Please, I jus' wanna go back to my folks!"

The woman waved off her question. "You needn't worry about that. I promise you will be much happier here than working in those horrible fields. Your parents should be ashamed to have made you do that."

Leona started to protest, but the woman said, "Hush now. Let me look at you." She crushed out the burning cigarette, immediately inserted another in the holder, and lit it as she studied the girl. She reached out and pulled Leona's brown hair back, scrutinizing her face. She grabbed each of Leona's hands in turn, clucking as she examined the callouses and scrapes she had gotten from handling cotton burrs as she plucked the fiber from the plants. "We'll have to do something about these. No more cotton picking for you, dear." Then she felt the girl's small, firm breasts, and Leona drew back. The woman uttered a deep, smoke-tinged laugh, then had her turn around. "I think you'll do nicely once we clean you up and get you out of those dreadful homespun calico clothes. You may call me Madam Trudy."

Another woman entered the room. Madam Trudy rasped, "This is Miss Jeannie. She will take you to clean up, and then we will make you pretty. Oh, yes, very pretty indeed."

Miss Jeannie was a tall, lithe woman who looked to be around thirty years old. Her brunette hair was carefully done in a Veronica Lake peekaboo style. Her grey, business-like slacks and a white silk blouse made her look very different from Madam Trudy.

Madam Trudy said, "Please don't get any notion of running off. The men who brought you here and others like them will always be watching you." She discharged them with a wave and said, "You girls run along now."

***

"Wha'dya want with me? Why'm I here? What is this place?" Leona's usually soft Texas drawl took on a strident tone bordering on panic.

Miss Jeannie spoke to her in a soothing voice. "It's all right, dear. You're in no danger. We're here to help you with a new and better life. No more trudging up and down cotton rows all day dragging a filthy sack. We'll dress you in beautiful clothes, do your hair, and make your life very comfortable."

Leona started crying and wailed, "I wanna be back with my folks. I don't belong here!"

"Just relax, dear," Miss Jeannie cooed. "In a little while, you'll be happy you've left that life behind. We'll introduce you to some very nice men and teach you how to make them happy. You won't have to work another day of your life. But first, you need to have some breakfast and settle in. Then we'll make you into the beautiful young woman you can be. I'll be right back with some food for you."

"I ain't hungry. I just wanna leave. Take me back to my folks!" Leona persisted.

But Miss Jeannie was already out the door of the room. Leona heard the snick of a lock, but she tried the door anyway; it wouldn't budge. There was no window in the room, nowhere for her to go. A half-hour later, she heard the lock open, and her new mentor returned with a tray of food.

"I brought you some nice, scrambled eggs with toast, dear. I hope you like them," the woman said. There is a vitamin tablet here for you, too. Taking it before you eat is essential, so it doesn't upset your tummy."

"I don't need no vitamins!" Leona objected.

"Oh, but you do, dear. You've been raised on a poor diet. You'll be amazed at how much better you'll feel. Our doctor says it's very important to feel your best." Miss Jeannie picked up the pill and handed it and a glass of water to her. "Drink the whole glass of water with it. Lots of water is important, too."

Obviously, Leona thought, *she's gonna stand there with that pill in her hand until I take it.* It didn't appear she had any choice. She sighed and swallowed it with the glass of water. Miss Jeannie sat with her while she ate her meal until Leona became groggy and passed out on the bed.

She woke later but didn't know how much time had passed. She was disoriented, and it was hard to focus her thoughts, but she felt strangely relaxed. The windowless room gave no clue whether it was day or night. Miss Jeannie was sitting on the edge of her bed, gently nudging her into wakefulness.

"Wake up, sleepy head," the woman chirped. "Don't want to sleep your life away. Time for a little dinner, a nice bath, and trying on your new wardrobe."

Leona sat up and surveyed her room for the first time: A small table with two chairs, a four-drawer dresser, a floor lamp, a full-length mirror on the wall, and a bed. There was a large mirror on the wall beside the bed, and another one on the ceiling. That seemed very strange to her, and he wondered, *why'd I need to watch myself layin' here on the bed?*

A plate on a serving tray held meatloaf, mashed potatoes with gravy, and corn. A small saucer held a slice of buttered bread. There was also another small pill beside the plates. It was a different color, shape, and size than the one she had taken earlier.

Jeannie picked up the pill and a glass of water and handed them to her. "This is the most important one for your health, dear. You are going to feel wonderful!"

Leona didn't care enough to protest, took the pill, and swallowed it. Miss Jeannie sat with her while she ate dinner. Leona was surprised to find hunger cutting through her fuzzy awareness. She was ravenous and wolfed down the meal. The rest of the evening was a blur to her. She had a bath, and her mentor showed her how to use various perfumes and powders. She wasn't sure why—she'd never needed those things before. Then she tried on several outfits: filmy see-through nightgowns, some baby doll lingerie, and a satin gown. They made her vaguely uncomfortable, but she was too disoriented to care.

Miss Jeannie said, "Oh, you look marvelous," the woman gushed. "These will do nicely. You will have your first visitor soon; I'm sure he will be very pleased. I know all your new friends will be very impressed."

Leona could barely keep her eyes open and stretched out on the bed. She felt warm and strangely relaxed as she lay there; her worry and fright from earlier were gone. Her head was swimming with all the new things Miss Jeannie had taught her. She wondered vaguely what her visitor would be like and what she was expected to do. She hardly noticed the metallic click of the door's lock when Miss Jeannie left, and quickly passed into a deep slumber.

Jeannie reported to Madam Trudy that she was sure the girl had never been with a man. Trudy smiled; the price the girl would fetch with her first client just doubled.

CHAPTER 4

Sean rode with a more experienced deputy for two weeks after finishing his training. Since he had no seniority, he would be working through the Christmas and New Year's holidays. His first day as an official deputy on his own was December 22, 1944.

He was awakened in the still dark hours of that morning with a warm tongue sliding over his face. "Sarge, enough!" he mumbled and pushed the big Labrador retriever away. Sean had been thrashing around on his bed when the dog started licking his face. The Sarge stayed by him, a puzzled look on his face. Sean was soaked in a cold sweat. It took him a few moments to gain his composure and realize he was home, safe in his bed. "Good boy, Sarge." The chocolate Lab finally relaxed as Sean scratched his ears.

It had been another disturbing dream of his time in the war. They were never the same, but they all repeated the theme of Sean's imminent death just before he woke up. The nightmares started while he was in the hospital in England.

One of the doctors, a psychiatrist, told him, "A dream has the power to poison sleep. That's a quote from an old English poet named Shelley. You might enjoy reading some of his work."

Sean replied, "Yeah, poisoned sleep. That's certainly true for me, Doc. What can I do about it?"

"The best thing you can do is to stay away from stressful situations and allow your body and mind to adjust to more normalcy in your life. The dreams are a sign of combat fatigue. It's a common symptom among soldiers who have been in high-stress situations for extended periods. They'll likely go away in time."

"How am I supposed to do that, doc? I'm a soldier fighting in a war! How can I stay away from stressful situations?"

"I am recommending you be discharged, Sean. The war here is nearing the end, and you will need more time for your injuries to completely heal."

"I can still fight! I'm no quitter!"

"No one thinks you are a quitter, Sean. You've done more than your part already. Accept that and move on with your life. I am prescribing a medication for you to help with your bad dreams."

Sean argued with the doctor, but he was adamant that Sean did not belong on the battlefield. The commanding officer in Leeds agreed, and Sean was discharged shortly after that.

The drug that was supposed to help with the dreams made him feel tired and lethargic. All he wanted to do was sleep. That would never do with his new job—he decided an occasional disturbing, "poisoned" sleep was preferable to feeling lifeless.

Sean unfolded his muscular six-foot frame from the bed and did a series of warm-up stretches. He had continued his workout routine since he'd been home and worked harder since he had started with the sheriff's department. Despite some lingering pains and stiffness from his war injuries, he felt like he was almost back in top condition. The face in the bathroom mirror looked back at him; it was like staring at the ghost of his father. He had his rugged features: prominently chiseled chin, wide cheekbones, and a naturally ruddy complexion. His green eyes had come from his mother, along with her blonde hair.

He still found it hard to believe that he survived that D-Day mission. Most of the haggard stress lines on his face were gone, and the shrapnel scars had faded, but they would always be with him. His hair had grown back where it had been shaved off to treat the head wound from the sniper's bullet. He thanked the powers that be once again that his helmet had blunted the force and trajectory of that sniper's bullet.

A fresh cup of coffee helped him clear his head. The sun came up and helped dim the images from the dream. Soon he'd go out on his first solo patrol and lose the war's memories in the job he felt he was born to do.

***

Sean's first dispatch call was to investigate a theft at a farm a few miles west of Avondale. A woman came out of the farmhouse to greet him when he arrived. She said, "They got into my wash house and stole my husband's new Lee overalls. I'd just sewed Albert's name on their front and washed 'em with two of his good shirts. They took all of 'em right out of the washer tub, too. I come out to hang clothes up to dry, and they was gone. Then I seen they stole two of my best layin' hens— stole 'em right out of the coop!" The woman stopped for breath, then continued to berate the young deputy. "This is the second time in two weeks we been stole from. And what has the Maricopa County Sheriff's Department done about it? Nothin', that's what!"

She looked expectantly at Sean. He figured she must have weighed close to three hundred pounds. Her face was deeply wrinkled and burned dark by long hours in the Arizona sun. She stood wheezing into his face waiting for his response, her small, porcine eyes boring into Sean's.

He nodded and said, "I'm sorry, Mrs. Anderson. Many people are coming and going for the cotton harvest. We can't check all of them. But I promise I will add your place to my regular patrol. I'll notify the other deputies to be on the lookout, too. We'll do the best we can."

"Harumph! Your best ain't amounted to much so far!" The woman stormed off and scattered a few chickens pecking around in the yard. Sean stood in her driveway, watching her walk back to her house with her vast skirt billowing like a ship's sail at sea.

A dispatch call on the radio gave him a welcome reason to leave. It was something about a missing girl near the village of Perryville. The dispatcher said to see the cotton weighmaster at the Miller farm. Sean quickly wrapped up his report on the burglary at Anderson's place.

The Miller farm was about 10 minutes away. He drove fast on Yuma Road toward the village. The patrol car's tires beat a rhythm over the expansion joints in the concrete pavement, reminding him of the rhythmic thumping of a train car moving down the track. The road was one of the few paved roads out that far from Phoenix. Most of the north-south roads were dirt, known by the same numeric designation as the lateral ditches that carried water from the main canals to irrigate crops.

  The cotton fields along the road shone brilliantly white in the bright morning sun. It felt like driving through a snow-covered landscape in some places. Recent frosty December mornings had caused the plants to drop most of their leaves; it was prime time for the harvest. Sean passed several crews picking cotton in the fields along his way. Cotton was the lifeblood of this area. Sean smiled, remembering the lesson he and every school kid in Arizona learned about the Five Cs of the state's economy: Cotton, Copper, Cattle, Citrus, and Climate.

  Cotton became important in Arizona during World War I when the Goodyear Tire and Rubber Company bought up more than thirty thousand acres of land west of Phoenix to grow long-staple cotton. It was made into fiber cord which was used in rubber tires, and the Salt River Valley was one of the world's few sources of the long fiber. The company called the project "Goodyear Farms." The town of Goodyear was formed to house labor for the farm operations, and the town was given Goodyear as its official name. A few small housing developments had been built, and the town had grown slowly, adjoining the town of Avondale.

Other farms grew up in the area, such as the one Sean was about to visit. Crews were busy working in the fields, dragging their long white canvas bags strapped over their shoulders as they plucked cotton from the rough cotton burrs. Many of the workers were from Texas and Oklahoma. They followed the harvest, most of them working their way to California with hopes of better jobs. A good picker might pick three or four hundred pounds in a day, earning two or three dollars per hundred. The fortunate ones who could make enough money could rent a shack in places like Perryville; those not so lucky camped by their cars along the roadways.

Sean pulled off the road and parked beside a cotton trailer being loaded on the Miller's farm. A hand-painted sign on the cotton trailer said, "NO ROCKS! GET CAUGHT—YOU'RE GONE!" A tall man was standing beside a tripod with a hanging scale. He was dressed in khaki pants, a red checkered flannel shirt, and a brown leather jacket. The brim of a tan felt fedora was pulled down over his eyes to shield them from the sun as he concentrated on entries in a large ledger. He was about an inch or so taller than Sean, but thinner. A half-smoked cigarette dangled from his lips.

"Good morning, sir." The man looked up with a scowl, irritated with the interruption of his work. "I'm Deputy Sean O'Conner. I'd like to ask you a few questions."

The man's coal-black eyes seemed to look right through Sean. He put down his ledger, smiled, and stuck out his hand. "Jim Kiefer. Pleased to meet you, Deputy. I'm the weighmaster here for the cotton pickers." He studied Sean for a few seconds, rubbed his well-trimmed beard, and said, "O'Conner. Was your father that O'Conner killed in a car wreck a while back?" Sean nodded, and the man said, "I'm sorry for your loss. How can I help you?"

Something about the man made Sean uneasy. Maybe it was his forced smile or the cocky angle of his short-brimmed fedora.

Sean said, "We had a report of a girl gone missing around here last night. Have you heard anything about that?"

Kiefer removed his hat, revealing thinning hair. He scratched his head, looking out into the field. "Yeah, I heard. Ol' man Peterson's been runnin' all over the place lookin' for her. He says she walked up to the market in Perryville yesterday evenin' and didn't return. My opinion, she's just another Okie girl who got all doe-eyed for some boy and ran off with him. Happens all the time with those folks."

"What can you tell me about the girl?" Sean asked.

"I'd say she's maybe fifteen or sixteen. Name's Leona. Been here pickin' with her family 'bout three days. Pretty girl, in a plain Okie way. Seemed kinda shy."

"What do you mean, Okie way?"

"Aw, you know. Plain homespun clothes, long stringy hair, sort of a lost look about 'em. All those women from Oklahoma and Texas look pretty much the same. We called 'em Okies during the Depression when they were all runnin' from the dust bowl. Still do."

"Can you tell me where to find her father?"

"I think he's back at their camp right now. Look for a beat-up old Ford with Texas plates by the cottonwood tree a little way east of here."

"Thanks for your time, Mr. Kiefer," Sean said. The man lit another Chesterfield and watched intently as the deputy drove away toward the Petersons' camp.

A man and woman with two young children were huddled around a small fire to keep warm. A beat-up coffee pot sat on a grill over their makeshift fireplace. A small tent with sleeping gear inside was pitched next to their old Ford sedan. Most of their belongings appeared to be in the car. The children, a boy, and a girl huddled behind their mother's skirt, peeking at Sean with wide eyes. They stared at the shiny deputy's star on his chest.

"Thank God you're here, officer," the man said. "Please, you gotta help us find our daughter!"

"We'll do our best, Mr. Peterson. What can you tell me about her disappearance?"

He pointed off to the west and said, "She jest walked off there towards Perryville long about sundown, and that's the last we saw of her." He paused and looked toward the village about three-quarters of a mile away. "Leona wouldn't jest run off, officer. She jest wouldn't. Not our Leona!"

His wife sobbed and said," Oh, Lord, I jest know somethin' awful's happened. I feel it in my bones! I said we shouldn' a left that run down ol' share crop place at Denton. At least we knowed where the kids was. Now, look!" She broke down sobbing and turned away from the men.

Peterson said they had sold their small interest in a share crop place near Denton, Texas. After the drought and the depression, they were never able to recover. They heard there were good-paying jobs in California, and they were working their way west. Sean took down all their information and told them he would be in touch.

He drove the quarter mile to the Miller farm headquarters and parked beside a white picket fence in front of a two-story house. It was a stately old building stuccoed in white with green wood trim. A large, grassy yard was ringed on three sides by now dormant Chinaberry trees with bunches of yellow berries hanging from their branches. A screened sleeping porch across the front was where the family slept in summer's suffocating heat. Several outbuildings and a barn stood behind the house. Four wood-sided cotton trailers were lined up along the adjoining field road, ready to be loaded.

A rust-colored Chow Chow dog stood at the gate barking at Sean until the farmer came out and called her off. He said, "Old Chow's gettin' cranky with age. I think she's about half blind and deaf, so we have to watch her when strangers come around. He opened the gate and said, "Come on in, Sean. It's good to see you."

"I guess she doesn't recognize me anymore," Sean said. He knew the Millers from his high school days. He had briefly dated Mr. Miller's oldest daughter, Lorna, once or twice, and recently learned she had married while he was away in the Army.

John Miller shook Sean's hand and said "We saw you had been wounded in the war. It was in the papers. Glad you made it back safe. The newspaper said you were awarded a Purple Heart."

"A lot of other men did far more than I did, sir. I was one of the lucky ones who survived."

"I'm happy to see you've joined the sheriff's department, but I expect this isn't a social call. How can I help you?"

"I'm following up on a report of a girl who disappeared from your farm last night. Do you know anything about it?'

"The girl's father came here earlier this morning and asked to use the phone to report it. We haven't heard anything since". Miller paused and continued, "This isn't the first time we've heard of a missing girl around here. There are rumors of two or three girls from pickers' camps gone missing since the cotton harvest has been in full swing this year. Come to think of it, there were similar rumors last year, too."

"None of those were reported to the Sheriff's department. Why do you think that is?"

Miller rubbed his chin and said, "Well, you know how it is with these folks. They're always on the move and don't like to involve the law in their affairs. For all I know, the girls may have turned up or run off with a boyfriend. Maybe that's why none of them were reported."

The two men talked about the weather and farming; then Sean took his leave. His interviews with other field workers on the farm didn't yield any other information about the missing girl. The weighmaster followed Sean's activities and watched suspiciously as he drove to the little hamlet of Perryville a half-mile away.

There were two grocery stores, two service stations, a pool hall, a bar, and a couple of meager homes in the settlement along with several laborers' shacks. The village sat at the intersection of Yuma and Perryville roads, two of the main paved roads in the area. Sean spoke to the business owners and any of their customers present who might have seen the girl.

The market on the north side of the street offered Sean's first clue. The owner came out from behind the meat counter and said, "Sorry for the bloody apron and all. It's just my wife and me here, and I pretty much do it all." He was a short, balding, and pudgy man, and he peered at Sean through Coke bottle glasses that made his eyes appear about three times larger than they were. "You're Frank O'Conner's boy, aren't you? We were terribly sorry to hear what happened to him. He was a good man." Sean thanked him and waited on his answer.

"Yeah, I remember that girl you're asking about. A nice girl, pretty, too. Leona, I think her name was. She came in yesterday evening, bought a few pieces of penny candy for herself and her brother and sister, then left. I believe her family is camped nearby, and she was walking. She had been in the store two or three times recently."

"Did she seem nervous or uneasy?"

The grocer scratched his head as he thought and said, "Not so I noticed. She always seemed happy to me."

"Was she by herself? Did you notice her talking with anyone in the store?"

"Nope. She came in alone, and like always, picked out the candy she wanted, paid, and left the store. I figured she was headed back to her folks' camp."

Sean lifted a Coca-Cola from the cooler, wiped off the bottle's moisture on a towel hung on the wall for that purpose, then sat it on the counter. He paid the owner a nickel for the soda and a penny deposit on the bottle. "Nice to meet you, and thanks for your time," Sean said. "Here's my card. Please let me know if you think of anything else that might help."

He drove back to his district office and put the empty Coke bottle in a wooden case by the door. The office donated the bottles to a local charity to cash in their deposit. Then he made his report to his district commander; the information was passed on to other deputies to be on the lookout for the girl. His boss told him there weren't any deputies to spare in looking for the girl and that he should continue to follow up on any leads he found.

***

The girl's disappearance was Sean's first major assignment. He still had to deal with petty thefts, traffic enforcement, and domestic disturbances. This opportunity to dig into something more serious gave him the motivation to deal with minor cases as quickly and efficiently as possible.

His investigation the day before had yielded the locations of farms where two other rumored disappearances had supposedly occurred. He stopped by the farmhouse at the first location. A large mixed-breed dog promptly blocked his exit from his car. The dog's fangs were bared; it looked like it meant business.

The dog's owner came out of the house and called off the dog, motioning Sean to come in. The man introduced himself as Bob Poston. "Sorry about the dog. We've had a lot of problems with theft, and I've trained him to be on guard."

The dog quieted and sniffed at the odor of Sarge on Sean's clothes. "Looks like you did a good job of it, Mr. Poston," Sean said with a smile. "I'm here to ask if you know anything about a young girl's recent disappearance from your farm. I heard she was camped here with her family while picking cotton in your fields."

Poston frowned and said, "Well, come on in out of the chill and have a cup of coffee, and we'll talk about it." Sean took the cup of black coffee and pulled out a chair at the kitchen's dining table.

"We heard about that girl," the farmer said. "It's hard to tell what's true with those folks. It was just before the crew wrapped up the harvest in our fields. There was a lot of coming and going, you know. The story I heard was that the girl had hitched a ride to the market in Perryville and never returned. Likely the girl's father didn't trust the police and didn't call it in." He took a sip of coffee and continued, "That made me a little suspicious of the story. I figured they should have called your office if they were really worried. They left a couple of days later. Don't know where they went."

Poston's wife had come into the kitchen. She looked like a woman who had done her share of hard work on the farm. But her face softened with a smile as her husband introduced her. She said, "You know, I don't believe anything I hear about those people. We've heard so many stories. There are always rumors of mischief floating around during picking season. All I know for sure is that a lot of them have sticky fingers. That's why Bob got that dog."

Sean asked a few more questions. It seemed odd that this girl, too, had been headed to the Perryville market when she disappeared. He thanked the Postons for the coffee and left. The dog in the yard gave him one more good bark as he was getting in his patrol car, letting him know who's boss.

A crew was picking in the fields at the next farm he visited. There was no one home at the farmhouse. Sean drove into the farm where the cotton trailers were set up and found the man in charge of the scales. He told Sean the same story he had heard at Poston's farm. A girl had supposedly disappeared from one of the roadside encampments when she went to the market. He weighed a picker's sack and made an entry in his ledger. "I took over this crew from Jim Kiefer, who was here then. It did strike me as odd that your department never came around to look into it. Maybe they didn't want to report it for some reason. These folks tend to be pretty skittish where the law is concerned."

"Is that family still working here?" Sean asked.

The man said, "Nah, they stuck around a few days looking for the girl and left. Guess they gave up trying to find her. I heard they were headed for California. Go figure. I would never stop looking if it was my daughter."

Sean spent an hour interviewing other pickers and got the same story. He noticed many of them seemed to be uneasy talking to him. The last man came dragging his cotton sack out of the field, and Sean asked if he could have a minute of this time. The man had an old, dog-eared, western-style straw hat pulled low on his face. Severely worn brogans the size of babies on his feet protruded out of what looked like a new pair of baggy coveralls about two sizes too big for him. He looked at Sean with beady suspicious eyes and said, "What d'ya want, officer?"

"I'm looking for information about missing girls in the area. Do you know anything about that?"

The man shook his head. "Nope. I jus' pick cotton and keep to myself. Don't know nothin' bout' no missin' girls."

He started to move away toward the scales. Sean put his arm on his shoulder and stopped him.

"What did you say your name was, sir?" Sean asked.

The man looked uneasy. "I din't, but it's James. James Peck. Now I need to get this here sack weighed and get back to work so's I can get paid."

Sean stepped in front of him and asked, "Then why does the name stitched on the front of your coveralls spell Albert Anderson?"

The man's eye's flicked side to side. "It's jest how they come to me," he said.

"Those pants were stolen yesterday. You are under arrest for theft and burglary, James."

The man dropped his sack and took off running. Sean caught him in five steps and tackled him to the ground. He held him down with his knee, pulled his arms behind his back, and handcuffed him. "You shouldn't have run," he said. "It's a bad sign."

The man repeatedly yelled, "I din't do nothin'! Lemme go!" Sean dragged the struggling man to his patrol car and shoved him in the back. A small crowd of pickers had gathered around the cotton trailer, watching the arrest unfold. He told the man at the scales why he had arrested Peck and to let any family the man had to know they could find him in the county jail. Sean got into the patrol car and said to the thief, "Show me your camp." The man grudgingly pointed off toward the edge of the field and Sean drove off in that direction.

"This is it," the thief said. Sean stopped beside a beat-up Model A Ford. It had assorted junk piled around it and a firepit with a grill over stones. He could see a bunch of chicken feathers scattered a little way from the camp.

Sean uncuffed his prisoner and said, "I'm going to let you out to get a change of clothes. Bring them with you. If you run, I'll catch you and add resisting arrest to the burglary charge. You'll be in jail for a long time." He opened the door, and the thief gave him a go-to-hell look. Then he rummaged around in the car and produced a shirt and a filthy pair of worn overalls.

Then Sean drove to the Anderson's place. Mrs. Anderson came out, and he took her to the car. He pulled his prisoner out and, keeping a firm grip on his arm, asked her if the man's coveralls were the ones stolen from her washroom.

She looked and exclaimed, "Land 'O Goshen! They shore are! I'd know my needlework anywheres. And he's wearin' one of the stole shirts, too!" Sean put the man back in the car and told her she could get her clothes back after he booked the man into jail at the Sheriff's office in Avondale. As Sean was getting back in his car, the woman said, "Did you find my chickens, too? I'd shore like to have them hens back!"

"No, ma'am. I'm sorry. I didn't see any chickens. Your stolen clothes were the best I could do. But it looked like some chickens had been recently cleaned around this man's camp. I'll add them to your complaint against him." The woman harumphed again and watched Sean drive away with his prisoner. He drove to the sheriff's department district office in Avondale and put him in a holding cell for booking on burglary charges. He told the booking deputy that the clothes the prisoner was wearing were to be held for return to their owner after he changed into a prisoner's uniform. He gave him the man's other clothes to be put with the prisoner's belongings.

***

Sean thought the consistency of the stories of the missing girls going to the market in Perryville was highly suspicious. He had also learned from his interviews that the same weighmaster, Jim Kiefer, had been in charge of the picking crews at the farms where girls had gone missing. Could those two things be coincidences? He remembered his father saying he put little faith in coincidences; his experience dealing with crime had shown him that there was usually a connection to known facts beyond a mere coincidence. Sean decided the facts he had led to a working theory — Jim Kiefer could be the key to the missing girls. He would focus his efforts on that and interviewing more people in the village and surrounding area.

His radio crackled to life with a report of a car in the Roosevelt Irrigation District's (R.I.D.) canal before he could begin his interviews. The canal was one of many in the Salt River Valley of Maricopa County and Sean sped off to the location the dispatcher gave him on Jackrabbit Trail.

He arrived to find several cars on the side of Jackrabbit Trail's bridge crossing at the canal. He jumped out of his car and saw a four-door Chevy sedan entirely upside down in the canal. It wasn't yet completely underwater, but there was no time to waste. The vehicle was crossways to the canal's current, damming the water flow and submerging the car further by the minute.

"I tried to get 'em out, but the water pressure on the doors was too great," one of the men looking on said. "Besides that, I think the weight of the car jammed up the doors against the car's roof when it hit the bottom of the canal. Gonna be tough gettin' 'em out!"

Sean saw a woman behind the wheel and at least two children in the car's back seat. The woman appeared to be unconscious. Water was gradually filling the passenger compartment; there wasn't much time left.

He ran to his patrol car and pulled it up on the canal's service road next to the wrecked Chevy. Sean opened the trunk, took off his gun belt and boots, and tossed them in the trunk along with his Stetson hat. He grabbed a crowbar and a length of rope from the trunk, then tied off the rope on his car's rear bumper. Waving a couple of men over to help Sean said, "You men hang on to this rope. I'll try and break into the car and pull them out, then tie this rope under their arms. You pull them out when I give you the signal."

He grabbed the crowbar and the end of the rope and lowered himself into the swirling water.

The frigid water created an eddy on the downstream side of the car. The car's plunge into the canal had indeed jammed the roof down enough that the front and back doors were stuck. He couldn't pry them open. The woman appeared to be unconscious; both children were alive and screaming in the back with their heads barely above water. The woman might not survive much longer—he would go after her first. More water began pouring into the car when he used the crowbar to break out the passenger door's window glass.

The children were screaming and beating on the rear door window. Sean yelled, "You kids keep your heads above the water, and I'll come back for you!" Since the car was upside down it meant they had to hold their heads at the floor of the car where there was still a pocket of air. He stuck his head out of the water, took a deep breath, and climbed halfway into the car through the window. He grabbed the unconscious driver, secured the rope under the woman's arms, and pulled her free of the vehicle. Two of the men on the bank grabbed the rope and pulled the woman onto the canal bank. Then Sean broke out the rear door window of the car and reached in to grab the first child, a girl around five or six years old. He pulled her out, sat her on top of the car frame, and told her to stay there. He did the same with a boy slightly younger than the girl. The men on the bank tossed him the rope; he tied it under each child's arms in turn, and the men pulled the children out of danger. Then they tossed the rope to Sean, and he pulled himself out of the canal.

The children were unharmed, but their mother lay unconscious on the bank. She wasn't breathing. Sean used his military first aid training to apply mouth-to-mouth resuscitation and help the woman expel the water from her lungs. She gushed a stream of water from her mouth, coughed, and started breathing again.

As soon as he arrived, Sean had radioed for an ambulance. It pulled up behind his patrol car and the medics loaded the woman and her two children into the back. Then they sped off with their siren blaring, heading toward Phoenix and a hospital.

The bystanders were all cheering and patting Sean on the back, telling him it was an amazing rescue. They figured all the family would have died if he hadn't gotten them out.

Sean called for a wrecker to get the car out of the water. He tried to help the driver when it arrived, but the combined weight of the water and the car proved too much for the wrecker's wench. The angle of the canal made it difficult to get any leverage on the car. The driver radioed to have another wrecker sent to help.

Sean said he couldn't stay any longer, and the wrecker driver thanked him for his help. No one else was around, so he stood on the canal bank, took off his wet clothes, and wrung out the water. It was the best he could do until he could get home and change.

He drove to St. Joseph's Hospital in Phoenix to check on the mother and her children. A nurse told him they were all okay, but the mother would likely be there for a couple of days to recover. She said the woman's sister was coming to get the children.

Sean spent the remainder of his shift at the district office filling out his report on the accident, his investigation into the missing girls, and his arrest of the thief.

At home that evening, Sean took off his boots, put on dry clothes, and relaxed into the comfortable old easy chair in his living room. He reviewed the events of his first days on the job; it was going to be more challenging than he initially believed.

He had stopped at the drugstore and bought a set of Black Diamond strings for his guitar. He spent a half-hour replacing the old ones and cleaning the accumulated dust on the instrument's frets and body with a soft rag. An E note on his musty old pitch pipe got him to the right pitch, and he tuned the other strings by ear, the way his Dad had taught him.

He had no idea how old the Martin was. His Dad had it for many years before passing it on to him. It had a mellow and distinctive tone, and Sean found it relaxing. He sat back and strummed a little of "Wildwood Flower," a song made famous by the Carter family. It was the first song his father showed him how to play, and it brought back many memories.

He and his father had been buddies as far back as he could remember. They had gone on summer camping trips to the White Mountains in eastern Arizona, up in the high pine country. His dad taught him how to catch trout in the clear mountain streams behind beaver dams, make a camp and fireplace, and cook the trout he had cleaned over an open grill. And, always, the Martin was nearby. His father would sit by the campfire and strum familiar songs far into the night. The instrument's gentle voice lulled Sean to sleep.

Sean was lost in the memories as he drank a beer and noodled around on the guitar until his fingers were sore. Sarge lay curled at his feet, seemingly relaxed by the old Martin's voice. Sean stretched and yawned, then called it a night. Sarge did the same and followed him off to the bedroom.

CHAPTER 5

Christmas Day arrived rainy and cold. Strong wind gusts buffeted Sean's patrol car, and rain squalls lashed at its windshield. It was typical of the winter storms that came out of California that time of year. Sean figured it was likely to leave a dusting of snow on Four Peaks in the mountains east of the valley; he'd always enjoyed seeing rare snow on the high mountains in the distance. He hoped the day would be a slow one; the combination of the rain, cold, and the holiday would keep the pickers out of the fields. *It's a tough way to spend Christmas*, Sean thought. He had continued his investigations into the missing girls the day before and was hoping to talk to some people he had yet to interview.

Annaleigh had invited him to Christmas dinner with her family. He planned to work around his interviews and at least have some time for Christmas cheer with Annaleigh.

He was on his way to Perryville to do more interviews when his radio came to life with an urgent all-hands-on-deck call. There had been an escape by prisoners from the Papago Buttes German prisoner-of-war camp in Phoenix. All available Sheriff's deputies were ordered to assist in the search. He was directed to coordinate with military authorities as much as possible.

So much for his plans. He learned that twenty-five prisoners had tunneled out of the compound. They were believed to be headed south for Mexico or possibly westward along the Salt/Gila River systems west of Phoenix to the Colorado River, then to Mexico. There was no word whether any of them were armed, and officers were told to proceed with extreme caution. Sean deemed it a terrible day for a prison break because of the weather. But, on the other hand, the conditions might work in the escapees' favor by reducing visibility and keeping most people in their homes.

His commander assigned him to patrol the area from the confluence of the Salt and Gila Rivers to the county line. It was a huge area, but he knew it well; it was where he had grown up. He stopped at the Chevron service station in Perryville and called Annaleigh to tell her what had happened, and that he wouldn't be able to join her and her family for Christmas dinner.

The Salt River flowed past Phoenix, then joined with the Gila River a few miles west of the city. The Gila then wandered further west past the towns of Avondale and Buckeye before gradually turning south. Its course meandered another twenty miles or so before turning back to the west and continuing toward the Colorado River near Yuma. The town of Gila Bend was appropriately named, situated at the top of the river's last turn.

Further information revealed that some prisoners had planned to cobble rafts from scrap rubber and wood. Their idea was apparently to float down the Salt to its joining with the Gila, and then on to its confluence with the Colorado River near Yuma. From there, they planned to make their way into the Gulf of California and escape to Mexico.

Sean had a good laugh about that. The Salt and Gila Rivers both had major dams upstream. There was only a trickle of water at the river's bottom, hardly enough to float even a tire's inner tube. He figured any escapees who had been foolish enough to try that plan would be on foot now. But they might try following the river's brushy course anyway to try and reach Mexico on foot. Dense stands of salt cedar along the bottom lands provided excellent cover. Sean decided to set up his patrol as close to the river as possible and coordinate with two other deputies assigned to the search area.

In the meantime, several hundred military personnel had been called out along with the Phoenix Police Department. They also hired several Papago Indian trackers to assist in the search. Several escapees were caught that same day. Under questioning, they revealed that all of them were headed for the border with Mexico. They reportedly had contacts there ready to assist them in returning to Germany.

The captured prisoners revealed that the escape had been planned and orchestrated by Captain Wattenberg, the highest-ranking officer in the camp. He had been captain of a German U-boat sunk off Trinidad and had a reputation as a troublemaker since his capture. In a short time, he became known as a "super Nazi" because of his fervent support of Germany and the war. Most of the other prisoners had been captured from U-boats and readily bowed to his authority. Other POW camps had repeatedly transferred him because he was such a rabble-rouser and agitator among the prisoners.

Sean stopped at several farmhouses near the river as far as Buckeye, about thirty miles from Phoenix. He apologized for disturbing them on Christmas Day. Everyone was concerned when he told them what was going on. They agreed to be on the lookout for strangers and any theft, especially food, and clothing. Sean cautioned them not to try and engage with any strangers and to notify the sheriff's department immediately of any sightings or losses.

Word of the escape spread like wildfire among the community. Farmers kept their shotguns loaded and handy by their front door in case the prisoners appeared. The community held much anger toward the Germans—many local people mourned the young men from the area who had been lost in the war in Europe. There was even talk of asking the sheriff to organize a posse comitatus to assist the official searchers, but the idea was quickly squelched.

The first break in Sean's search area came the next day. A farmer discovered a few chickens had been stolen the previous night near Avondale. A second call came in later that day from someone who had seen several men moving along the brush line of the river bottom several miles west of the first sighting.

The fast-moving Pacific storm had blown out during the night, and conditions were greatly improved but very cold, with temperatures near freezing. Sean assumed the men had nothing but their prison clothes, and they were no doubt chilled to the bone in the wintry conditions. He was glad for his heavy fur-lined jacket issued by the department.

Sean and two other deputies assigned to the same search area met at a coffee shop in Buckeye to discuss a strategy for that day's search. Sean said, "These men are probably getting weak now from the cold. It will slow them down. Fighting their way through the brush in the river bottom will slow them down even more."

Brad Jones said, "I agree. We should also be looking for smoke in case they were able to build a fire. I'm guessing they must be getting pretty desperate by now." He and Sean had become good friends when they went through the agency's training together.

The other deputy, Steve Riggs, chimed in. "The river forms a funnel downstream between those two buttes where Gillespie Dam is built. That might be our best shot at catching them if they make it that far."

They agreed on a plan: Jones would work down the river from Buckeye, Riggs would station himself at the bend where the river turned south, and Sean would keep watch from atop a butte by Gillespie Dam. They split up and began their search. There was no sign of the escapees by nightfall.

A farmer just east of Buckeye called the following day. Someone had broken into their house late at night and taken canned meats and beans, a can opener, a few pieces of silverware, and a box of matches. That meant the men were likely headed downriver and had enough food to get them through two or three days.

The deputies went back to their agreed search areas. Sean went to his overlook on one of the two black *malpais* buttes abutting Gillespie Dam. *Malpais* was a combination of two Spanish words, *mal*, and *pais*, which means bad country, generally covered by black rocks. It was an apt description of that area. The dam was a low structure, built to divert irrigation drainage water from fields upstream into a canal for use on farmland downstream near Gila Bend. The highway department built a bridge across the river below the dam to keep U.S. Highway 80 open when the river sometimes flooded. The highway was the main route between Phoenix and Yuma. The men would have to pass that point to continue their planned escape route along the river.

Sean positioned himself where he had a commanding view of the river bottom as it approached the site. He made a reasonably comfortable perch on one of the big black rocks and took out his binoculars to keep watch. A cold wind whipped along the river's course into the funnel created by the two buttes. The funnel's effect increased the wind's speed and power, making for miserable conditions for Sean. He sat shivering in his heavy service jacket, frequently taking short breaks inside his cruiser to try and warm up. The hours dragged by with no sign of the men. He had to give up when it became too dark to see; he would be back at this point by dawn the following day.

The other two deputies joined him the next morning as the sun began to put the first light on the buttes. The wind had died down overnight and the overlook was not as unbearable as the previous day. Sean said, "Man, these guys must be damned tough, or else they've found someplace to hole up. They surely built a fire somewhere to keep from freezing last night. They no doubt put it out at daylight to avoid the smoke giving away their position. Do you guys think they could have made it this far without us spotting them? It would mean they got around this dam in the dark because I was here until daylight was gone."

The men were silent as they considered it. Brad said, "I was thinking about this last night. There's a quarter moon now—they could have had just enough light to keep moving. The highway runs close beside the river through here. They could have gotten onto the highway and followed it over the butte to the bridge, then dropped back to the river bottom below the dam. There wouldn't have been much traffic, easy enough to hide from any passing cars."

The men were silent for a minute while they considered this possibility.

Sean said, "You're right, Brad. How about one of us staying here to watch the dam, just in case, while the others move on downstream? They can't be far if they did get past the dam."

Brad said, "Man, I wish we had some good tracking dogs. I checked, but they're all being used to track the main bunch of escapees."

"Yeah, it would sure make this job easier," Sean agreed.

"I'll stay here at the dam," Riggs said. "My butt's tired from sitting in the car driving around all day."

They all laughed, and Sean and Brad moved on downstream to alert the few farmhouses between there and the town of Gila Bend. Then they took up positions a few miles apart where they could watch the river's course.

Sean had long since decided these German POWs were very crafty; they had avoided capture for several days along miles of the river bottom. He wished for more men, but everyone was focused on pursuing the main group of escapees headed south to Mexico. It was on Sean and the other two deputies to find them.

Another day had passed when the deputies finally got a break. The escapees had eluded the deputies and made their way past the town of Gila Bend. Someone had reported three men walking along the edge of the canal bank north of town, headed west. The canal lay just south of the river, about a mile from the town. The three deputies converged on the area and positioned themselves a mile or so apart where they could see the canal's banks.

Sean was the first to spot them with his binoculars. The men cautiously emerged from the north side of the canal bank. They looked around, but he was too far away for them to see him. They scuttled down the canal bank out of Sean's view under a small bridge. He started his car and took off down the dirt road on an intercept path to where he last saw them. He radioed the other deputies to converge on the spot.

The Germans heard him coming and were hurriedly trying to put on their wet clothes and climb the canal bank at the same time. Sean thought it looked like something out of a Three Stooges movie; it would have been hilarious under different circumstances. They had been washing themselves and their clothes in the canal's water under the bridge. Sean skidded to a stop and jumped out of his car with his pistol drawn. The other two deputies' cars were almost on them as well. Two of the men threw up their hands and stood on the canal bank. They were half-dressed, shivering, and still dripping water. But the third took off back toward the brush along the river. Shawn walked across the bridge and yelled in German, "*Stopp oder ich schieße!*"– "Stop, or I'll shoot!" It was one of the German phrases he had been taught in the Army. He repeated it in English, then once more in German. The man kept running, and Sean took careful aim and fired. His shot hit the man in the leg and brought him down.

The men all spoke some English and made no further attempt to escape. They were haggard, exhausted, and hungry. Sean covered them while the other two deputies retrieved the wounded man. Brad tied a tourniquet around the man's leg to stop the bleeding.

Each deputy took one prisoner in their car to avoid any further attempts at escape as they transported them back to Phoenix. There was no doctor in Gila Bend, and Sean drove fast toward Buckeye with the wounded prisoner to get his wound tended. The men had gotten further than Sean imagined they could under extreme circumstances. He had to admire the Germans' tenacity.

Captain Wattenberg and the rest of the POW escapees
were eventually caught. They were all German officers,
highly intelligent and resourceful men. But three of them
hadn't counted on a desert river with only a trickle of water
and Arizona's rough and unforgiving terrain.

CHAPTER 6

The door opened on the side of the big C-46 Commando, and the roar of the plane's engine was deafening. Pitch blackness filled the doorway as frigid night air rushed in. The jumpmaster signaled to go, and Sean leaped out the door into the unknown night. He had a brief glimpse of scattered lights on the ground below. His static line jerked him upward, and the parachute briefly opened, then fluttered violently. He began spinning uncontrollably, grasping for the release cord of the emergency chute packed on his chest. It failed to open, and he was spinning and twisting toward the ground at one hundred sixty miles per hour. He would hit the ground in seconds, and his life would be over. His mouth opened for a scream that wouldn't come.

He woke up moaning and thrashing around on his bed, that same warm tongue again sliding over his face, and pushed the Lab away. The dog whined and stayed by him, a concerned look in his eyes. As always with the dreams, Sean was soaked in a cold sweat. It took him a few moments to gain his composure and realize where he was. "Good boy, Sarge," he said, patting the dog's broad head. The dog finally relaxed as Sean scratched his ears.

Germans! He'd been focused on the German escapees for a week. That must have been what prompted another dream of the D-Day invasion.

It was New Year's Day, 1945, and Sean's investigation of the missing girls had been delayed while he pursued the POWs. He was anxious to get back to it. There was a sense of urgency about it—if those girls were indeed missing, they might still be alive. He would do everything he could to find them.

His first stop was Perryville. It was a bustling village during the busy cotton harvest season, situated at the intersection of two main paved roads five miles from any other services. The field workers provided a major source of income for the businesses.

Sean concentrated on interviewing all the business owners and any residents he could find. The stores and gas stations were open in spite of the holiday—the workers celebrated by spending their hard-earned money with them. The only clear clue which seemed common to each disappearance was the market on the north side of the street and the fact they were possibly connected to Kiefer, the weighmaster. The owner of the market remembered two of the girls being in his store, but he wasn't sure about the third. Sean used this tiny thread of information to hone his questioning of others around the village: Had they seen the girls? Had they seen anyone suspicious hanging around the store? Had they heard any other rumors about the disappearances?

After several hours he didn't have any new information, but he knew the answer had to be there. It was beyond frustrating to keep hitting dead ends.

***

Kiefer was working nearby, keeping the crew busy despite the holiday. He had been hearing much discussion among the people picking cotton. The deputy's questions had generated all kinds of new rumors about missing girls; the number of missing was growing daily, according to the stories. He learned from a couple of his more reliable sources that the deputy had spent considerable time interviewing people in the village. The word was that he was concentrating on the north-side grocery in Perryville as the most likely scene of the disappearances. His sources also told him that his name seemed to come up regularly in the deputy's questions.

It was a problem that needed to go away. He stewed on this information for a couple of days and hatched a scheme to divert the focus away from Perryville. The deputy was a bigger issue, but he came up with an idea to solve that problem. It would require carefully picking the time to carry out his plan; it wouldn't do to have his little operation upset. It was too profitable. He called Madam Trudy and asked for her help.

***

The Orange Palace was known only to a very select clientele. No one came there without Madam Trudy's express permission.

The main building was a sprawling single-level house in the middle of forty acres of mature orange trees. She had acquired the property after the sudden and unexpected death of the last of several husbands she had over the years. His official cause of death was a heart attack, even though he was a relatively young man with no history of heart trouble. He was a prominent lawyer who had acquired the property as part payment for a large case he had settled for some clients in Detroit.

Those same clients had quietly bought up a significant acreage of citrus groves west of Phoenix and various other real estate, including office buildings and several businesses in Phoenix. They were an organized crime group in Detroit that was using their Arizona real estate holdings and businesses to launder huge amounts of money from their various criminal enterprises. Madam Trudy's husband oversaw all the legal transactions for the Detroit clients.

Madam Trudy, or Gertrude as she was officially known when she was married, had been unhappy with her husband. She considered him too cautious in his dealings—he should have made much more money, in her opinion. She pushed her ideas on him until it began to cause friction between them. He had asked her for a divorce just before he died. A doctor who was a personal friend agreed to pronounce him dead of a heart attack. The good doctor had provided her with a drug she put in her husband's coffee one morning. The drug mimicked a heart attack, and the man was dead within minutes. No one had questioned it. Dr. Biggs, as he was known, was a close associate of Gertrude's Detroit friends, and a key element in the Orange Palace operation.

Gertrude formed an alliance with her deceased husband's Detroit associates to assist with the operation she now controlled. She was a beautiful woman, and it didn't take long after her husband's passing for her to develop a relationship with the head of the Detroit organization—a man known only as "Johnnie O." Johnny arranged for his organization to provide trustworthy men for security and to help with any special problems that might arise. In return, they would take a small percentage of the operation's profits. All they asked beyond a piece of the profits was a place to stay and favors of the house when they visited the area. It was a very comfortable and profitable arrangement for both parties. The acreage of mature citrus the Detroit mob controlled surrounded the Orange Palace property and provided an additional layer of security. No one should be snooping around the orange groves who didn't have business there. The mob's property manager took care of the maintenance and harvest and proceeds from the crop were split equally between the parties.

Gertrude soon adopted the nickname Madam Trudy for herself. She went about slowly and methodically building a stable of young girls who would appeal to men with money and expensive tastes. Trudy carefully vetted men who were prospective clients before they ever set foot on the grounds. She considered the girls she offered as a commodity in a protected environment the men couldn't find elsewhere. The arrangement had proven profitable beyond her greatest expectations.

The men she catered to had an insatiable appetite for young girls. The younger, the better; a young virgin brought an incredibly high price. Providence had brought her the perfect source to keep a fresh collection of young girls in her stable— transient field workers. They were generally innocent, naïve, and inexperienced, making them

easily controlled with the drugs supplied by Dr. Biggs.
Perhaps best of all, their parents had very few resources to
try to find them. They were nameless and faceless people,
always on the move. The politicians had no reason to help
them; few, if any, resources were devoted to their
problems.

In the years she had owned the property, she expanded the
compound with several small private bungalows discreetly
placed among the trees. They were reserved for her most
exclusive clients and contained any convenience they could
possibly want. Sometimes a guest would reserve one for a
week and sample a different girl every night. She had also
added on to the main house. It had originally been a three-
bedroom house of around four thousand square feet. Her
additions doubled its size and included eight private rooms,
a beautiful custom-built walnut bar, and a large luxurious
lounge area to welcome her customers. Her lavish private
apartment was in a separate wing of the house.

She had coined the name "Orange Palace" as a reference
to the place's secluded location surrounded by the beautiful
orange grove on the property. She thought the name *palace*
gave it an aura of glamour and mystery. The fragrance of
the orange blossoms in spring was unforgettable. It was
secluded but conveniently located within easy driving
distance from Phoenix, and the other surrounding citrus
groves added to the privacy of the location.

She decorated the building's interiors to reflect the color
of the Orange Palace's name: sweeping draperies made of a
silky material with light orange color, custom-made

furniture pieces upholstered in coordinating colors of greens, cream, and brown, and table lamps with orange shades. It had the effect of making the large lounge glow in a soft orange hue. The specialty of the bar was an orange margarita when the fruit was in season. It was all very tasteful and added to the uniqueness of her carefully cultivated business.

A "bunkhouse" tucked away from the other buildings housed the guards for the operation. They patrolled the buildings and provided security around the boundaries of the property. Madam Trudy trained the men and paid them very well. Some of them rotated back and forth between the Palace and Detroit, depending on the mobsters' needs. But they were always anxious to come back to Madam Trudy's place; their service there also included the occasional bonus of sampling the business's inventory.

Two of the men had mysterious backgrounds with the mob before Madam Trudy recruited them as permanent security. They could be ruthless killers when needed and served as the main enforcers of the Orange Palace's needs.

Madam Trudy summoned the two men after Kiefer's call for help and gave them an assignment for a "special problem" that had to be carried out with the utmost secrecy. They were to meet with Kiefer later that day for detailed instructions.

CHAPTER 7

Kiefer pondered his options. He had assured Madam Trudy he would be supplying her with two new girls soon. He needed to change his methods to avoid bringing more attention to the operation and his plan for the next girl that should accomplish that.

The cotton harvest was winding down, and there was little else available when they finished on the farm where they were working. The military had cut a deal with the military to provide the damn German POWs for field labor; that had seriously cut into his available jobs. One of the POW camps was west of Phoenix, only a couple of miles away from Perryville. *The bastards were efficient as hell,* he thought, *working like it was some military exercise.*

Kiefer would soon have to find some other sources to keep the Orange Palace supplied. There were options in other counties, even in the towns and cities. But first, he had one more convenient opportunity to work. It should direct the investigations away from Perryville, and from him. That would give him a little breathing space.

He had once worked on a farm a few miles away near Buckeye and often saw a girl waiting for the high school bus at the end of a long lane from her house. She was the daughter of a local Presbyterian minister. He worked weighing cotton beside the road to her home and had spoken to her a couple of times when she walked by. She was a cute girl, with long curly blonde hair, and bright blue eyes. She was a little plump, but that could be overlooked. It might even make her more attractive to some of the

Orange Palace's clients. He remembered her name was Millie and hoped she would remember him.

Kiefer recalled that the school bus picked her up promptly at 7:30. He left his place Monday morning about twenty minutes earlier, trying to time arriving there a few minutes before the bus's scheduled stop. As planned, the girl was there waiting, bundled up against the January chill. He stopped beside her and rolled down the passenger side's window.

"Hi, Millie! Remember me?" She nodded her head a little uncertainly. The weighmaster continued, "I hope you can help me. I'm kinda lost. Somebody drew me this map on how to get to a farm near here, but I can't make sense of it. Can you take a look for me?" He got out, walked around the car, and laid a hand-drawn map on the car's warm hood. "See here?" He pointed to a spot on the map. She took a couple of steps closer so she could see the map. "It's supposed to be here," he said. He laid his finger on the map, and she leaned in to look closer. The weighmaster had already taken the cap off a syringe and placed it carefully in his coat pocket. He quickly slipped it out of his pocket, shoved it into her neck, and pushed the plunger.

A shocked expression froze her face as her eyes glazed over. He caught her as she slumped against the car, then opened the passenger side door, and shoved her onto the seat. She moaned a little, then went quiet. Kiefer jumped back in the car, laid the girl down on the seat with her head on his lap, and sped away.

He had never grabbed a victim out in the open. It was
risky, but it would be worth it if it took the deputy's
attention away from him. There were no other cars on the
farm road, but he passed the school bus going in the
opposite direction. He pulled his hat down so his face was
in shadow and hoped the driver couldn't make out his face
as they passed. He had taken the precaution of removing
the car's front license plate to make the vehicle less
identifiable.

He slowed down and took some back roads to get to his
place. It was about a half-mile north of Perryville near the
R.I.D canal. He had purchased the small two-bedroom
house and forty acres several years prior. Raising alfalfa for
hay and keeping a few cattle was a perfect cover for his
more secretive and lucrative operation. There was a small
garage and a wooden storage shed behind the house. Bales
of hay were stacked in a barn further back; a few white-
faced Hereford cattle were in corrals nearby.

There was no other traffic nearby as he pulled into his
driveway. He eased his car close to the storage shed, got
out and unlocked it, then looked carefully toward the main
road and along the canal's service road for anyone who
might see his car there. Seeing none, he opened the car's
passenger side door and carefully lifted the unconscious
girl out. She gave a slight convulsion and shook her head
side to side, then was still. He didn't notice a small item
that fell from her hair into the loose dirt as he carried her
into the shed. He gently laid her on a filthy mattress on the
floor and covered her with old heavy wool blankets. The
padlock on the door's chains gave a satisfying click when

he closed it, then he moved his car out of sight into the garage.

Inside his house, he dropped into his easy chair to relax. He poured a splash of Jim Beam bourbon into his coffee, then sat back to consider his next moves. *My plan is a good one*, he thought. *The girl won't be missed until she doesn't return home from school this evening. The bus driver would have assumed she was ill and missed a day of school. That leaves the rest of today to put the rest of my plan in motion.* He waited until late morning to call Madam Trudy; he had learned through experience that it was not a good idea to call her before eleven. She was a little testy when she answered but agreed to arrange a pickup later that night.

***

"What's your name, dear?" the woman with the raspy voice asked. Millie blinked in the light. They had just removed the hood from her head. She still felt woozy from the drug the weighmaster gave her, and rubbed the sore area around the injection site.

"I said, what's your name? Are you deaf?" This time the voice was more demanding.

"M M M Millicent" she stammered. "Most people call me Millie."

"That's better, dear. You may call me Madam Trudy."

The woman emerged from the shadow, and Millie could see her more clearly; she was embarrassed to look at her. She could see through her flimsy gown, which left most of

71

her breasts uncovered. Madam Trudy certainly didn't look like the kind of woman she was used to in her associations. The ladies who belonged to her father's church wore dresses with muted colors, collars buttoned up to the neck, and hems extending to their ankles.

The woman chuckled at Millie's obvious discomfort. She fitted a Phillip Morris cigarette in her long silver holder, struck a flame from her gold covered lighter, and took a deep drag of the smoke as she studied Millie with an appraising gaze. "How old are you, dear?"

"Fi fi fifteen," the girl stammered again.

"Don't be afraid, dear. We won't hurt you. Just the opposite—we will take good care of you. Very, very good care."

Her words didn't reassure Millie. There was something about the woman—her smile didn't match the evil look in her eyes. "Why am I here? What do you want with me?" the girl asked.

"You'll learn soon enough, Millicent. I prefer that name to Millie, by the way. It adds to your innocent charm. You will be 'Lady Millicent', the preacher's daughter."

Millie was shocked. "How do you know about my father?" she blurted.

Madam Trudy exhaled a cloud of smoke. "Oh, we know everything about you, dear. You are going to be one of our greatest assets!" She motioned to another woman in the room. "This is Miss Jeannie. She will see to getting you settled. And don't get any ideas about running away. There are guards here inside and out, night and day. Run along now."

Madam Trudy smiled to herself. This girl would make a fine addition to her stable of young ladies. And a preacher's daughter! No doubt a virgin to boot! She already knew the perfect client to introduce her to—a de-frocked priest with a secret taste for young girls. The irony of it was delicious! She would fetch a high price, indeed. She knew the priest was currently out of town—this girl would be kept on ice until he returned.

***

Sean was frustrated with the lack of progress in solving the missing girls' case. He worried the missing girls would join the ranks of many other unexplained disappearances of girls from the fields. The consensus among the other deputies was that they probably ran off with boys, hoping to escape the drudgery of the fields. The department had recognized him and the other deputies for their work in apprehending the POW escapees, but he was anxious to find a break that would lead to the missing girls.

His commander called him into his private office on Tuesday morning as soon as he arrived at the office. As always, the commander's desk was neat and orderly, a cup of coffee in a large mug off to the side of his papers. There was a notepad in front of him with what appeared to be voluminous notes.

He looked at Sean and said, "Another girl has gone missing overnight. This time it's the daughter of Pastor Billings, a respected member of the Buckeye community with a large church following. I had an urgent call from Sheriff Roach early this morning to find her. He said this was to be our highest priority." He studied Sean intently and continued, "I want you to drop everything else and pursue this."

Sheriff Roach had taken over from Sheriff Jordan, whose term had expired at the end of the year. Sean had not yet met him.

He made careful notes on what was known about the situation, got in his patrol cruiser, and sped to the girl's parents' home. He found both parents in tears, barely able to speak.

Pastor Billings wiped away tears and said, "The last time we saw our daughter was when she left to walk down the lane from the house to the school bus stop. She didn't come home last night. I called the school superintendent and learned she had not been in school that day."

Sean inquired gently as to whether she had a boyfriend. Her parents adamantly shook their heads no.

Her mother sobbed and said, "Millicent is only fifteen years old. She's never been allowed to date anyone. In fact, she's never even mentioned any boys at her school. She's a good girl and wouldn't have run away like this!"

Sean nodded and asked, " Have you seen any strangers around here? Anyone who looked suspicious?"

"We've seen no one," the father replied. "We seldom see strangers about— our home is a bit isolated from the road."

Sean then asked if they shopped at the north-side market in Perryville. They seemed puzzled by the question. After a moment, the mother said, "We occasionally shop at the other market there. The owner is a member of our church. Why do you ask?"

"There seems to be a connection between the market and three other missing girls," Sean replied.

The mother got a look of shock and horror on her face and said, "You mean there are others? Why haven't we heard about this?"

"Ma'am, to our knowledge, all the other girls were from families who were here following the cotton harvest. There hasn't been any publicity about it—only one of the girls' parents had reported them missing. I've only recently learned about the other two when I began investigating the missing girl whose parents contacted us. The only clue seems to be a connection to the market in Perryville."

He got a more detailed description of their daughter, what she was wearing, and who her friends were. "I have one other question," he said. "Do you have any knowledge of a man named Jim Kiefer? He may have been a weighmaster with cotton picking crews nearby?"

The pastor replied, "It's hard to say. We don't have much association with those folks. They come and go. What does this man look like?"

Sean gave him a description of the weighmaster. "You know," the pastor said, "I do have a recollection of a man like that working on the farm next door, maybe a couple of years ago. I remember he wore a hat like you described when I saw him, with the brim always pulled down over his eyes. Do you think he took our daughter?"

"I don't know if he is involved. All I can tell you is he is a person of interest in my investigation, but there is no evidence directly connecting him to the other girls' disappearances."

Sean stood to leave and said, " We will do everything we can to find your daughter. Do you have a photograph I can post at the station?"

Mrs. Billings rose and took an eight by ten black and white photo of the girl off the fireplace mantle. She handed it to Sean. "Will this do?" she asked.

"Yes, ma'am, it will help a lot. I will get it back to you after we find your daughter. Please contact me if you think of anything else that might help." He gave them a card with his contact information, then asked to use their phone to call the high school in Buckeye. The superintendent said he would arrange a meeting with the girl's bus driver in his office at ten o'clock that morning.

Sean parked in front of the school's main building. It had a red tile roof and beige-colored stuccoed walls. Well kept, as always, with manicured grass, a low hedge across the front, and a couple of stately date palm trees in front. He sat in his car for a couple of minutes, awash in memories of his time there. They had been mostly good years: wide receiver on a winning football season, classes he had enjoyed like math and biology, and the excitement of dating several different girls before he met Annaleigh.

He introduced himself in the superintendent's office. The secretary smiled at him and said, "I remember you, Sean! I'm glad you came home from the war in one piece. Go on in; the superintendent and Gloria, the bus driver, are waiting for you."

They exchanged a few pleasantries, and Sean asked Gloria about her route yesterday morning. "Did you see anything out of the ordinary? Any strange people hanging around?"

"There was nobody else around. Millie has always been on time at her stop," she said. "I waited there a couple of minutes in case she was late for some reason, then went on with my pickups. I figured she must have been ill." She paused, thinking, then continued, "But you know I did pass a strange car on the road about a mile before Millie's stop. The driver had his hat pulled low, and I couldn't make out his face. But he was driving extremely fast, unusual for that area."

Sean perked up and asked, "Think about the car. Why was it unusual? What kind was it? What color? Any small detail might help."

The driver thought some more and said, "Well, it was a pretty nice car for that area; it looked new. And it was unusually clean, which is a little odd on those dirt roads. It was a bright green color, which is also a little uncommon here." She paused briefly and continued, "One other thing. It had a lot of chrome on the front. The bumper and grill were all shiny. I noticed that before we passed—it was almost blinding in the morning sun. And when it was closer, I saw it had one of those fancy hood ornaments that looked like an Indian's head. We passed, and I couldn't see anything else."

"You've never seen that car in the area before?" Sean asked.

Gloria shook her head no. "I'd remember a car like that. I've never seen one like it."

Sean took careful notes and thanked them for their time. He stood up to leave, and Gloria said, "I sure hope she's all right. Such a sweet girl. I'd hate for anything to happen to her." They shook hands all around, and Sean left. He tipped his hat at the secretary; she smiled sweetly back at him and continued tapping away on her typewriter.

The description of the hood ornament sounded like what Pontiac used on their cars. That meant they were looking for a well-kept late-model Pontiac painted bright green. It was more than he had in his other investigations so far. There could not be many cars matching that description in this area—probably not many in the entire county. Especially few that would have been out on a dirt road at seven-thirty in the morning.

He returned to Perryville to try to find other people who may have seen that car. He started with the owner of the northside market. He came around the store's meat counter to greet Sean, again wiping fresh blood off his apron. "Mornin,' Deputy O'Conner. Good to see you again."

Sean said, "Good morning, sir. I'm checking some possible leads concerning the missing girls. How often do you see Jim Kiefer in your store?"

The grocer considered the question and said, "Well, sir, all I can tell you is Mr. Kiefer is a good customer. He's usually in here two or three times a week, buys his groceries, and such. He always pays cash, too. I don't have many customers like that. Most of 'em want credit. Is he a suspect or something?"

"Not at this point. We're just following any possible leads concerning people who are around here fairly often."

The grocer shook his head knowingly as if he were asked about that sort of thing every day.

Sean asked, "Does Kiefer always buy groceries or just hang around the market?"

"Sometimes he comes in for a soda or maybe an ice cream bar. I think he keeps an eye out for new people coming around. Those cotton pickers come and go; this is a good place to find replacements."

"Did you ever notice him talking to young girls in your store?"

The grocer looked at his feet and said, "Well, I don't really know about that. He may have once in a while. As I said, he always needed new hands to pick in the fields. Some of them may have been young girls, but I don't know for sure."

Sean persisted. "Have you ever seen him leave with a young girl?"

"I don't recollect ever seeing anything like that— I doubt that he would have done so." The man gazed off into the store for a few seconds and added, "As far as I know, Mr. Kiefer is a good person and has helped many people hereabouts when they needed it. He even once gave me a tow when I had car trouble down the road a couple of miles."

"Do you know if he owns a late-model green Pontiac?"

"I couldn't say. Only thing I've seen him drive is a pickup truck."

Sean thanked him for his time and left. He walked around the outside of the store, looking at the layout. The entrance was highly visible from the street. There was a house on the west side of the market's building. The east side was more secluded. A tall oleander hedge appeared to enclose the owner's living quarters which jutted out to the side of the store. He thought a car parked in that area at dusk would be tough to see in the waning light of dusk.

A row of laborers' shacks was across a broad driveway from the market. They appeared to be simple one-room shanties with slightly sloped roofs and a stove pipe sticking out of each one. An outhouse sat behind each shack; Sean could smell their pungent odor as he approached a woman hanging up clothes beside one of the ramshackle cabins. She had a haggard look, a threadbare homespun dress, and skin that had seen too much sun and hard times. A toddler peered at Sean from the doorway of the shack.

Sean said, "Afternoon, ma'am. Could I have a few minutes of your time?"

She peered suspiciously at his deputy sheriff's uniform through her stringy dishwater blonde hair. "S'pose so. But make it quick. I gotta lot of work to do."

Sean pointed back toward the market and said, "I wonder if you have ever noticed a newer green car parked over there on this side of the market?"

The woman perked up and said, "Why shore! There's a shiny new green car that belongs to the weighmaster that's workin' at the farm down the road a half-mile or so east of here. I see it there in the evenin' by the store reglar like, and sometimes his truck, too. Sometimes other folks park there if the store's real busy, like on a Saturday evenin'."

"Have you ever seen a young girl get in the car or truck with Mr. Kiefer?'

The woman hesitated, her eyes shifting around everywhere but on Sean. Finally, she said, "Waal...what if I did? Why d'ya want to know?"

"I'm looking into the recent disappearance of a young girl who had been camped near here with her family. Anything you can tell me would be a big help."

She rubbed her chin and said, "Yeah, I heard somethin' bout that. You think he grabbed her?"

"I don't know, ma'am. I'm just checking on any possibilities. We're doing our best to help that family find their daughter," Sean replied.

"Waal don't ever let it get out I told ya, but I saw a girl come outta the store a while back and talk to the man. He kinda waved her over to the car, she got in, and they drove off. That's all I know."

"What did the girl look like?'

"Aw, ya know, it was purty near dark, and I couldn't see the girl very good.

"Are you sure you haven't seen the girl around here before?"

"Like I told ya, deputy, it was too dark to see her clear."

"Do you know anyone else who might have seen a girl get in the car?"

"Maybe the folks stayin' next door, but they're all workin' in the fields right now."

"Thank you very much, ma'am. I appreciate you taking the time to talk with me. I'll come back later to talk to the folks next door."

The woman's information made Sean's suspicions about Kiefer much stronger. He had a call of another burglary in the area and went to investigate. He was glad for the reprieve from the eye-watering odor of the nearby outhouses and chuckled to himself remembering something his dad sometimes said—*there's nothing finer than a fresh breeze in an outhouse*!

The weighmaster had noticed Sean's patrol car parked by the workers' shacks. He pulled into the market's parking area across the street and watched the deputy's movements with interest. *This had to stop,* he thought to himself. *Stop now*!

***

The woman at the laborers' shack described what sounded like the same car the school bus driver had seen. Sean needed to find someone else to confirm what she had told him—someone, who had seen a girl get into the car at the grocery store. He found two people who had seen the car, but neither recalled seeing a girl get into it—or would admit to it if they had. Sean was surprised at how suspicious of the police these people seemed to be. He desperately needed at least one confirmation to justify a search warrant for Kiefer's place.

He returned to the district office to find the commander and two detectives waiting for him. The commander motioned the three men into the small conference room. A phone and two big, amber-colored ashtrays sat on a table surrounded by six chairs. A picture of Sheriff Roach was the only decoration on the whitewashed walls. Weak daylight from a single small window filtered through cigarette smoke haze.

The commander introduced the men to Sean as Detectives Johnson and Harper. The commander said, "These detectives will be leading the investigation of the missing girls in our area from now on. We appreciate all the work you've done so far on the disappearances, Sean. Now we need to put more effort into building on what you've done. This last missing girl has brought a great deal of attention to the problem. The sheriff is genuinely concerned about the disappearance of the daughter of a prominent community member."

Sean nodded and said nothing but considered it ironic that the other missing girls had not warranted this level of attention.

The commander continued, "I want you men to work closely and share everything you learn about this. I want daily updates on progress from all of you."

As Sean went over his notes, the men made their own. He started to describe the incidents of the other missing girls, and the men quickly lost interest.

Johnson, the lead detective, said, "We will focus on this most recent case. The clues are fresher. They'll be the best place to start. You continue the work you are doing with the field workers. We'll meet back here every morning to coordinate our work." They stood, and the two detectives walked out of the room.

Sean was struck again by the lack of interest in the other disappearances. It was obvious that missing girls from cotton pickers' camps didn't count for much. There were no politicians who might look bad if they weren't found. That meant there was little or no priority in finding them. Sean seethed inwardly at the injustice of it; he resolved to do anything and everything he could to find those girls, too.

CHAPTER 8

Sean awoke the next morning from yet another stressful dream of the war. Sarge was again licking his face and whining with concern. Sean had raised him from a pup before he went into the Army. He was a beautiful chocolate Labrador retriever with a short, dense coat. His deep brown eyes were kind and expressive, with slightly pronounced eyebrows, giving him an inquisitive look. He had grown into a powerful, muscular companion, highly protective of Sean. The dog's name was an inside joke with Sean's father, who had disliked a sergeant in the sheriff's office. A neighbor of his parents had taken care of the dog after his parents' car accident until Sean's return. His reunion with the dog was one of the few bright spots when he arrived home. It was like he had never left.

Sarge had started licking his face when Sean began thrashing around on the bed. He told the dog he was a good boy, scratched him behind his ears, and hugged him. He shook himself awake, made his morning coffee, and ate a couple of biscuits with ham left over from dinner at Annaleigh's place the night before. Then he headed out for his day.

He met the detectives at the district office. Sean related more of what he had learned about the possible owner of the Pontiac the bus driver had identified. They agreed on a plan to pay an informal visit to Kiefer and headed for Perryville to have a talk with the weighmaster.

Kiefer acted surprised to see the deputy and two plainclothes detectives show up to question him at the farm where he was working. He waved to his assistant to take over weighing the pickers' sacks while he talked to the police officers.

Detective Johnson asked the first question and Kiefer replied, "Yes sir, I own a green Pontiac. Why do you ask?"

Johnson answered, "We have reason to believe a car fitting that description may have been involved in a crime in this area. Yours seems to be the only one local people have seen. Can you tell us where you were last Monday at about seven thirty in the morning?"

The weighmaster rubbed his short beard and replied. "Well, sir, I would have been on my way to Phoenix. I had an appointment with my doctor at 8:30 that morning. I've been having some stomach trouble."

Johnson asked, "Can you give us the doctor's name?"

"Sure! His name is Doctor Biggs. He's been my doctor for years. Call him up, he can confirm I was there."

"We'll do that," Johnson replied. "In the meantime, we'd like to see your Pontiac. Is it here?"

"Naw, I keep it in the garage at my house. It's only a couple of miles away. Let me give my assistant some instructions, and I'll be happy to show it to you."

Kiefer got in his work-worn black Dodge pickup truck and led the little caravan to his house. *What the Hell,* he thought. *How had they made this connection*? He would have to be very, very careful now. He opened the garage door and said, "Help yourself, Officers. Ain't she a beaut? About the only time I take her out is when I go into town. Otherwise, I use this old truck."

Sean watched as the two detectives went over the car. It was indeed a beauty. A top-of-the-line Pontiac Torpedo model. Its green paint almost glowed, even in the dim light of the garage. They got out flashlights and examined the interior thoroughly: the folds of the seats, floor mats, and underneath the seats. The car's interior was spotless. Finally, they looked in the trunk and found nothing there, either.

Detective Johnson said, "Thank you for your time, Mr. Kiefer. We may have additional questions later." The detectives told Sean they had some more people to talk to in Buckeye and that they would see him tomorrow morning for his day's report.

Kiefer went into his house and called Dr. Biggs. The doctor agreed to support Kiefer's alibi that he had seen him on Monday morning. Then he called Madam Trudy and roused her out of sleep. She was angry to be disturbed at an early hour for her.

"What the hell do you want, Kiefer? She spluttered. "You better have a good reason for calling me at this ungodly hour!"

She came fully awake when the weighmaster explained why he called.

"Things have taken a turn for the worse. We have to move on the deputy now," he said and explained what had happened. She agreed to move quickly.

Sean went back to Perryville. He had another hunch to check out. He sped back to the farm where Kiefer had left his assistant in charge. He hoped to ask him a few questions before his boss returned.

Sean said, "I was just with Mr. Kiefer. He was showing his car to the other officers and me. I didn't get a chance to ask him if he ever drove it to his jobs."

The man was on his guard, clearly uneasy talking to a policeman. "Well, about the only time he'd do that was if his truck was broke down. That don't happen much. He usually only uses the car when he's off work. He drives it to the Perryville market in the evenings sometimes or when he's going into town." The man abruptly stopped, thinking maybe he'd said too much. About that time, Kiefer pulled up next to the cotton trailer, slammed the door on the pickup truck, and stormed over to the two men.

"What's going on here, deputy?" the weighmaster growled through clenched teeth. "Why are you bothering my man?"

Sean said calmly, "A couple of things occurred to me I forgot to ask at your place. I figured it would save time if I stopped and asked this gentleman."

Kiefer's face turned into a scarlet scowl. He bared his teeth and snarled, "Anything you want to know about me, you ask me. Understand? I catch you bothering my help again, I'll report you to the sheriff for harassment. Now go on and let us do our work!"

Sean politely thanked him and his assistant for their time. Then he smiled to himself as he was getting into his patrol car. He knew he had hit a raw nerve with the weighmaster. The information from his assistant about Kiefer driving the Pontiac to the Perryville market confirmed a significant piece of the puzzle of the disappearing girls. He made careful notes of the conversation before driving away.

Kiefer thoroughly cursed his assistant. When he learned what he had told the Deputy, he was ready to explode. He told the man that if he ever talked to the police about him again, he'd fire him on the spot.

***

Sean lay awake till midnight that night, thinking about what he had learned. He was sure there was a connection to Kiefer. He had an eyewitness account of him leaving the market with a young girl, a similar description of the car the school bus driver had seen, and the reaction of the weighmaster himself that morning. But he didn't have enough evidence to arrest him for the girls' disappearances. He would go over it with the commander at their meeting in the morning. He finally drifted off into a restless sleep.

Sarge's low growling woke him a couple of hours later. Sean was instantly awake, rubbing the sleep from his eyes. A sliver of a waxing moon's weak light through his bedroom window showed the dog standing at the bedroom doorway. He was looking out into the house, his hackles raised and continuing a low growl. Sean spoke quietly to calm him, then picked up his pistol from the nightstand. He had slept with the Colt .45 automatic near at hand since the early days of the war.

He slipped into the living room, stopped, and listened. He hissed at the dog to stay quiet when he started another low growl. Then he heard a slight noise from the doorknob on the front door. It was an old brass entry set with a keyed deadbolt on top. A scraping sound of metal on metal was coming from the deadbolt's lock. An intruder was trying to jimmy it! Sean kept his left hand on the dog to quiet him; his right hand leveled his pistol at the door.

He tensed as the lock turned and Sarge gave a low growl. Whoever was outside slowly pushed the door inward. That was too much for Sarge, and the dog lunged at a man standing in the doorway. He clamped onto the man's calf, causing him to stumble and nearly lose his balance. Sean called off the dog, and the man staggered out into the yard.

"Stop and raise your hands!" Sean commanded. The man spun around, and Sean saw a hand with a pistol rise toward him. His reflexes from his military training took over, and his .45 automatically centered the man's chest. The big pistol barked and the man went down, firing a single wild shot that lodged in the door frame above Sean's head.

The muzzle flashes from the guns momentarily blinded Sean and he stepped carefully toward his assailant, keeping his pistol trained on the inert form. His vision cleared and he saw no further movement from the man. He kicked his assailant's gun away as a car on the street raced off, but

Sean couldn't get a good look at it in the dim moonlight. Sarge stood over the man on the ground, growling. Sean scratched the dog's ears and said, "Easy, Sarge. It's okay. Good boy! You're a really good boy!" The dog sat down nearby and watched the scene carefully.

The intruder had not stirred. Sean could see the dark blood stain on his chest and bent down to take his pulse. The man was dead. Sean's aim was deadly; the .45's slug had likely ripped through the man's heart and torn a huge exit hole in his back. Sean's training in the Army with both a pistol and a rifle had made him a deadly adversary fighting the enemy during the war—and it did so again here in his front yard with a different kind of enemy.

There were no city police in Goodyear, so Sean called the Sheriff's department dispatcher to report the incident. A deputy arrived on the scene about twenty minutes later, followed by an ambulance. By then, most of Sean's neighbors were outside their homes to see what all the commotion was about.

The investigating deputy took down all the information. "You'll have to be interviewed and fill out the paperwork for an officer-involved shooting in the morning." He bagged the dead man's revolver for evidence and said, " Help me cover the body and rope off the area as a crime scene for the department's investigators. I'll stay until they show up."

"Thank you for your help, Jim. This is a big mess."

"No problem, Sean. Glad that guy didn't get the drop on you!"

"Yep. My dog's warning saved my ass." He put Sarge back in the house, then reassured his neighbors and explained what had happened. All he could do then was wait. The ambulance would stay until the coroner arrived.

Detectives Johnson, Harper, and the county coroner showed up at about four a.m.

Johnson, the lead detective said, "We got a call that this might be related to the case we're working on. Can you think of anyone who might have a death wish for you?"

Sean recounted what he had learned that day. "I believe this could be connected to my investigation of Mr. Kiefer. He was pretty angry with me for talking to his assistant at the cotton field. I questioned him after we checked out Kiefer's car. Maybe I'm too close, and he called in reinforcements. I can't think of any other reason anyone would come after me. We need to turn up the heat on Kiefer."

Johnson nodded and said, "We'll need more than vague witness accounts, but it's a start. Let's meet at the division office at nine and work out a strategy. Try to get a little sleep, and we'll see you then. You're gonna be busy most of tomorrow with reports and being interviewed yourself." The coroner gave the go-ahead to load the body in the ambulance after all the shooting scenes had been photographed. A broad, dark stain had spread where the dead man had fallen—the blood looked black in the moonlight. Sean got his garden hose and washed most of it away.

  There was no chance Sean could sleep now. His body was still flushed with adrenaline, and his hands shook slightly as the spike started to subside. He made a pot of coffee and sat at his kitchen table, his mind roiling with questions: *What was this about? Who was the man? Who sent him? Would there be others?*

CHAPTER 9

Madam Trudy was livid. "What do you mean Eddie didn't make it? I sent you to do a simple job with some hick deputy sheriff, and you tell me you not only failed, but Eddie didn't make it?"

Billy Bones, the subject of her ire, looked at his feet. "He musta' been ready for us or somethin'—there might've been a dog, too."

Trudy glowered at him and yelled, "A dog! How in God's name did you two survive on the streets of Detroit?"

The man said nothing. He was a veteran of many assassinations and other jobs for the mob in Detroit. He and "Fast" Eddie had been partners for years. *This should have been a quick and easy job*, he thought to himself. But they had messed up. They didn't do enough background work. And Kiefer didn't do enough surveillance. He should have warned them about the dog. The damn mutt must have tipped off their mark when Eddie was jimmying the front door's lock.

Trudy screamed. "I should send you back to Detroit and have Johnny O deal with you. A dog, for God's sake! Get out of my sight!"

Nobody wanted revenge more than Billy Bones for the loss of his partner. *I'll get the sonofabitch if it's the last thing I ever do,* he said to himself. *I'll never live this down if I don't.* Avenging Fast Eddie's death was the only way he could redeem himself with the bosses in Detroit.

Madam Trudy sensed that the missed hit on the deputy increased the risk of exposure to her operation. There would be much more focus on the investigation now, with more cops snooping around. She had to take more aggressive action to prevent that exposure and the problems that would come with it.

The deputy was still an obvious problem. But now she suspected that Kiefer was becoming a liability as well. An idea took form in her mind for a way to get rid of both issues. She picked up her phone and called Detroit on her private line. She had insisted there be no party lines on the phones at the Orange Palace. Johnny "O" answered, and the two exchanged a few pleasantries before getting to the call's subject. Johnny had started an affair with her right after her husband died. They had maintained the relationship for several years when he often visited Arizona on business. He always looked forward to the opportunity to spend time with Trudy. She was a woman who knew what a man liked. He had helped her get started in her business and only took a small percentage to cover the cost of the help he provided her. The real sweetener was the girls. Young girls spent a while at the Orange Palace being trained in the "trade." Trudy had a steady supply of new blood, and the girls who had been there a few months were sent to Detroit and integrated into the mob's prostitution operations. It kept both operations fresh. It was a cozy arrangement, and Johnny was always there for Trudy to help with problems she couldn't handle.

She explained the problem. Johnny O said, "Damn. I'm sorry to hear about Fast Eddie. He'd been with us for years. How'd a local cop get the drop on him?"

"Billy Bones said a dog in the house jumped Eddie when he opened the door and caused him to stumble backward. The cop was already alerted by the dog and ready with a pistol. Shot him before he could recover. Eddie and Billy should never have made that kind of mistake."

Johnny O agreed. "I've got just the guy to help you out. I'll get him to you on a plane. We call him Lucky Lenny. But luck don't have much to do with how he does things. He's a kind of standoffish guy, but he's damn good at what he does. I'll have him contact you when he gets there. You tell him what you need. He'll get the job done."

"One more thing," Trudy said. "Kiefer is a liability now, and we need to get rid of him, too. I'd like to have Lenny deal with that while he's here. It would solve two problems at the same time."

Johnny O said, "Yeah, I agree. Loose ends are always a problem in our business. I'll have Lenny take care of both things."

"What do we do about Eddie? Can the police connect him to you?"

"Not likely. They won't learn much if the cops identify him from his fingerprints. He only had a few small-time arrests from years ago before I recruited him. There's nothing since to tie him to us."

"Thanks, Johnny. I owe you one!"

"You owe me several," he laughed. "I'll be out there to collect soon enough!"

The call ended, and Madam Trudy started refining her plans.

***

The weighmaster was nervous. He figured he was on thin ice with Madam Trudy after the very public failure of his plan for the deputy. The diversion would have worked if the assassins had done their job right. But that excuse, he knew, wouldn't hold water. After all, he had supplied the information on the deputy's schedule and his address. He had watched his movements after work and followed him to his house. But he hadn't looked hard enough. He should have found out about the dog. The damn dog! It had screwed up the hit. And it cost Madam Trudy's organization one of her most trusted enforcers.

He pondered what he would do in her shoes. The cops were going to turn up the heat very quickly. She couldn't afford to have loose ends that led back to her. It was a simple solution—he would have to go. So would the deputy. The cop was still the closest to the truth in the investigation. With him and the deputy gone, there wouldn't be any more loose ends.

She no doubt had many options, given her connection to the Detroit mob. His part in supplying girls was convenient so long as it didn't cause problems. Now those problems had come home to roost. He was expendable.

 He hatched a scheme to protect himself— if he was extremely careful. If that didn't work…well, he had his stash and house in Mexico. He would run. Run, and hope they couldn't find him.

CHAPTER 10

Sunrise found Sean lying on the bed, fully dressed and awake after a sleepless night. He showered, shaved, and put on a clean uniform. His stomach was still tied up in knots, but he forced himself to eat some toast. He fed and watered Sarge, then left for the district office and what he knew would be a very long day.

He met with the department's investigators after a short briefing with the commander and the detectives. The investigators' job was to investigate any officer-involved shooting. They had an endless stream of questions about the previous night's shooting: No, he had never seen the guy before. Yes, he gave the man a warning before shooting—told him to stop and raise his hands. Yes, he saw the guy raise his weapon and feared for his life. No, he couldn't think of anything else he could have done.

They asked the same questions over and over in slightly differing ways for what seemed like hours. And the paperwork! That and the interview took up most of the day. The investigators told him they would make a report to the Sheriff, and he would be notified of their findings. He just wanted to be done with all of it and start looking for why he was a target.

That night Sean tossed in bed, trying to think it through. He might be dead if it weren't for Sarge warning him of the shooter's presence. That was no ordinary hoodlum off the street he had shot, and he had an accomplice waiting in a car on the street. Sean knew in his gut that it was related to his investigation, and he must be getting close to a break. The weighmaster must have sent those guys to stop him.

But, in the back of his mind, he had doubts that a guy working on his own in the cotton fields had the connections to bring in professional hitmen. There was something larger at work. He was sure it wasn't about some pervert kidnapping those missing girls. There was something else going on. He had heard about human trafficking in the big cities where women were forced into prostitution. Could there be something like that going on here? He had never heard of it around Phoenix. These were all things to discuss with the detectives. He believed the weighmaster was the tip of the iceberg.

Sarge curled up on the bed beside him. He stroked his head, scratched behind his ears, and told him again what a good dog he was.

The next morning Sean and the detectives met and explored all the possible angles. They had sent the dead man's fingerprints by overnight air express to the FBI in Washington, requesting to rush and call with the results as soon as possible. They hoped that might give them a break they desperately needed.

Detective Johnson said, "Sean, we agree there's a bigger picture here. And you are a target. You should stay somewhere else for a while to protect yourself from another attempt to kill you. Do you have someplace you could do that?

Sean thought about it and replied, "It has to be someplace I can take my dog. I have a friend who might help me with that. I'll call him when we're done here."

"Good," the detective replied. "We'll get a warrant to shake down Kiefer again, search his property. In the meantime, keep working on your contacts and see what you can find out. We'll let you know about the search warrant. We'd like to have you there when we do the search."

The commander came into the room as the meeting broke up, and asked Sean to stay. "I've spoken to the Sheriff about your shooting. The investigators called it justified in the defense of your life. There will be no further action on it."

"Thank you, sir. I just want to get back on the job."

"Be careful, son, and watch your back."

The commander left and Sean tried but couldn't reach his friend Ricky. He was sure he'd be able to help him out with a place for him and Sarge to stay for a while. He would try to connect with him later.

The dispatcher sent Sean to investigate a disturbance at a place called "Froggy Bottom." Sean knew of the spot by reputation but had never been inside the building. It was supposedly a brothel that catered mostly to the black population. He was immediately on guard due to the events of the last couple of days; he didn't want to walk into a trap.

He drove through Perryville and continued on west. The pavement ended when he crossed Jackrabbit Trail. A mile or so further, he crossed a bridge over the R.I.D.'s canal. Only open desert was on this side of the canal; all the cropland was on the opposite side. In another half-mile, he came to a run-down-looking bar in the desert with four ramshackle shacks behind it. The place backed up to the north side of the canal, which ran at an angle to the road. There was a tall neon sign advertising A-1 beer in front. Sean had seen it at night, its red glow visible from long distances. There were a couple of older cars parked in front. Sean pulled in beside them and noted their license plates, just in case.

He radioed his location to dispatch. Loosening the holster strap on his pistol, he got out of the patrol car and looked carefully around before heading to the door. He saw nothing of concern, opened the old weather-beaten door, and walked in. The room was dim, and his vision took a few seconds to adjust.

There was a bar against the back wall with a few tables and chairs scattered around in front of it. No one was behind the bar—no drinkers that early. A chair scraped, and Sean tensed. Then a large black woman stood up in the shadows and approached him. She had a smile spread across her face that lit up the room with a mouthful of gleaming white teeth. She was wearing a colorful red dress that barely covered her enormous bosom. Several gold-colored bracelets adorned her right wrist, and a similar number of silver ones jangled on her left ankle. They all jingled and clattered when she walked. She was barefoot and moved with a grace that belied her size.

"Good mornin,' officer," she said. Her voice was deep, loud, and strangely melodic. "My name is Melvira. This is my place. Thank you for comin'."

Sean introduced himself, and she motioned him to sit at one of the tables. He was careful to seat himself with his back facing the wall.

"O'Conner. Would your Daddy have been Deputy Frank O'Conner?" she asked. Sean replied that he was.

She said, "I was dreadful sorry hearin' about him and your mama gettin' killed in that accident. He was always truly kind to me when I called on him for help. I heard you was off in that war fightin' Germans when the accident happened. I'm very sorry for your loss."

Sean was at a loss for words. He finally cleared his throat and said, "Thank you, ma'am. It was a hard thing. I'm glad you knew my father. He was a great law officer. What can I do for you?"

She shifted her bulk, and her chair groaned. She studied Sean with intensely black eyes and said, "We had big trouble here last night. A man with a knife cut up one of our best customers. He lived, and I drove him to the county hospital. He's still there. We rassled the knife away from the other man. Got him locked up in our broom closet over yonder." She pointed off to the other side of the room. "I'd 'preciate it if you could take him off our hands," she said with that same gleaming smile.

Sean took down all the information, including the names of witnesses. He said, "I'll book the man into the county jail for assault with a deadly weapon. There will likely be more questions— you and other witnesses could be called on if there is a trial."

"I'll do what has to be done. We try to take care of our own problems here. But this is different—this here man's white. It's unusual for a white man to be here, you know, 'cause this ain't a white folks sort of place. The man he cut up is black; he was jus' mindin' his own bidness when that white man picked a fight. He's cut pretty bad, and he might die. So, you see, we need this handled right by the law."

Sean said he understood and assured her he would handle it right.

Melvira said, "It's gettin' on time for lunch. Let me fix you somethin' to eat. Folks say I make the best fried chicken this side of the Mississippi!" Before Sean could object, she hurried off into the back. He sat there alone, thinking about what his Dad would have done in this situation, and decided his Dad would have taken the fried chicken and enjoyed it. He told him to always make the best of any situation. It couldn't hurt to be on good terms with Melvira, either. He guessed she knew as much about what went on in this part of the county as anyone.

She was back in a little while with a big plate of golden fried chicken, some mashed potatoes with white gravy, and a couple of slices of white bread. She beamed at him and set it down in front of him, then seated herself across from him and watched. Sean took a bite of chicken, and his eyes grew large as he chewed.

"This is unbelievable!" he said between mouthfuls. "I've never tasted anything better in my life!"

Melvira's smile seemed impossibly wider, and she nodded her head at his pleasure.

He continued to wolf down the food. The mashed potatoes with gravy made the meal even better. She told him about some of the times his father had been there to help with an occasional problem, just as Sean was now doing. Then she asked him if there was anything she could do for him.

Sean said, "Ma'am, this meal is the best I've had since I got home from the war! Thank you! How much do I owe you?"

"Your money ain't no good here. I appreciate the sheriff's department heppin' us when we truly need it. Mos' white folks pretend we ain't here."

Sean thanked her again. She studied him for a moment, and said, "I been hearin' rumors of several white girls disappearin' lately. And I hear you been tryin' to find 'em. Folks 'round Perryville been talkin' 'bout it when I buy my groceries."

"Yes, ma'am, we are looking into that," Sean replied. Her comment put him a little on edge. "Do you know anything that might help us find those girls?"

Melvira's deep-set, piercing eyes didn't waver. "I can tell you this. We had another white man in here 'bout a month ago. Didn't look like he belonged here, either—most of 'em don't. He was dressed purty fancy, you know, looked like a big bidnessman with money. We don't get much trade like that. He drank too much beer and said he was lookin' for a girl. I asked him why he come here, and he told me he'd been in a fancy restaurant in Phoenix the day before and heard some men talkin' at a table beside him. Said they was laughin' 'bout the price of some young girls and one of 'em said it was a bargain at any price, and they all laughed some more. The only other thing he said he heard was 'bout somethin' he called an Orange Palace. He said the men got up to leave, and he asked one of 'em 'bout it. But the man told him he didn't look like he had enough money for it, and all the other men laughed as they went on out the door." She paused for breath and continued, "He said he heard 'bout our little place and come here to see what we had to offer."

Sean wanted to ask if she fixed him up, but he bit his tongue. Instead, he asked, "Had you ever heard of the Orange Palace?"

"Well, I been hearin' rumors of such a place for a while now, but that's the first I heard of that name. The only thing I know is it's supposed to be some secret and mighty fancy place rich white folks go for some entertainment, if you know what I mean."

Sean pressed, "Do you know anything about where it is?"

"All's I know is the rumors say it's somewheres west of Phoenix or Glendale. Nobody I know's ever been there." She studied him and said, "I thought the part 'bout there bein' young white girls might be somethin' that'd interest you. If I learn anythin' else, I'll let you know. It ain't right, kidnappin' young girls and doin' 'em that way, if that's what's happenin'."

Another man came in while they were talking. Sean watched him carefully as he busied himself behind the bar and watched Sean curiously.

Melvira said, "That there's Frenchy. He's been with me long as I been here. Tends the bar and watches over things." She paused a few seconds and continued, "One other thing I heard. There's s'posed to be some big money from back east buyin' up citrus fields and other lands around. They're doin' it quiet like, too."

Sean perked up. "Do you know where these people are from back east?"

"Rumor I heard was maybe Chicago or Detroit. I don't know nothin' else 'bout it."

Sean thanked her again for the information and the lunch. Then she led him to the closet and unlocked the door. A disheveled man got up. The front of his shirt was covered in dry blood, and his face was swollen and bruised. He immediately started cursing Melvira. Sean told him to shut up, forced his arms behind his back, and put on handcuffs. He continued yelling and cursing as Sean pushed him out the door. Then he locked him in the back of his patrol car.

Melvira was standing in the doorway. Motioning him over, she handed him something wrapped in a towel and said, "This is his knife. It's one of them fancy switchblades. He dropped it when a couple of people jumped him. I picked it up with this here towel and never touched it." Sean got an evidence bag from his car and placed the knife in it. He thanked her again, and as he was getting in his car, she called out, "Come back anytime, honey. You always welcome here!"

Sean was glad he was in his car, and she couldn't see his face turn red. He booked his prisoner into the district office's holding cell, then booked his knife into evidence. He called the county hospital to inquire about the man who had been stabbed—they informed him he was dead. It was now a murder case which would likely make his life a lot more complicated. It would be the first time he had dealt with a case like that. He filled in his district commander and then called Melvira to let her know.

He had some very useful new information to discuss with the detectives now. The strangely named Orange Palace could be the lead they were looking for.

***

Sean called his friend Ricky again after finishing his paperwork.

"Hey, *como esta, amigo?*" Ricky said when he heard Sean's voice.

"Ricky, I need a big favor. Someone tried to kill me at my house last night—they might try again. I need someplace where Sarge and I could sleep for a few nights in case they show up again. Could we stay with you and your parents until this all blows over?"

Ricky exclaimed, "Somebody tried to kill you? *Madre Dios*! Of course, you can stay with us. There's a spare bedroom since my older sister got married and moved out. My parents will be happy to have you here."

"*Gracias*, my friend."

"*De nada, amigo*. I'll get it set up and you can stay with us tonight."

"Let's get together for a beer, and I'll tell you all about it. I'll take off work a little early. How about 5 o'clock at the Wishing Well in Cashion?"

"*Órale*! See you there, *amigo*!"

Enrique Martinez was Sean's best friend. Sean called him "Ricky," as did all his Anglo friends. Ricky was the same age as Sean, and they graduated high school the same year. He had been a star linebacker on the Tolleson high school's football team; Sean's Buckeye high school team was a friendly rival. The two men became friends when Sean saw three older boys ganging up on Ricky in the school parking lot after a game. He stepped into the fray, and the fight soon left Ricky's attackers. He and Sean had been best friends since that night.

Ricky had joined the Marines after high school and was sent to fight against the Japanese in the War of the Pacific. His left leg was severely injured by a mine on a beach during the invasion of the island of Tinian. He was transported to a hospital in Hawaii for treatment and had recently returned home.

He was a couple of inches shorter than Sean but outweighed him by a good twenty pounds. As always, Levi's jeans, a multi-color striped western shirt with snap buttons, and Justin cowboy boots were his daily outfit. His black hair was combed over with a severe part, the same way he wore it in high school.

They ordered beers and settled into a booth in the bar. Ricky told Sean that he had asked to be sent back to continue to fight in the war with Japan after his hospital recovery, but his commanders refused. They told him he needed more time to heal from his injuries and feared he would be a liability on the battlefield. He had spent several weeks in the hospital and now walked with a pronounced limp on that side.

"It makes me angry," he told Sean. "I could hold my own with any of them. But it was an argument I couldn't win."

Sean said, "I know how you feel, *amigo*. I felt the same way." He reflected on his war experience for a minute and continued, "You know, maybe it's for the best. We did our parts and survived. I feel like I'm doing good things here in my job, and I'm lucky to have it. I imagine you will be doing good in whatever you do from now on."

The men sipped their Coors in silence and watched a couple dancing to a song on the jukebox called "I'm Losing My Mind Over You." The song ended and Ricky said "You're right, Sean. My parents are both having health problems and can use help right now with their store." His parents owned a market in Avondale that catered mainly to the Mexican community. They had been there for years and were highly regarded in the area.

Sean told him what he was involved in with his job. He explained what he knew about the missing girls and asked him to be on the lookout for any information that might be helpful. Then he explained the attempt on his life and the possibility it could happen again.

"Man, that's scary. You're right to go somewhere else until you find out who it is and why they want you dead. You should stay at our place tonight!"

"You sure your parents won't mind?"

"You know better than that, Sean. Get what you need and come back to the house. We'll wait dinner for you."

"Thanks, Ricky. I appreciate it."

Sean drove back to his house and packed up what he would need for a few days' stay at Ricky's parents' house. Then he packed dog food, dishes for food and water, and a leash for Sarge in a cardboard box. The dog was watching him intently. He said, "Come on, Sarge. Let's go!" The dog was up instantly and waited by the door. When it opened, he headed to the truck, wagging his tail. Sean opened the truck's door and the dog jumped in. He loved going for rides and immediately stuck his head out the window in the brisk night air, excited for an adventure.

The entire Martinez family came out to greet them when they arrived. Ricky took Sarge into the house while his parents hugged Sean like a long-lost son. He had spent a lot of time in their home as he and Ricky finished high school.

Sean stepped inside and instantly felt at home in the rambling old adobe structure. Ricky's grandfather had built it in the twenties. The walls were thick unfinished adobe brick with a warm, brown color. It was an effective insulator, keeping the house at a comfortable temperature year-round, with a small fire needed only on cold nights. A swamp cooler in one window kept a cool breeze circulating in summer. Its third bedroom was vacant, and Sean stowed his things in its closet. Sarge found a cozy rug and curled up on it to watch the people.

They sat at a big mesquite wood table in the dining room for dinner. The table and ten matching chairs were the centerpieces of the house. The set, along with most of their living room furniture, had been made by Mr. Martinez's brother in Mexico using native mesquite and ironwood. It took four strong men to move the table. A painting of Jesus on the cross and another of the Virgin of Guadalupe overlooked the dining set. Both pieces were in ornate gold gilded frames, separated by a large intricately carved wooden cross.

Mrs. Martinez had big plates of beef enchiladas with salad and a pot of black beans ready for dinner. They were the best enchiladas Sean had eaten in years, and he complimented the cook. She beamed broadly and told him he was always welcome at their table.

After dinner, the men sat in front of the living room's fireplace, smoking cigarettes. The small fire gave the adobe a warm glow, making the room cozy. Sean mostly only smoked on social occasions, but he lit his second Camel as he talked. Camel cigarettes had been distributed in ration packs during the war and became Sean's preferred brand.

Sean explained again what had happened with the attempt on his life. It was good to talk about it. "Sarge saved my life. That guy would have jimmied the lock on the front door and shot me while I was sleeping if Sarge hadn't warned me." The dog looked up expectantly, beating his tail on the rug at the mention of his name.

Ricky and his father had heard the rumors of missing girls but didn't know Sean was investigating it. They said they would be on the alert for any information which might help.

Sean and Ricky talked long into the night. Ricky said, "That Orange Palace thing you mentioned is curious. Do you suppose it has anything to do with orange trees? Maybe an orange grove? Seems like an odd thing to call a place."

"I don't know, Ricky. That's an interesting idea. I hadn't considered it," Sean replied. "Do you have any ideas about how we could find out more?"

"The orange harvest is just getting started. I can ask some people I know who work in the groves if they have heard about it. I'll let you know."

The two men talked war stories for a while and agreed that one battle was as bad as the other. Ricky said he received excellent care in the hospital on Oahu, Hawaii, recuperating, and he'd love to go back to Hawaii someday when he could enjoy the islands. Sean talked about his time recovering in the British hospital; the men agreed they were fortunate to have survived and gotten excellent care for their injuries. Sean said he had an early morning coming up, and the men headed for bed.

***

The following morning Sean met with the detectives and the commander. He told them about his talk with Melvira at Froggy Bottom and her mention of a place called the Orange Palace.

The commander asked, "What did she know about the place?"

"Well, sir, the only thing she knew was that it's supposedly located someplace west of Phoenix or Glendale. According to her information, it is an expensive brothel that caters to wealthy men." He paused and continued, "She also said she had heard from a man who said the place is supposed to have young girls available and wondered if there is a connection to our missing girls."

115

The other men looked at each other and were quiet while they digested this new information. Sean felt like the whole atmosphere in the room had changed. He said, "Another thing Melvira mentioned is that she has heard rumors of a lot of money from back east buying up land and businesses here. She thinks it may come from Detroit or Chicago."

"I'll ask the sheriff to contact the Phoenix and Glendale police chiefs to see if they have any information about it," the commander said. "In the meantime, I want you detectives to coordinate with the Phoenix and Glendale police departments to share this information. Sean, you stay focused on running down any leads you can find about that place and the missing girls. It will raise the stakes tremendously if it turns out there's a connection."

CHAPTER 11

Two days later, the commander called Sean into his office and said, "I had a call from Sheriff Roach about you this morning." The commander sat stony faced and waited for a little before continuing, enjoying watching Sean squirm, trying to figure out what he might have done wrong. Then he smiled and said, "Seems you've become a local hero." He could tell his new deputy was especially confused now. "That woman and her two kids you saved in the canal are from a prominent family in Buckeye. The town's mayor told the Sheriff they want you to be the grand marshal for their big rodeo parade next weekend. Then they want a little ceremony at the dance that night at the American Legion Hall to honor your service and thank you for saving that family."

Sean was speechless. Finally, he stammered, "I…I was only doing my job, sir. I don't deserve any of that. Anyone in our department would have done the same. And, sir, I don't know if it's a good idea for me to have that kind of publicity right now."

"I understand, Sean. But the Sheriff thinks this will be very good for our department. You are a war hero *and* a local hero. That's a hard combination to beat. I want you to make any necessary plans — I'll make any needed adjustments to your schedule. Take that weekend off. Spend some time with that pretty gal of yours. We'll watch your back."

Sean understood the decision had already been made for him and reluctantly agreed. The men shook hands, and Sean left to join the others.

***

Lucky Lenny was shown into a back room at the Orange Palace. He had just arrived from Detroit and Madam Trudy and Billy Bones came in to brief him. He looked nothing like what Trudy was expecting. He was small and wiry and dressed like he was going to Hawaii with a flowered aloha shirt topped off by a white, narrow-brimmed Panama straw hat. His beady eyes were wide set above a narrow nose, reminding Trudy of a weasel. He had a high, tinny voice and a nervous tick in his upper lip.

Lenny gave a short, barking laugh and said, "Hey, Bones! Long time no see! I didn't know you were here."

"Heard you were comin, Lenny. Good to have you here. We can use the help."

Madam Trudy said, "Enough good old boy chit-chat. Let's get down to business." She laid out the situation in detail.

Billy Bones told him what had happened to Fast Eddie, and Lenny shook his head and said, "How the hell did you two make a greenhorn mistake like that? Jeez!" Billy Bone's face flushed red, but he bit his tongue and stayed quiet.

Lenny said, "The dog is a complicating factor, no doubt. I'm glad to know about it—it eliminates the house for the hit."

"This is a very high priority and needs to be done quickly," Madam Trudy said. She handed him a slip of paper. "This is my personal phone number. Anything you need you call me day or night. Anything!"

Lenny said he would find a motel near the deputy's office and would let her know how to get in touch with him.

Billy tossed him the keys to the Chevy sedan parked by the door. "There's a local map in there, too," he said. Lenny tipped his hat to Madam Trudy and left.

He found his way to Avondale and located the sheriff's department division office. It was growing late, but he sat and studied the building and surrounding streets in detail. He'd do a daytime reconnaissance in the morning; Billy had given him a detailed description of the deputy and the pickup truck he drove. He wanted to be nearby when his target showed up.

Lenny had seen a sleazy-looking motel nearby. Its gaudy neon sign had a flashing arrow pointing at the office and advertising the 'cheapest rates west of Phoenix!' He returned and took a room, two dollars a night, and maid service once a week. He asked for and received a room far away from the flashing sign. It took less than two minutes to unpack his small suitcase and toss the clothes he wore over a chair back. He placed his .22 revolver along with its screw-on suppressor on the bedside table, stretched out on the bed, and was instantly asleep. His uncanny knack for knowing the time, even in a different time zone, was like an internal clock that woke him at six the next morning. He quickly dressed and left the room. He stopped at a greasy spoon café down the street and got two stale donuts and two large cups of coffee to go. Then he cruised the area around the police station and found an alley close to the building that afforded a good view of the street approach from both directions. He backed the Chevy into the alley's early morning shadow and settled in to eat his donuts and wait.

The Ford step-side pickup he was looking for showed up at five minutes to seven. He watched Sean get out, gather his things, and head for the door. Lenny studied his movements in detail through a small pair of binoculars. Experience had taught him to learn everything he could about a mark he was stalking. He noted that this man moved with effortless, fluid grace, like an athlete, and seemed very aware of his surroundings. He also noted the .45 automatic in its holster on the man's hip.

Several other people showed up, including what looked like a couple of plainclothes cops. About two hours later, his target, another deputy, and the two plainclothes men came out. The two deputies left in separate marked patrol cars while the two other men left in an unmarked Ford sedan.

Lenny didn't come by his nickname "Lucky" by accident. He was a meticulous and methodical killer. He studied a mark very carefully and tried to leave nothing to chance when he made a move. His success as a paid mob hitman came from being patient and picking precisely the right time and place to do his job. If others believed his success came from luck, that was all right with him. It kept him employed.

  This job would be no different; he would do his homework. It was a departure from the typical environment where he operated. His usual targets were invariably in a large city where he knew what variables to expect. But here, it was different. Small towns, farms, and country cops were a new experience. He would enjoy and learn from the experience. It was something else to add to his resume and make him more valuable to his employers.

  He spent the rest of that day wandering around the small towns of Avondale and Goodyear, familiarizing himself with their simple layout, and making notes of any significant features. It was not always clear when he passed from one to the other—basically, they were divided by a main street. A drugstore, a bank, a couple of restaurants, a Goodyear tire store—he wondered idly about the significance of the company name of Goodyear to the town of the same name. Then he noticed a large manufacturing facility with the company's name on the west side of town. It was near an airport with a sign that said Naval Air Facility, Litchfield Park. It seemed strange for a naval facility to be this far from any water; it was another detail he would investigate. He drove around the base's perimeter and saw several planes near some big hangers and others that appeared to be stored in another area. He never knew what kinds of information might prove useful.

  He had lunch at a diner and asked the waitress about the Navy's air facility. She had lived there all her life and was a wealth of information. She told him the base's original purpose was to test aircraft modified for the Navy by Goodyear Aircraft Corp. during the war. It was rumored, she said, that after the war, its purpose would be to preserve military aircraft they didn't use anymore.

In mid-afternoon, he returned to the same alley he had used that morning and backed in. The late afternoon shadows from adjoining buildings provided him with good cover while he waited for the deputy's return to the police station. The cop returned at about four p.m. and went inside. He came out an hour later, got in his pickup, and left. Lenny waited a few seconds and followed.

Sean immediately noticed the car in his rearview when it pulled out of the alley and headed in the same direction he was. He was sure he had seen that car parked in the alley's shadows that morning when he left the district office. All his senses warned him of danger. He couldn't go directly back to his friend Ricky's house where he was currently staying.

He made a series of right turns and came back out onto the street where he had started. Sure enough, the car emerged from the same place he had just come from. *Okay*, Sean thought. *Let's see how determined this guy is!*

He accelerated east out of town, braked, and made a hard right turn just before the bridge over the Agua Fria River's dry bed. He floored the truck and raised a cloud of dust as he sped down the dirt road. About a mile further, he came to another dirt road that intersected the one he was on. Another right turn took him to an intersection with the next road, which led back to town. He stopped and looked back; there was no sign of the following car. To be safe, he took several back roads before arriving at Ricky's parents' house. He drove around into the side yard where he normally parked; it would be hard to spot from the street. Then he called the office and told the commander what had happened, gave him a description of the suspicious car, and asked him to put out an alert.

Lenny knew he'd been made when the deputy sped out of town and made that abrupt right turn. His instincts told him there was no sense in following any further. He had seen a decent-looking restaurant and went there to have dinner and plot his next move. He picked up a local paper by the door and took it to a table to read while he ate. A piece on the front page of the paper caught his eye. He was indeed lucky! There, at the top of an article, was a picture of the deputy he was after. The headline blared: LOCAL WAR HERO TO BE GRAND MARSHALL AT RODEO PARADE. The article gushed about the man being a war hero and Purple Heart recipient and went on about him being a local hero for saving a woman and a couple of kids from drowning in a canal. The town of Buckeye was about to have its annual Hellzapoppin Rodeo days with a big parade, rodeo, and dance. The deputy was to be the parade's grand marshal and receive an award at the dance that night.

Lenny could not have wished for a better setup. All that commotion should provide him with many opportunities and plenty of cover to complete his job. Even better, he could move on to his next assignment with Kiefer as soon as the first job was done. He smiled—the sooner it was done, the sooner he could get out of this hick town and back to Detroit. He took his map from his pocket and found the town of Buckeye about fifteen miles west of his present location. Tomorrow he would spend the day there to familiarize himself with its layout. He was sure he would find an ideal place for what he had to do. The festivities were only three days away.

CHAPTER 12

Kiefer expected to see the police swarm his place at any time. He took the old mattress and the slop bucket out of the tool shed, rinsed the bucket thoroughly, and then tossed it in his barn. The mattress was tossed out back of the barn, doused with kerosene, and burned. He swept out the floor of the shed, scooped up the material and put it in his garbage can, and brought in a few tools from the barn.

The weighmaster went back into his house and went through every room with a fine-tooth comb, looking for anything that could possibly incriminate him in the girls' disappearances. None of them had ever been in his house, but he couldn't be too careful. Then he got a flashlight and went over every nook and cranny of his Pontiac's interior and trunk. He had always meticulously cleaned the interior of the Pontiac after a kidnapping—wiped down all the surfaces, carefully brushed off the seats and checked for any lingering bits of hair and washed the floormats. There was nothing to be found now in the house or the car.

His nerves took away his appetite, and he couldn't eat anything. There was a nearly full bottle of Jim Beam on the counter. He grabbed a glass and the bottle of whiskey and carried them to his easy chair. The first glass of amber liquor relaxed him, and his mind wandered back to the events in his life that had brought him to this point.

He'd had a respectable hardware business in Kansas and a good marriage. Or so he thought. One day he closed up his store early and came home to find his wife in bed with a passing salesman. He went after the man with a baseball bat, and the salesman barely escaped with his life. He chased his half-naked wife as she ran screaming down the street to her sister's house. He tried to get into the house, but the sister had hurriedly locked all the doors and called the police. They arrested him and hauled him away in the back of a black and white police car. He spent the night in a cell with a couple of drunks, seething over what his wife had done. The police released him the next day, and he found his wife had left town overnight. Her sister wouldn't talk to him and threatened to call the police again if he kept bothering her.

Something snapped in his brain—he couldn't stand to stay in that town anymore. He sold his house and business at a fraction of their value and then headed west to start a new life. He eventually landed in California, and then Arizona, where he found a profitable business as a labor contractor and weighmaster during the cotton harvest.

At first, he kidnapped a couple of girls for his own use. When he was done with them, he strangled their life away, then buried their bodies far out in the desert. It made him feel good to take revenge on women—they were all untrustworthy and no good as far as he was concerned. Each girl he killed felt like revenge for the way his wife treated him.

Then he discovered Madam Trudy and the Orange Palace. He had made her an offer that fit in perfectly with her needs, and they made a deal that was profitable for them both. It opened a whole new path for his revenge— kidnapping young girls and selling them into a life of prostitution. In his mind it was the ultimate payback for his wife's treatment of him— he had a feeling of great satisfaction each time he took another girl. The only downside was that he could not sample the merchandise. Madam Trudy paid him a premium for young virgins.

He lost track of how many more glasses of the amber liquid he drank. Passed out in his chair, he knew nothing until his rooster crowed at dawn. He awoke with a splitting headache. Waves of nausea came when he stood up, and he stumbled to his bathroom to throw up. His face in the mirror looked even worse than he felt. Deep worry lines and bloodshot eyes told their tale. His head finally cleared, he made a pot of coffee, then sat at his kitchen table, pondering what the day would bring. *The best course of action is business as usual*, he thought. *Don't let the cops see I'm worried.* He shaved and dressed in clean khaki pants and a flannel shirt, then headed for the new farm where he was working. He was lucky to have gotten this job, but he was too distracted by what he knew was coming to care.

There was no surprise when a Sheriff's Department police car pulled up next to the cotton trailer by his scales. He was making notes in his ledger when a deputy he had not seen before approached him and asked if he was Mr. Kiefer. The weighmaster nodded his head.

The deputy said, "Sir, I've been asked to escort you to your home. Please gather what you need and come with me."

"Give me a minute to get my assistant here to take over", Kiefer replied. He gave a loud whistle and waved over a man standing by the trailer. He, along with several of the cotton pickers, had been watching what was going on. "Take over here," the Weighmaster said. "I don't know how long this will take. I should be back before the end of the day."

The deputy told Kiefer he would follow him to his house. They pulled into his place behind several other marked and unmarked police vehicles. Detective Johnson walked out to meet him. He handed Kiefer a document and said, "Mr. Kiefer, this is a court warrant allowing us to search your property. Please come with me." The weighmaster followed him inside. He saw O'Conner, the deputy who had been hounding him, standing to the side, watching him. The detective pointed to an easy chair and said, "Please have a seat. Do not go anywhere else unless we tell you to. We need keys to any locked doors, or we will be forced to break into them."

Kiefer took the key for the padlock on the shed off his key chain. He said, "This fits the tool shed. It's the only outside lock." The detective took the key, put it in a small paper bag, and labeled its contents with his pen.

The weighmaster sat in his chair, watching. He couldn't tell how many cops were there. At least four were going through his house and belongings. The deputy had gone outside to join the others. The empty whiskey bottle lay on its side on the table by his chair, along with an empty glass.

The bottle's still-damp contents glistened on the table and floor where he had spilled them when he passed out.

***

Sean was particularly interested in the tool shed. He figured it would be an ideal place to stash a kidnapped girl. It would be nearly impossible to escape through the heavy padlocked door, and there were no windows. He waited until the detectives finished their search of its contents, then stepped inside. His first impression was that there weren't many tools stored in it for a shed its size. Secondly, it looked like the few tools saw little use and were arranged too carefully—the space was way too clean to have farm tools stored in it. Sean believed the weighmaster had likely cleaned it and staged the scene to make it appear like what he wanted the searchers to think it was.

He unhooked his flashlight from his belt and began to move its strong beam around the walls. Something white in a far corner stood out in the light, something different from the small amount of dirt and debris elsewhere. He stooped and looked closer. It was a small piece of whitish-grey fabric the Weighmaster had missed in his cleaning. Sean got one of the detectives to come in to photograph and bag it. They had missed it in their search.

Sean then looked around inside the barn but saw nothing of interest. He walked around it and found a still smoldering pile a little way in the back of the building. Whatever it was had burned beyond any recognition. Then he spotted something in a weed next to where the fire had been—it was the same whitish-grey color of the fabric he had found in the shed. He brought one of the detectives around to bag it for evidence.

"We already examined this burn, but looks like we didn't look hard enough," the detective said. He photographed the piece of fabric from four different angles.

Sean said, "It was easy to miss in that weed. The light was just right when I walked up to it." The detective nodded, smiled at Sean's tact, then walked away to join the others.

The detectives thoroughly went over the green Pontiac in Kiefer's garage for the second time. That search again yielded nothing. Sean looked around the garage when they were done but saw nothing of interest.

It was well after noon when the detectives completed the search. It had yielded almost nothing. The men gathered outside the house to discuss their next steps. Sean said, "I have a question about what was burned behind the barn. I found a scrap of unburned material beside it which looks like the same material I found in the shed. The piece by the fire looks like it has a little bit of ribbing similar to what you would see on a mattress. Can we compare them?"

Johnson nodded and had one of the detectives lay out a piece of clean cloth on the hood of one of their cars. Using tweezers, he carefully laid the two pieces side by side. They did indeed look like they came from the same source, possibly a mattress.

The detective replaced the material in the evidence bags. Johnson and another detective went into the house to question Kiefer. He had sat in the chair for several hours and now looked decidedly uncomfortable. He said, "Well, at least this deputy you left here to watch me let me go in the bathroom to take a leak. I was about to bust. Are you finally done? I got work to do!" He scowled at the detectives. Sean was standing behind them, and Kiefer glared daggers at him.

"Mr. Kiefer," Detective Johnson began, "what did you burn behind your barn?"

"Aw, it was just some old cotton sacks with rotten fabric. They were no use, and I got rid of them," he replied.

Johnson said, "The ashes are still warm. You must have burned them yesterday evening. Why do it now?"

"I was just cleaning up a little bit. Something wrong with that?" Kiefer replied.

"Did you recently have a mattress in your shed, Mr. Kiefer?" the detective asked.

Sean watched the man's eyes shift around the room to anything except his questioner. "Hell, no!" he exploded. "Why would I have a mattress in there? That makes no sense!"

Sean thought he was putting on quite a show. So did the detective.

Johnson shifted the line of questioning to Kiefer's recent activity. He didn't deviate from what he had told them before. It was clear the detectives would get nothing more of use from him. Johnson told him not to leave the county and that they would have more questions for him later.

The weighmaster went back to his job site to relieve his assistant. He told his helper he would need to be there the next morning and possibly all day while he took care of business in town. The assistant knew better than to ask what was going on. The weighmaster never said anything about what he did with his own time.

***

Kiefer sensed that things might be coming to a head, and he could be in the greatest danger of his life. He made a phone call to his long-time attorney that evening, told him it was an emergency, and made an appointment for the following day. Writing quickly, he wrote out detailed instructions for his attorney, folded the paper, and put it in an envelope. The secretary in his attorney's office could notarize it in the morning before he sealed the envelope. His neat printing on the envelope said: OPEN ONLY IN THE EVENT OF MY DISAPPEARANCE OR DEATH.

It was signed James Kiefer. He would also have the attorney redo his will.

He slipped his Smith and Wesson .38 police special into the Pontiac's glove box the following morning, backed the car out of the garage, and headed to Phoenix to meet with the lawyer. He told him what he wanted him to do and asked to have his secretary notarize a document. The attorney asked what the document was, but all Kiefer would tell him was that it contained final instructions to be followed in the event of his death or unexplained disappearance. The lawyer believed it was all very suspicious, but he could see nothing illegal about it. Kiefer said the document would be placed in a safe deposit box at the Valley National Bank in Litchfield Park and could only be accessed by himself or the attorney. The lawyer would need a certified death certificate and his will appointing him executor to do so. Then he had the attorney redo his brief will and had the secretary witness it. The only change was to make the attorney his executor upon his death. The last item of business was for the attorney to draw up a standard retainer agreement in the amount of three hundred dollars to provide the service. Another two hundred in cash would be left for him in the safe deposit box as a final payment upon Kiefer's death. He paid him in cash and left with the sealed envelope and carbon copies of the other documents.

The last piece of the weighmaster's preparation was to stop at the bank and place the documents in his safe deposit box. Then he headed for the Orange Palace.

The guard stopped him at the metal gated entrance to the lane leading to the Orange Palace. He said, "Hey, Jim – You're here kinda early, ain't ya?" It was three in the afternoon, and Kiefer knew Madam Trudy would just be getting ready for the evening's activities.

"I need to see Madam Trudy on urgent business. I don't think she'll mind," Kiefer said.

The guard nodded and opened the gate. "Suit yerself," he said and waved him through.

He parked at the side of the main building, out of sight of any guards who might be watching. The .38 Special fit snugly under his shirt in the small of his back; he fervently hoped he wouldn't need it. He approached the front of the building where Billy Bones stood at the door blocking the entrance. Billy said, "What are you doing here this time of day, Jim? Is Madam Trudy expecting you?"

"No, Billy, but I have urgent and important business to discuss with her. Please let her know I'm here."

"Go in the lounge and wait. I'll see if she's available." Billy disappeared off in the direction of Madam Trudy's apartment.

Kiefer sat on one of the fancy orange-hued chairs and waited. He knew his life was in jeopardy; the greatest danger he had ever faced. A strange sense of peace settled over him despite the risk he was taking. His preparations were the best he could do to protect himself—he would learn soon enough if they were sufficient to allow him to leave this place alive.

Madam Trudy swept into the room about a half hour later. Kiefer noticed that Billy Bones hovered nearby in the shadows of the room. The weighmaster knew him to be a dangerous man.

"What's this about, Kiefer?" Trudy snarled at him. "You know better than to show up here unannounced. What's so damned important you interrupt my day?" This was the first time he had seen her dressed in anything but an evening gown. She wore striking black palazzo pants with white polka dots, her trademark high-heel shoes, and a white blouse. Even early in the afternoon, her hair was done in its signature victory roll style, and her makeup was impeccable.

He drew a deep breath and said, "I believe you may think I have become a liability to our operation. If that's true, and I think it likely is, my future doesn't look very bright here."

The woman said nothing as she stared at him with a wary look.

"I want to offer you an alternative to removing me, a way we can continue our arrangement that benefits both of us."

"Get to the point, Kiefer. I don't have time for this." The woman's voice dripped venom, and her eyes blazed with anger. The weighmaster knew his life depended on what he said next.

"First, I want to describe an insurance policy I have put in place to protect me from any plans you might have for me." He described in detail the arrangements he had made. "The document I have in a secure place describes every aspect of our operation, from my part up to you and our friends from Detroit. In the event of my death or disappearance, that information will be made public by a trusted associate of mine. It will go to all the local police organizations here and in Detroit. It will also go to every newspaper here and in Detroit." He paused to let all that sink in.

She sat speechless for a few seconds, her mouth agape in anger and surprise. He could see the blood rise on her face, even through the heavy makeup.

"You son of a bitch!" she spat. "You'll never get away with this. You think you can blackmail me, you little pissant?"

The weighmaster tried to appear calm and cool. "This isn't blackmail, Trudy. I am simply protecting myself from how I know you and your associates do business. There's no reason we can't continue our operation. I can do what I've always done for you. All this does is establish a greater degree of trust between us. There will be no misunderstanding about where we stand with each other."

She studied him while she got her anger under control. Kiefer could see the wheels turning behind her now placid face. Her eyes were cold and calculating. *It's now or never*, he thought. He shifted slightly so he could easily reach the pistol tucked at his back. *I pray I don't have to use it.*

Finally, she said, "How do you think you can continue to operate with cops crawling all over you?"

Kiefer exhaled. He knew he had won. "They have no evidence to tie me, or you, to anything. They searched my place and my car and found nothing. All they have to go on is a description of a car that may or not have been involved in the last girl's disappearance. My car is not the only one in the county that might fit that description. I think that one deputy is likely the closest to finding any other information; the same one that killed Fast Eddie. He has all the local contacts, and their entire investigation will fall apart if we get rid of him. In the meantime, I'll move my operation to a different area and continue supplying your needs."

Madam Trudy did the mental calculations of what he proposed and said, "All right. We will proceed. The deputy will be taken care of. I expect you to deliver two new girls to us in the next two weeks. But be warned: If you screw up again, it will be your last. Now get out of my sight."

CHAPTER 13

Sean was embarrassed thinking about his day even before it started. The big rodeo event in Buckeye was beginning in a couple of hours. He was scrubbed and shaved and even had his hair cut yesterday. His new white Stetson hat topped off his clean and pressed deputy's uniform, and his boots had a mirror-like sheen. The embarrassment came from the thought of parading in front of all those people. He was no hero. Didn't want to be. But he would do what he had to and represent the department to the best of his ability. It was as nerve-wracking as going into battle.

Annaleigh would help him through it. He picked her up on his way to Buckeye. She bounced into the cab of his pickup, leaned over, and kissed him.

"Wow! You look like a million bucks!" Sean said.

She had on new jeans, a fancy western shirt with embroidered designs of red roses and frilly lace across the front and back, and expensive new grey ostrich skin boots. She topped it off with her grey felt Stetson which matched the color of her boots.

She laughed and tossed her head, causing her ponytail to bounce over her shoulder. "You're not so bad yourself, lawman! You clean up real nice."

Sean couldn't help blushing a little, and she laughed at him again.

"I'll be so glad when this is over, Annaleigh. I hate all this attention. Riding in a car at the head of a parade is not my idea of fun. I'm glad you'll be there with me."

"I still worry about how it will look. This is your day, and I don't have any business there with you.

"You're my girlfriend. That's all the business you will need. Besides, you were the rodeo queen three years ago. That ought to be credentials enough!"

She laughed. "Well, you'll have to explain it to the current queen. Leading the parade is one of the biggest perks of the job."

They planned to attend the rodeo after the parade. Afterward, she would accompany him to his day's final embarrassment for the ceremony at the American Legion Hall dance after dinner. It felt like the day would never end for Sean. He loved spending time with Annaleigh, but not like this.

The parade would travel the length of Main Street, east to west. A large crowd was already lined up along the route when Sean and Annaleigh arrived. The local Chevrolet dealer had provided a shiny new maroon Chevy convertible for them to ride in at the head of the parade. Sean and Annaleigh sat in the back while the mayor was in front with a town councilman driving. The mayor had a megaphone he was using to shout instructions at parade organizers.

The current rodeo queen glared a burning look at Annaleigh as they moved into position ahead of her. They were followed by a string of assorted floats, horse-mounted honor guards, farm equipment, the high school band, more new cars from the local dealership, a couple of clowns, veterans' marching groups, and assorted prize-winning livestock in cages on flatbed trailers. Sean and Annaleigh sat on top of the convertible's back seat and convertible cover. He was busy watching people on the street for any sign of a shooter, his eyes darting from one side of the street to the other.

She leaned over and whispered in his ear. "Relax, honey. You're supposed to be enjoying this. Put on a smile and wave at the folks like you want to be here."

Sean did his best as the parade moved down the street. He felt highly exposed, even though he could see several of his fellow deputies and a couple of Buckeye's police officers scattered in the crowd. The mayor was in the front of the car with his megaphone extolling Sean's virtues in between hawking various businesses in town which had contributed to the festivities. Men were holding young children on their shoulders and people were jostling for a better look at a bonafide hero each time he mentioned Sean. They stopped occasionally, and the crowd cheered and applauded. Sean waved, but he figured his face must have gone beyond red to crimson—he couldn't wait for it to be over.

They finally reached the end, and Sean heaved a sigh of relief. The mayor and town dignitaries shook his hand and told him how much they appreciated all he had done. Then the councilman drove them back to Sean's pickup on the other side of town.

When they were alone, Sean said, "See! I told you there was a good reason I wanted you here! I would never have gotten through that without you! Besides, most men in the crowd were looking at you!"

She turned pink with embarrassment and punched him good-naturedly. "Well, most of those men know better. We'll see if I can do anything else for you later!" They both laughed.

They had burgers and fries for lunch, then headed to the rodeo arena. The Hellzapoppin Rodeo had been a Pro Rodeo Cowboys Association event since 1929. It drew participants from around the country and spectators from around Arizona and California. It was a sold-out crowd, but Sean and Annaleigh had reserved front-row seats. He was uncomfortable having all those people behind him. It was irrational, he knew. No one would try to shoot him with all those people looking on. At least, he hoped not.

An angry bull was chasing a couple of clowns around the arena while the rider it had thrown off ran for cover. The crowd was laughing and applauding. The bull charged one of the clowns and he ducked behind a protective barrier in front of where Sean and Annaleigh were sitting. The animal bellowed and hit the barrier with a loud thud hard enough to shake it before moving off to chase another target.

Sean leaned over to Annaleigh and said, "You know, I can think of all kinds of ways to have fun…but none of them involve climbing onto an angry bull with blood in his eye for me."

"I don't think you need to worry, sweetheart. No one's going to strap you on one of them," she said with a grin.

Annaleigh gave him a blow-by-blow critique of each event's participants. Sean said, "You ought to be in the announcers' booth. You'd do a better job than those guys."

She laughed a deep laugh. "I tried it once. They never invited me back!" They had a good laugh over that. Annaleigh had been into rodeo since she was a girl. She had won the calf roping event for her age group at several local amateur rodeos, then graduated to barrel racing when she was older. That became her main competitive event, and she had several trophies and big silver belt buckles to show for her winnings. Sean was awed by her horsemanship and competitive spirit. He had never been much of a horseman and only rode when Annaleigh badgered him into it.

After the last events, they returned to Annaleigh's parents' place. Sean used their small guest house to clean up and prepare for the dance. He was glad he brought a clean uniform; the one he had worn all day had the sour/stale odor of nervous sweat.

They had a pleasant steak dinner with Annaleigh's parents. She had coached them not to ask about the war and tried to direct the conversation to horses and rodeos, but her parents wanted to know about the rescue of the woman and her children from the canal.

Her father said, "Tell us about that rescue, Sean. I heard the family was trapped in the car upside down in the canal. How did you get them out?"

Sean was embarrassed again. "All I did was break out the windows with a crowbar and tie a rope around the passengers when I got them out of the car. The men on the canal bank pulled them to safety. That's about all there was to it."

Annaleigh's mother said, "That must have been incredibly difficult, Sean. We heard the car was nearly underwater when you got there, and no one else had been able to reach them. What was it like being in that water?"

Sean chuckled and said, "Well, ma'am, what I mostly remember is how cold the water was. I was wishing for a fire to warm up and dry my clothes when it was over. I undressed there on the canal bank and stood shivering while I wrung out my clothes. I was too cold to be embarrassed!"

Everyone laughed, and Annaleigh changed the subject. They sat at the table, making small talk until it was time for the couple to leave for the dance.

The American Legion Hall in Buckeye was already crowded when they arrived. They parked in the only lighted space Sean could find, even though it was a good way from the building. He didn't want any surprises lurking there when they came out later. He took Annaleigh's arm, and they headed inside. There was a deputy sheriff near the door and Sean thanked him for being there.

The local country band was already cranking out Bob Wills' "San Antonio Rose" when they entered the crowded room. Couples packed the floor, twirling to the Texas swing music. Tables with chairs were arranged along each wall, leaving a large clear area for the dance floor. The stage was at the opposite end of the entry door, and the mayor was standing there waving them to a reserved table in front. Sean held Annaleigh's hand as they threaded their way through the crowd. It was a little hard to carry on a conversation over the band's loud and enthusiastic interpretation of the country song.

The mayor escorted Sean onto the stage when the band took its first break. There was loud applause, and Sean was embarrassed all over again as he looked out at the crowd. The mayor tapped the microphone and started speaking with his mouth too close to the mic; the speakers screamed with feedback. He stepped back a little, and the squealing stopped. He said, "Ladies and gentlemen, it is my pleasure to introduce you to a great American hero tonight. Not only is he a Purple Heart recipient for his heroic actions fighting Germans in Europe, but he is a life-saving hero for a family right here in our town!" The audience erupted in cheers and applause. Sean was sure his face was glowing fiery red by now. The mayor continued, "Mrs. Atkins, would you stand, please?" A woman who was seated next to Annaleigh rose from her seat. "Adele," the mayor continued, "would not be with us had it not been for this man's heroic actions. Neither would her two children. We're glad you're with us, Adele!" The crowd again cheered and clapped. Sean wondered if it would ever end.

"And now, ladies and gentlemen," the mayor said with all the flourish he could muster, "let me introduce Deputy Sean O'Conner, the pride of the Maricopa County Sheriff's Department! Sean," he said and waved him to the microphone. Sean felt utterly humiliated by the public praise. What could he possibly say to these people?

He also got too close to the microphone, causing another ear-splitting squeal. He stepped back and said, "Sorry!" The crowd laughed at his obvious discomfort. "I am at a loss for words to thank you for your support," he continued. "I think I can speak for every soldier who has fought for our country. We appreciate you supporting us." He waited for more applause to quiet down. He looked at Mrs. Atkins at the front table and said, "Mrs. Atkins, I am thankful you and your children are well. I am honored to have been able to help you." More applause. "Any deputy in our department would have done the same or more than I did. When you see a deputy, I hope you will also thank him for his service." More applause and cheers. Sean looked over the crowd, broke into a smile, and said, "Now, let's dance!" He walked off the stage with the mayor as the band returned and swung into Tex Ritter's "There's a New Moon Over My Shoulder." Couples quickly filled the floor.

Sean grabbed Annaleigh, and they danced through the song. It was the only way he could escape the backslapping and glad-handing from well-wishers in the crowd. They stayed on the floor after the first song and danced through a waltz while the crowd's energy died down. "That was a wonderful speech, dear," Annaleigh said in his ear. "You are a natural." Sean was embarrassed yet again.

They stayed and danced until the band's next break. Sean stood to leave and shook the mayor's and other dignitaries' hands again. Before they left, he walked up to Mrs. Atkins, shook her hand, and told her again how glad he was that she and her family were all right. She nodded in thanks, then burst into tears and hugged him. There was more cheering and applause from the watching crowd. Then they made their way to the door through the throng of admiring people. A Buckeye town police officer was standing just inside the entrance. Sean shook his hand and thanked him for being there.

The sheriff's deputy was still standing outside by the door, watching the parking lot. He saw Sean, nodded, and said, "Thanks, Sean." Sean shook his hand, too, and thanked him for his help. Then he offered his arm to Annaleigh, and they walked out into the night toward his pickup. They were passing a waist-high hedge when Sean caught a flicker of movement to his left. His battle-honed sixth sense told him something was wrong, and he reacted instantly, shoving Annaleigh forcefully away from him.

A small man stepped out of the darkness behind the bushes and took two steps toward them. Sean saw him raising a gun; it was as if the whole thing was playing out in slow motion. Annaleigh's scream registered on the fringe of his awareness; he was operating strictly by instinct as he spun toward the man. His left arm reached out and batted the pistol away from him just as the assailant's finger closed on the trigger. The sound of the suppressed gunshot made a spitting sound, lost in the noise from the music and crowd in the building. The bullet flew into the sky. Sean continued to turn toward the gunman and punched him squarely in the throat with his right fist. The man staggered back, gasping, but still trying to bring the gun to bear. Sean could hear Annaleigh screaming for help somewhere in the far recesses of his awareness. He stepped into the man's gun hand, grabbed his wrist, and twisted his arm toward his back. His shoulder dislocated with a loud pop and the gun fell to the ground. The man was gagging and gasping from the blow to his neck but, amazingly, slashed at Sean with a knife in his other hand that had come out of nowhere. The attacker's blade was aimed at Sean's throat, but he stepped back, and it ripped into his shirt, cutting a gash across his chest. Sean reflexively grabbed the arm with the knife and, in one smooth maneuver, twisted it and shoved the knife into the man's side. His assailant collapsed onto the ground, gasping for air and bleeding from his side, the knife's pearl handle protruding from his side. Sean kicked the gun far away from the man's reach and removed the knife. It increased the flow of blood from his side, but Sean didn't care. *This guy's tough*, he thought. *Don't need him making a last ditch effort to stick me with that blade.*

It was over. What felt like an eternity to Sean had happened in a matter of seconds. Annaleigh's screams had alerted the deputy and the town policeman; they came running up just as the man fell to the ground. Both men drew their pistols to cover him and pushed Sean back. The attacker lay writhing on the pavement, clutching his side and trying to breathe.

It was the first chance Sean had to get a good look at his assailant. He would certainly have stood out had he come into the dance hall. He was maybe five and a half feet tall with a slight build. His gaudy Hawaiian-style shirt, slacks, and black loafers looked completely out of place; everyone else wore boots, jeans, and western shirts and hats. The man's Panama hat lay off to the side of where he had fallen. Sean picked it up and tossed it onto the man's chest. The attacker's face was twisted into a mask of pain; it was hard to make out his features in the poor light.

The deputy was handcuffing the man while the Buckeye officer covered him. Annaleigh rushed to Sean and said, "My god! You're bleeding!"

Sean hadn't noticed the slashing cut on his chest. He looked down and saw his shirt was soaked in blood. He knew it was only a flesh wound and looked worse than it was. "Damn! This is a brand-new shirt!" he chuckled.

Annaleigh didn't think it was funny. She said, "Oh, Sean!" and hugged him tight despite the blood covering his chest.

He kissed her on the forehead and said, "It's over now, sweetheart. We're safe."

The other deputy had radioed for backup and an ambulance. They could hear sirens approaching in the streets. "You ever see this guy, Sean?" he asked.

"Nope. Sure doesn't look like he's from around here. I hope he lives long enough for me to question him."

By then, the attacker had passed out, still wheezing and gasping on the ground.

A large crowd had gathered by the time more deputies and the Buckeye police chief arrived. The ambulance pulled in shortly after, its siren blaring and lights flashing. The medics worked to stop the bleeding from the hit man's side where Sean had stabbed him with his own knife. Then they loaded him into the ambulance and bandaged Sean's wound before leaving. Sean ensured that one of the deputies would ride in the ambulance with his assailant.

Sean pulled the lead deputy aside and said, "This man proved himself to be resourceful, and full of surprises. We need to have a guard put on him when he arrives at the hospital. If he lives, that is."

"Yeah, you did a pretty good number on him, Sean. I'm really glad you and Annaleigh are all right. This could have gone a lot differently if you hadn't been alert. I'll call dispatch and have a guard posted on him.

"Thanks. I appreciate you being here." Then Sean turned his attention to the inevitable questions.

The deputies dispersed the crowd that had streamed out of the dance hall at the sound of sirens. The babble of concerned voices made it difficult for the Sheriff's deputies and the town police chief to sort out responsibilities for the inevitable paperwork to follow. Sean didn't care who would be in charge so long as he could question his attacker later. He answered their questions and said he knew nothing about the man. That wasn't exactly true; he had a fairly good idea where the man had come from.

Sean and Annaleigh left, headed for her house. She laid her arm on his and said, "Let's go to your place. I don't want either of us to be alone tonight. I'll phone my parents and let them know what's happened and where I am."

They were both still shaking from the adrenaline when they got to Sean's home. She made some coffee, and they just sat together on the couch for a while. She said, "Sean, I was so scared. I didn't know what was happening. I saw that man's gun and I was so scared of losing you. I love you, Sean. I'd die if anything happened to you."

Sean reached over and put his arm around her. "I love you, too, Annaleigh. All I could think about was protecting you when that guy jumped us. I would never have forgiven myself if you had been hurt."

They sat like that in silence for several minutes, sipping coffee. Sean reached over and kissed her, then looked deeply into her eyes and said, "I want you with me forever, Annaleigh. Will you marry me?"

She kissed him back and held his face in her hands. "I thought you'd never ask! Of course, I'll marry you! Why do you think I've waited all this time?"

"I'm sorry I don't have a ring, but I'll get you one soon as I can," he said.

"A ring can wait. Right now, I want you to be safe. Find out what's going on and who's trying to kill you. Everything else can wait."

It was the first night they had spent together. Her gentle love wiped away the memory of the near miss of the assassin's bullet. He didn't even notice the sting of the knife wound on his chest and slept peacefully for the first time in months.

CHAPTER 14

Madam Trudy flung the morning edition of the Arizona Republic across the room. The incident at the rodeo dance in Buckeye was front-page news. It displayed Sean's official Sheriff's Department photo under a bold headline: LOCAL HERO SAVES ANOTHER LIFE. The article went on to gush about him disarming and disabling a would-be assassin.

She was barely controlling her anger. "What is this? What the hell is going on?" she said through clenched teeth.

Billy Bones was the only one in the room with her. "I don't know," he said. "We ain't heard from Lenny since he left here. Does it say the cops know who he is?"

She snorted. "If they do, they're keeping it to themselves. If they don't, they'll find out soon enough." She stopped for a breath and considered the news. "Do you think he'll talk if he lives?" she asked.

Billy said, "I doubt it. Lenny's a pro. He's been loyal to the organization for as long as I can remember. If I was in his shoes, I'd figger they already got me for the attempted murder of a police officer. I'm gonna go to jail regardless of what I tell 'em. I think Lenny would clam up and take the consequences."

"You may be right. I hope so. It sounds like the cop injured him quite badly. If he dies, it's one less worry. But now that damn deputy is an even bigger pain in our side. How in the hell did Lenny miss him?"

"Well, ma'am, from what we know, the guy was some kind of badass in the Army. Commando training and stuff. He got shot up pretty bad and lived to tell about it. Now he's like a big hero or something." He pulled on an ear lobe while he thought and continued, "My guess is he's got that fighter training, great reflexes, and maybe some weird sense for danger. I've heard that men who've been in battle have some kind of edge like that. We underestimated him twice, and it's pretty clear the direct approach ain't workin'. We're gonna have to try another angle to get rid of him."

Trudy sat for a long time, twirling a curl of hair on her shoulder around her forefinger. Finally, she said, "We need to forget about that deputy for now. This has gotten far bigger than him. That public hit Lenny screwed up will bring a lot more heat down on us. It's only a matter of time before the cops start putting pieces together and the Palace becomes a target. We need to plan how to protect our operation now."

"What do you want me to do?"

"Right now, that dumb ass Kiefer is our weakest link. He thinks he has blackmailed me with a threat of making everything public. I'm working on a plan to change that. We will act on him as soon as I have the right information. For now, I want you to increase our security. Make sure all our men are alert and ready if needed."

Billy nodded and left. He was seething inside. Maybe she was content to let that deputy go. But he had killed his best friend. Billy couldn't let that pass. He decided he would act on his own when the time was right and worry about the consequences afterward. Fast Eddie deserved no less.

Madam Trudy picked up the phone to call Johnny O. She hoped he was home from church with his family.

***

Annaleigh invited Sean to dinner at her parents' house Sunday evening. He looked forward to a relaxing time with her and her family. It was a perfect time to ask Mr. Childs the big question. They retired to the living room after dinner. Annaleigh's parents sat on a couch facing Sean, who sat on a big easy chair; Annaleigh perched on one of the chair's arms with her hand on Sean's shoulder.

Sean was nervous. He had rehearsed this moment a thousand times in his mind. But the reality ate away at his confidence. Finally, after a break in some small talk, Sean said, "Mr. Childs, Annaleigh, and I are deeply in love. I want to ask you for your daughter's hand in marriage.

Childs studied him for a minute and replied, "Sean, I would be honored and happy to have you as my son-in-law. I'm sure Mrs. Childs will agree."

Mrs. Childs was nodding vigorously with a big smile on her face. "Oh, Sean, I always knew this moment would come. You two are made for each other. I will be thrilled to have you as part of our family."

Sean heaved a big sigh of relief. He had a distinct impression that Annaleigh's parents knew this was coming and were already prepared. It made him feel good to know

154

how they felt about him. He smiled at his bride-to-be sitting beside him. She had a big smile, too, and was practically glowing. He marveled at what a beautiful and impressive woman she had become, and her cowgirl ways made her even more attractive to him.

 Annaleigh and Sean talked late into the evening, planning their wedding and future lives together.

CHAPTER 15

Sean arrived at the district office Monday morning and immediately knew something was up. The Sheriff's official car was parked in front of the door. The two detectives Sean worked with were already there, too. He doubted it was a sign of good news.

The division commander waved him into the conference room as soon as he walked in. Sean seated himself at the table.

Sheriff Roach said, "Before we get into this, I want to thank you, Sean, for your actions over the weekend. I heard you did a great job with all the festivities in Buckeye. The mayor called me at home to express his pleasure with your terrific job. You're a credit to the department, son." Sean squirmed in his chair and said, "Thank you, sir." He hoped his embarrassment over being singled out again didn't show.

"Now," the sheriff continued, "I want to know everything there is to know about what's going on here. Everything. Commander?"

The commander started with an overview of how the case developed and what had been done to date. Then each of the detectives summarized what they knew. It eventually came around to Sean, being the lowest seniority. He detailed how the case started with the report of a missing girl from a field worker's camp, then progressed through every step he had taken to the present.

The room was silent as the sheriff digested the information. He said, "Sean, the first man who tried to kill you at your home was from Detroit. Do you think this man who attacked you Saturday night might also have been from there?"

Sean considered it. "It seems likely. The guy sure didn't look like he was from around here, the way he was dressed and all. He looked like he was going to a Hawaiian luau instead of a rodeo dance. He seemed to be a professional hitman. He planned the ambush to catch me off guard while I was with my fiancé, and his pistol was a .22 revolver with a suppressor. They told us at the academy that was frequently a weapon of choice for professional killers because it's quiet and deadly at close range. The guy was also quick and tough. He came back at me with a knife despite a blow to the throat and a dislocated shoulder that should have disabled him. There was no ID on him, which also made me think he was a pro. So, it seems possible that the same people sent him that sent the first hitman to my house. I can't think of anyone else who would have done it."

Sean paused for a breath. "I feel lucky to be alive, sir. If I'd been looking away I would be dead now. He might have killed my fiancé, too."

The sheriff nodded. "We're glad you're both alive, Sean. Now let's talk about this so-called Orange Palace. The Phoenix Chief of Police told me the name was unknown to them, but they had heard rumors of a high-end brothel somewhere on the county's west side. He's putting the word out to his people and the other local police departments to be on the lookout for any other information." He looked at each man in turn. "If these missing girls are somehow connected to that, we have a very big problem on our hands."

The room was hushed as the men considered the possibilities. "There's one other thing," the sheriff said. "The Phoenix police chief also told me his intelligence people were investigating what appears to be significant amounts of money flowing into the city from Detroit. He said they also have information that the same people are buying up large tracts of land here, including a substantial acreage of citrus groves. That fits with the information Sean mentioned. It seems likely that this Orange Palace could be connected to that; it might even be in one of those citrus groves. I want you men to find it, and quickly. Let's put a stop to whatever operation they are running."

The sheriff stood to leave and shook each man's hand in turn. He was a long-time department veteran, well-liked, and highly regarded by the men.

The men got down to work. The commander directed Sean to focus on Kiefer. He was their strongest suspect so far. They didn't have enough evidence to arrest him, but if they kept the pressure on him, he might make a mistake and give them what they needed.

The two detectives were assigned to coordinate with the Phoenix police intelligence staff. Their first task was to run down any recent land purchases with Detroit connections at the county recorder's office. Two other deputies were assigned to patrol the citrus groves' vast acreages west of Phoenix, looking for anything out of the ordinary.

***

Sean discovered the cotton harvest was done at the farm where the weighmaster was last working. No one seemed to know where he might be now; he hadn't been seen for several days. Sean drove to his property north of Perryville but saw no activity. The Dodge pickup he had seen the man use was not there. He decided to have a look around and pulled into the driveway. He would come up with some pretense for being there if Kiefer happened to show up.

He looked in the one-car garage and saw the Pontiac still there. Sean figured the man wouldn't have gone far without the car. It seemed to be his pride and joy. He didn't see anything else of interest, but as he walked past the tool shed, his boot kicked up something in the dirt. Using the toe of his boot, he moved the loose soil around for a better look. It appeared to be a small hair clip that a girl might use to hold her hair in place.

He carefully walked around and saw nothing else of interest near the shed. If the hair clip might be evidence, he had to proceed very carefully. He got his Kodak camera from the car and photographed the clip from various angles around the shed. Then he returned to Perryville to find a pay phone to call the district office. He explained what he had found to the commander and asked him how to proceed. He told him to go back and sit on Kiefer's place until he let him know otherwise. They had to do this right,

159

and that meant a search warrant. He said he would try to make it happen as quickly as possible.

Finding a judge willing to expedite a warrant didn't take long—a missing pastor's daughter garnered a lot of attention, and the sheriff had made it known that finding the girl was a high priority. The two detectives were directed to pick up the warrant at the courthouse and get to Kiefer's place as quickly as possible. They found Sean parked on the side of the road where he could keep an eye on the weighmaster's place. They pulled into its driveway, and Sean directed them to his find.

The detectives carefully photographed the scene again and then used tongs to pick up the hair clip and put it in an evidence bag. They would rush it back to the department's lab in Phoenix to have it cleaned and dusted for fingerprints. Sean hoped this might be the lead he hoped for to tie Kiefer to the girls' kidnappings.

The weighmaster was on his way home and spotted the cars parked beside his house before he got there. He stopped and studied what was going on. He was sure the cops could see him; if he ran, things might go from bad to worse. He decided to pull up next to his house and work up a good case of indignation.

He jumped out of his truck, slammed the door hard, and shouted, "What the hell is going on? Why are you back on my property?"

Detective Johnson approached him and said, "Mr. Kiefer, we have a duly authorized search warrant which allows us to search the premises. We are looking for additional evidence we may have missed in our earlier search."

"Evidence of what?" the weighmaster yelled. He was getting red in the face and sweating despite the cool day. "There ain't any evidence for anything 'cause I ain't done anything illegal. I demand to know what this is all about!" He was angry and shaking, glaring at all the officers—Sean in particular.

Johnson stayed cool. "Sir, we are looking into the disappearance of some young girls in the area. You were seen with possibly one of those girls before her disappearance. We are doing our legal duty to follow up on any leads related to that." He handed Kiefer a copy of the search warrant, and the men prepared to leave.

Kiefer stood there spluttering, threatening to go to the governor, the sheriff, and even his congressman. The officers ignored his threats and left.

When they were gone, the weighmaster stood there in his driveway, thinking. "What the hell?" he said aloud to himself. The cops had searched his place from top to bottom already. What were they doing back? Did they have something on him? He couldn't think of anything they might have found. He decided that if they had anything, they would have hauled him off to jail. He still had time, but the vice was tightening.

He went into his house and called his lawyer. "Remember that document I put in my safe deposit box and told you to retrieve if anything happened to me?" he asked the attorney. He said he did. "Well," Kiefer continued, "some unpleasant people may come knocking on your door. They will want that information, even though I may still be alive. I'd suggest you get out of state for a while until things blow over."

"What in hell have you gotten me into, Kiefer? Am I in danger?"

"Yes, you are. They'll want that document awfully bad and will go to almost any lengths to get it. I think I can settle things down in a few days. In the meantime, you should make yourself scarce."

The weighmaster wouldn't give him the details of the document. He would only say that it was an insurance policy for himself. But it would only protect him if it stayed in his safe deposit box."

The attorney was upset. "You shouldn't have done this to me. I have a family to worry about."

"You're my lawyer, and I've paid you well for this. Take your family and get out of town, preferably for a couple of weeks. Take a surprise vacation. You'll be fine."

***

The lab had carefully cleaned the hair clip. They found two small fingerprints, likely belonging to a child or young teenager. There was nothing else. Sean and the detectives gathered back at the division headquarters to discuss what to do next.

Detective Johnson said, "We need to see if we can get any fingerprints of the missing girls to compare. Sean, can we find any of the girls' parents?"

"I don't know about the field workers," he said. "It looks like the cotton harvest is pretty much over, and they may have moved on to California. I'd suggest starting with the pastor and his wife. I'm sure they are available and would provide us with anything we need."

"All right. That's a good starting point. See what you can do."

"Yes, sir. I'll also see what I can find out about the other families, too. One question: Can I take the hair clip to show the parents? It has some unique decorations, and they might recognize it."

"You can take it but handle it only with gloves. We don't want to disturb the prints. It's our only piece of real evidence. Be damn careful with it."

"Yes, sir. I have gloves in my patrol car." He took the evidence bag with the clip and left. The other officers went back to their assigned tasks.

Sean was excited. Finally, there was something solid that might break this case. He headed directly to the preacher's house, driving fast with lights on and siren blaring. He wanted to keep this investigation moving as fast as possible, get a confirmation of the prints on the hair clip— he had a good idea who it belonged to.

The pastor and his wife were both at home. They had anxious looks on their faces as they invited Sean in and motioned him to a chair. The living room was the perfect picture of a pastor's home: Conservative floral print furniture coverings, beige carpet, a painting of Jesus feeding the masses, a large carved Presbyterian cross, and a substantial bible with an embossed cover on the coffee table. A photograph of Millie sat on a side table beside one of three comfortable chairs arranged in front of a table and a sofa.

"Have you found her, deputy? Have you found our daughter?" the preacher asked excitedly.

His wife said, "Please tell us you have some news. We are worried sick."

Sean replied as gently as he could. "I'm sorry to say we haven't yet found your daughter." The air went out of the couple like a ruptured balloon. "But we are doing everything we can. I have an item of evidence that could be linked to your daughter. I want to show it to you, If I may."

"Of course!" the couple said in unison. They leaned toward him expectantly.

Sean put on his gloves and reached into the evidence bag. He took out the little hair clip and held it in his cupped hand to show them.

The pastor's wife gasped and fainted. The pastor held her up and fanned her face. She came to in a minute or so and reached for the clip in Sean's hand. He pulled it back and said, "I'm sorry, ma'am. This is evidence, and we can't let you handle it. It has fingerprints we are trying to identify."

She said, "There's no need for fingerprints, officer. That's Millicent's hair clip. I'd know it anywhere because I helped her paint and decorate it."

"Are you sure enough to testify to it in court if it comes to that?"

"Of course! There couldn't possibly be another like it. You can see her initials in tiny print on one of the flowers if you look carefully. Where did you find it?"

Sean hadn't noticed that detail but could now see the tiny MB letters with close inspection. He said, "I have no doubt you are correct, Mrs. Billings. But to have it serve as unquestionable evidence, we need to compare it with your daughter's fingerprints. Do you have something I could take to our evidence lab to do that"?

"I'll see what I can find," she said and started toward the girl's bedroom.

Sean stopped her. "Please wait, ma'am."

He handed her a pair of latex gloves and said, "Please wear these gloves before you pick up anything. It will avoid any potential confusion at the lab with your fingerprints."

She sobbed loudly as she put on the gloves and went into Millie's room.

Pastor Billings asked again, "Where did you find her hair clip? Do you know who is responsible for this? Will this evidence lead you to her?"

Sean nodded. "We have a potential suspect. We should be able to arrest him based on this evidence if it matches any of your daughter's fingerprints you can provide. That's all I can tell you right now. We will let you know as soon as we learn anything more."

His wife returned with a large hairbrush and a small mirror. She was careful to grasp them only by their edges, even with the gloves on. "Will these do? Millie used them every day." She handed them to Sean. He thanked her and placed them in two separate evidence bags.

He did his best to console the anguished couple and assured them again that the department was doing all it could to find their daughter. He took the two items and raced back to the department's lab in Phoenix with his lights flashing and siren wailing. He wanted the information to confirm the fingerprint samples before the day's end.

Sean met the two detectives back at the station. They talked about what they had found in the county's land records while they waited for a call from the lab.

Johnson said "We've begun to identify a pattern in the records of what appear to be shell companies buying up real estate in the county, much of it in the western part. There are signs of dirty money, possibly from Detroit, but it's tangled up in a complex web of the companies being used. It's gonna take a while to sort it out."

The office phone rang shortly before five p.m. The secretary said it was the lab. Johnson picked up the phone in the conference room and listened. He hung up with a big smile on his face. "We've got a match," he said. "They confirm a definite match on all three items." The men looked at each other in silence for a few seconds.

"Let's go get Kiefer!" Sean said. "I've waited a long time for this!"

Johnson said, "Not so fast. We have to do this exactly right. We need an arrest warrant to make it official."

"Hell!" Sean said. "It's after five. How are we going to get a warrant now? Can you get a judge to act on it as an emergency?

The detective said, "The best thing to do is see the county attorney first thing in the morning. We'll run the evidence past him and get a warrant if he thinks we can make a case. The last thing we want to do is let Kiefer get off because of some legal technicality. He would disappear for sure!"

Sean was dejected. He knew the detective was right. But it worried him that Kiefer would somehow slip through their fingers before they could arrest him.

***

"Lucky" Lenny regained consciousness Thursday afternoon after the surgery to repair his liver. The surgeon had been able to stop the bleeding and said the patient would likely recover. The breathing tube had been removed and the doctors said his larynx would heal with time and proper care.

A nurse came in to check his vital signs. She asked him how he was feeling, and he croaked, "Lawyer."

She wasn't sure she'd understood him and said, "What?"

"Law-yer," Lenny croaked again, louder. Then he started coughing and passed out.

The nurse found the doctor in charge and relayed what the man had said. Then the doctor approached the deputy guarding the door to Lenny's room and told him what had happened. The deputy thought that it was an amazing thing that a man who had been on death's doorstep would have a lawyer on his mind first thing when he came to. He asked the doctor to wait in the room while he made a call. His supervisor told him it was too late to do anything about it that day, and he would pass it on to the sheriff in the morning.

***

Madam Trudy called the hospital that evening and was connected to the nurses' station. She said she thought the unidentified man who had been stabbed might be her brother, and she wanted to know his condition.

The nurse said, "He has recovered from surgery." She paused and said, "Ma'am, you're the first person who has contacted us about him. We don't know his name or any other information about him. Please come to the hospital to identify him and provide more information."

Trudy asked, "Will he live?" The nurse said she couldn't provide more information over the phone and that she would have to come to the hospital. Trudy hung up.

She considered her options. If Billy Bones were right, it was unlikely Lenny would tell the police anything. But she also knew that sometimes people babbled all sorts of information when they were under the influence of drugs. It was a possibility to consider. She could do two things: Send her lawyer to deal with the hospital and represent Lenny or send someone else to take more extreme action to ensure Lenny never said anything ever again. She decided on the latter option. It was a clean and final solution. It was time to act.

Madam Trudy had called Johnny O as soon as she had learned what had happened with Lenny. She told him she wasn't sure her men were up to what had to be done; Billy Bones was too close to another of his old friends to act. Johnny O immediately put two men on a red-eye flight to her that he said were pros and completely reliable. She put them up at a hotel in Phoenix to await her instructions.

She dressed in her business suit the next morning and drove to Dr. Biggs' office. The doctor had gotten his medical training in Chicago before moving to Detroit to take over a private practice. He had specialized in anesthesia and considered that as a career. But the deal to take over the established practice in Detroit was too lucrative to pass up. He had done well, and his reputation as a general practitioner had grown.

A couple of years after relocating to Detroit, he got a strange call. Someone representing another person wanted him to make a house call. He responded that he didn't make house calls. The caller replied that this was a special patient who would gladly pay triple his fees. Biggs was intrigued and agreed to visit the patient that evening.

He drove up to the address he had been given. It was an imposing home in one of the wealthiest parts of the city. He rang the bell, and a huge, muscular man answered.

"I'm Doctor Biggs," he said.

The man studied him for a moment. He had a very intimidating attitude. The doctor was reminded of a villainous professional wrestler he had once seen crush his opponent in a match at the arena.

"This way," he said in a deep but quiet voice, leading the doctor up a beautiful spiral staircase, through a sitting area larger than most people's living room, and into a luxurious private bedroom suite. It looked like pictures he had seen of living quarters used by wealthy royals in Europe. A pair of ornate sitting chairs beneath what appeared to be an expensive original oil painting graced the side of the room opposite the bed. The room's carpeting was the deepest, softest material the doctor had ever stepped on. The patient lay on the most enormous canopy bed Biggs had ever seen.

He was coughing loudly and waved the doctor over to the bed. The giant doorman stayed one step behind him.

The man stopped coughing long enough to introduce himself in a rasping voice. "Call me Johnny. Thank you for coming to see me." Then he started gasping for breath and coughing again.

The doctor set his black bag on the edge of the bed and took out his stethoscope. He said, "Tell me what's going on. How long have you had the cough?"

"About a week," Johnny said.

Biggs listened to his lungs and heart, then put a thermometer in his mouth. The man had a temperature of 104 and severe congestion in his lungs.

"Well, my friend, you have an advanced case of pneumonia. It's a wonder you're alive from the sound of your lungs." He reached into his bag, took out a small medicine vial, and filled a syringe with its contents.

The hulking giant laid a hand on his shoulder and said, "Wait." His voice sounded like a lion's growl. "What is that? You don't put it in Johnny until he says it's okay."

The doctor was taken aback thinking *What was this, anyway? Who were these people?* He said, "This man has pneumonia. He will likely die without an antibiotic. This is penicillin. It's the best thing available to treat his condition."

The hulking bodyguard looked at Johnny, who nodded his head. "Go ahead," he rumbled.

The doctor administered the injection and said, "I should see you again tomorrow. Your condition is extremely dangerous."

Johnny nodded again, and the giant escorted him back downstairs. "Johnny said to give you this," he rumbled, handing the doctor a plain white envelope. "Come back tomorrow at this same time." He opened the door, and the doctor quickly went out and down the stairs to his car. The hulking man stood in the doorway watching him.

Doctor Biggs was too shaken to look in the envelope until he got home. He went inside, poured himself a tall scotch on the rocks, and sat in his easy chair. He opened the envelope to find five crisp, one-hundred-dollar bills. It was many times what his normal fee would have been.

That was the beginning of what turned out to be a long and profitable relationship with the man known to his friends and associates as "Johnny O." The doctor's background in anesthesia proved quite valuable on many occasions, and he formulated several drugs for his client's use. He developed severe problems with arthritis, and the harsh Detroit winters took a toll on him. Johnny O told him they were creating some extensive operations in Arizona and asked if living there would help his arthritis. He said it would, and they arranged to for him to open a new private practice in Phoenix. His only patients were those in Johnny O's and Madam Trudy's organizations. He was on call twenty-four hours a day if needed.

Madam Trudy's current request of him was simple. He had prepared it without knowing its purpose—he didn't need to know and didn't ask. He had it available when she arrived. She thanked the doctor, took the package, and left. Then she drove to the hotel where the two men from Detroit were staying. They met in a hotel room, and the men introduced themselves as Robert and Paul. Paul seemed to be in charge. Trudy said, "This job has to be done fast. I hate having to do it, but it's unavoidable."

Paul said, "Johnny O told us about what happened. We only know Lenny by reputation. It's not a job we will enjoy, but we'll get it done. Tell us what you know about the setup."

"Lenny is in a large hospital called Good Samaritan here in Phoenix," she began. "His room is guarded by a cop twenty-four hours a day. What I have in mind is a two-man job," and she outlined her plan.

Paul nodded thoughtfully and asked a few questions. "We'll need a little time to look the place over. But we'll get it done soon. Tonight, if we can. We'll be in touch when it's finished."

Trudy felt relieved and confident that these men would take care of it. Then she left for an appointment with her attorney not far from the hospital.

This was only the second time the woman had been to the attorney's office. He had always come to her at her place in the citrus grove. He liked it that way, too, because there were some excellent fringe benefits for him when their business was concluded.

He said, "It's delightful to see you."

"Tell me what you've found out," she replied without preamble.

"None of my associates know who represents the man. But I finally found a connection on a real estate document at the county recorder's office: an attorney who represented him through a negotiation when he bought a small farm and house west of Goodyear. I looked it up—it's near a little burg called Perryville. It was the only legal reference I could find. My guess is that he is the attorney you are looking for."

"Is that all you can tell me?"

"I called his office. He has a small practice operated from a remodeled house in west Phoenix. His secretary said he had left on a last-minute vacation to Mexico, and she wasn't sure when he'd be back. At least a week, she said. Then I asked if she knew James Kiefer. She said, oh, I can't tell you that. It's private information."

Madam Trudy waited for him to go on. "I could tell by her tone of voice and her reaction that she knew the man. I'm reasonably sure he's the attorney you want. I left a message with her to have her boss call me as soon as he returns."

She stood up to leave and said, "Call me immediately if you hear from him or get any other information about him. It's extremely important."

The lawyer didn't ask any more questions—he knew better than to pry into Madam Trudy's affairs. She thanked him and left. *Kiefer*, she thought. *He must have gotten spooked and tipped off his attorney.* She needed to find out what was up with him. The more she considered it, the more obvious it became that it was time for him to go away permanently. She would deal with his attorney when it was done; some very persuasive methods had served her well in similar circumstances in the past. In the meantime, she'd have Billy Bones pay Kiefer a visit.

***

Paul and Robert had worked together in Detroit for many years. They specialized in the art of creating a diversion to cover whatever their assignment was. This hospital would be just another in a long list of public hits the men had carried out. They had studied its layout and visited the floor where Lenny was being treated. Their plan was simple.

Paul walked up to the nurse's station on Lenny's floor at the hospital. He asked the nurse for the room number of a fictitious name.

"I'm sorry," she said. "There's no one on this floor by that name. Are you sure you're on the right floor?"

"This is the third floor, right? That's where I was told to go."

The nurse picked up a phone. "Let me call downstairs and find out where he is. It will only take a minute."

Suddenly the fire alarm bells started ringing. There was instant confusion: Nurses and doctors rushed to their assigned emergency tasks, patients and visitors poured out of the rooms, and everyone was yelling over the clanging of the alarm. The deputy guarding Lenny rushed to the nurse's station and asked what he should do, and a nurse told him to get out of the building as quickly as possible.

No one noticed Paul slip into Lenny's room. Lenny was awakened by the alarm and looked up in surprise when Paul walked in. "Who are you?" He croaked. "Are you getting me out of here?"

Paul walked up to his bedside and said, "Yep, you're getting out of here, buddy." Then he quickly plunged the syringe Madam Trudy had given him that morning into Lenny's neck. The drug hit him almost instantly. Lenny got a surprised look on his face and took a deep gasping breath as his heart stopped beating. Paul lingered a minute, checking for a pulse with his finger on the carotid artery in Lenny's neck, and watching for any sign of breathing. He slipped out the door when he was sure the man wouldn't recover.

He calmly made his way through the chaos and down a crowded stairwell of panicked people trying to leave the hospital. No one noticed him. He met his partner in the lobby. "Perfect timing with that alarm, Robert. The cop guarding the door never saw a thing." The two men returned to their hotel. Paul called Madam Trudy as soon as they were in their rooms to tell her the job was done.

***

The detectives were meeting with the county attorney at the same time Lenny breathed his last. They laid out all the evidence they had for arresting and prosecuting Kiefer. The attorney listened carefully, then sat tapping his fingers on his desk while he pondered the possibilities. Finally, he said, "All your evidence is circumstantial. The description of the green Pontiac near the kidnapping scene is not strong enough. His attorney could argue that there are dozens like it in the state."

A secretary brought in coffee for the men, then the attorney continued. "The hair clip is compelling, and the additional items' fingerprints certainly confirm it belonged to the girl. But an argument could be made that the hair clip had been stolen, and the thief had somehow lost it on Kiefer's property. You told me the man did business with transient laborers and was in charge of paying them. Is it possible one of them could have stolen it and lost it at Kiefer's house?"

"That's quite a reach," Johnson said. "Sure, I suppose it's possible. But it is highly unlikely."

"You have to think like a defense attorney," the county's lawyer said. "If I can raise that question, you can bet a defense attorney would raise it in a trial. It's enough to sway a jury and kill the case." He looked at the men's dejected expressions. "I'm sorry, but we have to have more. If you arrest him, his lawyer will have him back on the street in a few hours. Worse, you would have tipped your hand. The man might run, and you'll never find him. Bring me something that definitely links him to the girl. We need to have evidence that can't be challenged."

The two detectives left the county attorney's office muttering and cursing under their breath until they were out of the building. "Damned attorneys!" Johnson spluttered. "This case is plain as day. We were lucky to get the evidence we have. Now what?" He looked at his partner. The man just looked down and shook his head.

CHAPTER 16

The weighmaster's biggest worry now was Madam Trudy. He knew she had people watching him. It wouldn't take long for word to reach her that he had been visited by cops at his house again. He figured it might cause her to act irrationally, despite his insurance ploy. The mob had ways of sweeping many things under the rug.

She owed him for the preacher's daughter he sent her. He'd call her and see how she sounded. If her voice dripped honey, he'd know to stay away.

He decided to speed up his liquidation process for his personal belongings and the car. It would be too late if he waited until she sent one of her goons after him, or if the law were breaking down his door to arrest him. He had made a deal with Buster Mason to buy his house and farm at a fraction of what it was worth. The old coot owned the farm adjoining Kiefer's and had been after him for years to sell. His attorney could handle the transaction with the sale and get the money to him later.

The weighmaster had buried eight two-pound Hills Brothers' coffee cans in various places in his yard and marked each with a small circle of stones. They were stuffed with large bills; the can's lids were on tight and sealed with paraffin wax to keep moisture out. He had been hoarding the cash for years because he didn't trust the banks and didn't want any questions or paperwork about it. It was his emergency stash for when the day came he might need it in a hurry. All his instincts told him that day had now arrived. He dug them up and put their contents in a suitcase, then carried it to his barn. A small space hollowed out in a stack of hay bales made a perfect hiding spot for the suitcase full of cash.

He dialed the number for "Jimmy's Fine Used Goods," a used furniture and assorted junk store in Buckeye. Jimmy had been a friend for years. "Come on out and make an offer, Jimmy," Kiefer said. "I'm moving to California, and I'm not taking any of my household stuff with me. I'll be gone this morning, but I'll leave the place unlocked. Look around, and we'll talk later." Then he called Buster Mason and reached a deal to include his cattle, farm tools, and equipment in the farm's sale for an additional three hundred dollars.

His phone rang as he headed out the door. He went back and answered, surprised to hear Madam Trudy's voice this early in the day. She said, "Jim, I don't think it's a good idea for you to come here for payment for your last delivery. There's so much attention from the police right now. We wouldn't want them to follow you here. I am going to send Billy to your home tonight with the money. Would eight o'clock be all right?"

The weighmaster knew instantly that something was wrong. She had never been that cordial in a conversation as long as he had known her. His mind was churning with possibilities. He answered as calmly as he could, "Sure, Trudy. That would be fine. I'll be here."

"Thank you so much, dear. I knew you would understand," the woman said sweetly and hung up.

That sealed the deal, Kiefer thought. He had to get ready.

He studied his room's layout. It was a typical old farmhouse arrangement with the living and dining area in one room and a small kitchen in an adjoining room, a front door, and a back door. Two bedrooms and a bathroom were in the back of the house. The floor was covered in worn and scuffed linoleum with a faded green checkerboard pattern. Not much furniture, just his easy chair, a side table, and a beat-up old couch against one wall. A small yellow Formica-covered dinette table with four matching vinyl-covered chairs sat off the kitchen door.

Billy would probably come to the front door. He wouldn't likely try anything until he was inside the house. And it would come quickly.

He made a plan and rehearsed it over and over in his head. *What if Billy did this? What if he did that?* Kiefer figured his plan would provide good options for all the possibilities he could think of. He hoped. He made the necessary arrangements to carry it out.

Then he went out to his garage. The last thing he needed to do before he disappeared was to sell the car. He backed the Pontiac out of the garage and headed to Phoenix. He pulled into the General Motors dealer's lot where he had bought the car and asked to see the owner. It had cost him $1800 two years earlier. The man remembered selling him the car and asked him if he wanted to trade it for a new one. Kiefer said, "No trades this time. I want to sell the car for cash. Make me an offer." The car dealer knew the signs of desperation, and this guy had them in spades. He chewed on a stubby cigar, tugged his suspenders, walked around the car, looked inside, and checked the odometer. "I can give you five hundred as it sits," he said. Kiefer countered with seven hundred and fifty and a ride back to his farm. The dealer smiled, and the deal was done.

One of the dealer's salesmen drove him back to his house. "This is a great car," the man said. "How come you sold it?"

"Just need cash," Kiefer replied and looked out the window to discourage more questions.

The weighmaster had long ago purchased a house on a beach near the town of Guaymas, Mexico, far south down the coast on the Gulf of California. It was a livable place where he could be comfortable for a long time. He had gone into partnership with a local Mexican fisherman to buy a boat for deep-sea fishing. Kiefer had to supply half the boat's price and pitch in his share for maintenance and upkeep on it. His partner took care of the business, and it provided Kiefer with a tidy income year-round. Kiefer usually made the trip from Arizona to Guaymas during the off-season of the harvest in Arizona. He occasionally took the boat out between commercial bookings for deep-sea fishing.

He would go there—if he survived the next few hours and days. It had always been his plan to retire and live there, anyway. He had never told anyone in Arizona about it, and it was doubtful anyone would find him in Mexico.

He sat in the house to await his fate. Dinner time came and went— he was too nervous to eat anything. It seemed like the wall clock's hands were moving twice as fast as usual, spinning inexorably toward a reckoning. He felt ill-prepared; soon, he would face a seasoned gunman with many killings behind him.

The crunch of tires on gravel in the driveway brought him to full alert. Kiefer looked out the window and saw that Billy was alone. That, at least, was in his favor. Then he slipped his leather jacket back on and waited.

He heard Billy's footsteps on the porch, followed by a heavy knock on the door. Kiefer positioned himself carefully, reached with his left hand to open the door, and stepped aside. He kept his right hand on the S&W .38 pistol he had placed in the right-side pocket of the jacket.

"Come on in, Billy. Good to see you!" Kiefer said cheerfully. He hoped he looked calmer than he felt.

"Yeah," Billy said, "you too."

"Good timing. I just walked in a couple of minutes ago. The heater went out in my truck. Damn cold night. Stuff always seems to happen at the worst time."

"Yeah. Sorry 'bout that. Madam Trudy sends her regards. I got your money right here." Billy reached under his coat with his right hand.

Kiefer knew he carried a pistol there in a shoulder holster. He had seen it many times when Billy wasn't wearing a jacket. *Hell*, he once thought, *he probably sleeps with the damn thing.*

He saw Billy's hand grip the weapon. In that split second, he fired the snub nose .38 special from his jacket pocket. They were only four feet apart, and the round hit Billy in the stomach. Billy's hand came entirely out of his jacket gripping his pistol, but Kiefer quickly pulled the pistol from his still smoking jacket pocket and fired all five of his remaining rounds at point-blank range before Billy could bring his revolver to bear. He couldn't miss; the bullet wounds formed a bloody erratic pattern from Billy's stomach up into his chest. The man had a startled, faraway look in his eyes. His pistol dropped to the floor as he staggered back against the door and slid down onto the floor. Dark blood stains seeped and spread across the linoleum flooring.

Kiefer picked up Billy's pistol and watched him for a minute. He wanted to be damn sure the man was dead. There was no chest movement indicating breath in his lungs, his mouth hung slack, and his eyes were rolled up into their sockets. Finally, Kiefer was satisfied Billy Bones was finished.

Billy's pistol was also a .38 revolver. Kiefer opened the cylinder and shook out the cartridges in his hand, then dropped them into his pocket. He rolled the body slightly onto its side and retrieved Billy's wallet from a hip pocket. It contained a hundred dollars cash, which Kiefer also pocketed. There was a Michigan driver's license, but no other identifying information. He kept the license—it would burn with the rest of his garbage in the morning. He took the wallet and pistol outside and laid them on the seat of his pickup. Then he backed the truck around to the front porch.

He collapsed into his easy chair, shaking fitfully, waiting for the adrenalin to subside. He had survived this test. He suspected there would be more.

It was time for the second part of his plan. Billy was a big man, too heavy to lift, so he dragged him out the front door by his feet. A bright trail of blood followed the body from the living room as Kiefer dragged him to the side of the porch. He dropped the tailgate on the truck; its bed was only a foot or so lower than the porch. Then he stepped into the pickup's bed, grabbed Billy's legs under his knees, and yanked as hard as he could. The body dropped down into the bed, and Billy's head gave a sickening thud when it hit the edge of the tailgate. The weighmaster pulled the body all the way into the pickup's bed, jumped down on the ground, and closed the tailgate. Then he turned on the faucet to a garden hose and washed off all the blood he could see in the glow of the porchlight. The floor inside the house was a mess. He filled a bucket with water, grabbed some rags, and scrubbed it down as best he could. It took two buckets of water and all the rags he could find.

He allowed himself a big swallow of Jim Beam before the next phase of his plan. He drove the short distance north of his house to the R.I.D. canal, turned onto its dirt access road, and traveled about a mile down the dark canal bank. There was no one nearby, no farmhouses in sight. He killed the headlights and turned off the truck's engine. The only sounds were the ticking of the vehicle's engine as it cooled and the soft murmuring of the water flowing past in the canal. The dim glow of stars in the black night barely provided enough light to see by.

 The weighmaster dragged the body out of the truck and dumped it unceremoniously on the ground. Then he stepped up into the truck bed and hefted out two one-hundred-pound tractor wheel weights. He shoved them into position side by side at the edge of the canal's bank, then looped some long lengths of heavy wire cable he had cut earlier through the wheel lug holes in the weights. He strained to drag Billy's corpse onto them. After a little maneuvering, the body was positioned so that one weight was behind Billy's chest and the other at his backside and upper legs. Kiefer looped the cables around the body and tightened them down with some big open-jawed pliers. When all was ready, he sat on his butt beside the body, positioned his feet at each weight, and pushed. The combined weight was probably four hundred pounds, and it took all his strength to move it a few inches. But, after three tries and much grunting, he inched the body close enough to the edge for it to tip over the side of the canal bank and slide down into the water. Its weight and inertia carried it to the bottom at midstream. Kiefer shined his flashlight into the water and was satisfied that the body was well settled onto the bottom. Any random passers-by would not be likely to see it. With luck, it would not be found for many months, maybe even years. Billy's arms moved slowly up and down in the water's current as if waving a final goodbye. He drove a little further along the canal, stopped, and tossed Billy's pistol into the dark water; the wallet went into the water a little further down, before Kiefer reached a crossroad where he could turn around.

One thing left, Kiefer thought. He returned to his house, parked his truck, and hosed the blood off the bed. Then he got into Billy's car, drove it to Perryville, and parked it behind some other vehicles on the side and toward the back of the bar. No one would likely pay it any mind for at least a couple of days. Then he walked back to his house, keeping off the road so as not to be seen, and chucked the car's keys far out into the cotton field he was walking beside. He had a fifty-five-gallon drum behind the shed he used to burn trash. He tossed Billy's driver's license in with the other garbage, poured a little kerosene into it, and tossed in a match.

He was finally able to relax. He set a half-full bottle of Jim Beam and a glass on a side table and settled into his easy chair, trying to make sense of recent events. *How had everything gone so wrong so quickly?* Billy Bones had been a friend of sorts, and he had killed him. *How had it come to that?* His clean and simple operation had come to a screeching halt. Now he faced the likelihood of prison if the cops got him, much worse if the mob got to him first.

He lit a Chesterfield and watched the smoke curling away. *That damn deputy sheriff! This all started because of him,* he thought. *All his snooping and prying. He was like a dog with a bone that refused to give it up. Two men had died trying to silence him. Two! Professional hitmen. Now,* he thought, *it is only a matter of time until they find the Orange Palace, and everything blows wide open. When that happens, I will become a prime target of the police— and the mob. I know too much. My "insurance policy" doesn't mean squat now. They'd probably already gotten to my attorney, anyway.*

The more he drank, the more he focused on the deputy as the cause of his troubles. *Everything was fine until he came along*, he told himself. *He should pay for the trouble he had caused.* The bottle was nearly empty. The last whiskey-fogged thought the Weighmaster had before passing out was that he would make that deputy pay. *If it's the last thing I ever do—I'll make the man pay. Oh, yeah. I'll…*he blacked out and his arm on the table went limp and knocked the bottle over. The remaining few drops of whiskey dribbled out onto the floor.

CHAPTER 17

Sean and Annaleigh met Ricky and his girlfriend Rosa for dinner at a popular steakhouse in Phoenix. It was Saturday night, and the place was crowded. They finally got a table and ordered dinner and a bottle of wine.

Ricky stood up, holding his wine glass high, and said, "A toast to Ricky and Annaleigh's engagement! May you always be happy and have many beautiful children!" They all laughed and clinked glasses as he sat down. Several people seated nearby applauded. Sean, as usual, was embarrassed by the attention.

The couples chatted for a while. When the women went off to the powder room, Ricky said, "I have some information that might be useful. I've talked to several people working in the citrus harvest, and a couple told me about a strange place. They said they could only work there between the hours of ten in the morning and four in the afternoon. One of them said there was a very large house with a bunch of other buildings around it right in the middle of an orange grove. He also said that some of the men there looked like guards, but he had never seen anyone else there. The other odd thing about it, my friend told me, is it has a big, locked gate on the only road in or out of the place, and there was always a guard there." He took a sip of wine and continued, "I've never seen or heard of any place like that. Why would they have guards? And such crazy hours for harvest crews to work. Seems like they must be hiding something."

"Did your friend say where the place is located?"

"Yeah. It's like this." Ricky sketched out a rough map on a paper napkin. "One other thing my friends said," he went on. "They have never seen so many no trespassing signs."

The women returned, and the men changed the subject. They finished their T-bone steak dinners and another bottle of wine before heading home. Sean was sure that the place Ricky described must be the Orange Palace. He would relay the information to the detectives on Monday morning. There had to be a way to get a better look at the place.

***

Monday morning brought chilling news to the group meeting at the district office. The commander came in and said, "I just got off the phone with the sheriff. The man who tried to kill Sean died in the hospital last Friday night. The doctors said the man was recovering after liver surgery and was expected to live. Their examination found a fresh and unexplained needle mark on his neck. They said it was suspicious and speculated that he was injected with poison or a drug that killed him. He's at the county morgue now. The medical examiner will run tests today to try and identify it."

The commander left the room for another telephone call. The men were silent. This was yet another link in a strange chain of events. They had started discussing how the hit in the hospital had happened when the commander returned. He said, "That call was the FBI. They identified the man as Leonard Jones, also known as Lucky Lenny. His last known location was Detroit."

190

Detective Johnson said, "Sounds like the guy's luck ran out."

There were a few quiet chuckles, and the men grew silent. Finally, Sean said, "Why would the Detroit mob send hit men after me? This must somehow be connected to Kiefer and the missing girls."

Then he relayed what he had learned from field workers about the strange citrus grove. "That could be the mysterious Orange Palace we've heard about. Why else would a citrus farm need that kind of security?"

Detective Johnson said they had found something in the county real estate records that was likely related to the same place. "There was a long string of transactions for land planted to citrus groves in the county's west side. A few years ago, one of the shell companies involved transferred a deed to forty acres to a lawyer named Delbert Coburn. His name also appeared on numerous other documents related to various real estate deals. Mr. Coburn died a year or so after that transfer, and the land is now owned by his widow, Mrs. Gertrude Coburn." He paused and lit a cigarette. "The money behind all these deals appears to have come from Detroit. The Phoenix police are trying to get more information on it because the same outfits are buying up land and businesses in the city."

The commander had stayed and listened to the discussion. He said, "It seems clear that all this is somehow connected to Detroit. It can get much more dangerous if the mob senses we are onto them. Sean's close calls show that they will do anything to protect their interests. I want you men to tread carefully with this. I don't want to lose any of you. Focus on getting to the bottom of it. Request any assistance or backup you need."

Johnson said, "If we find out they have taken any of those girls from here to Detroit, the FBI will get into it. That could be the way to break them. Kidnapping, interstate human trafficking, money laundering, and who knows what else. Drugs probably. The FBI has a lot more firepower to throw at it."

"We'll cross that bridge when we get to it," the commander said. "Focus on the leads we have. Let's try to find those girls and run those bastards out of Arizona."

The men spent the rest of the morning plotting their next moves. Sean continued working the area around Perryville for any additional information or clues. He could not locate any of the other families whose daughters were missing. They had moved on to California or possibly elsewhere. A couple of them left notes on bulletin boards in the markets that said what areas they thought they would be in. Sean copied that information and would relay it to the appropriate police in California. That left only the pastor and his wife directly connected to one of the missing girls. He knew they didn't have anything else that would aid their investigation.

Two other deputies were charged with patrolling the area around the suspicious orange grove. The commander hoped the increased attention might put enough pressure on the operation for someone to make a mistake. Sean had his doubts about that. He was impatient to move on the place because time was likely growing short to find the missing girls— if they were there. He had to take action. He called Ricky from a payphone on his lunch break.

"We're getting more information about the orange grove you told me about. The problem is that we can't get into the place without a warrant and don't have grounds yet to get one. I'm going to go in alone, and I need your help."

There was a long silence, then, "*Muy peligroso, amigo.* You could lose your job if you don't get killed first. What do you want me to do?"

"I need you to drop me near the grove, and I'll go in on foot. We can arrange a place to meet when I come out."

"You may need backup, my friend. You sure you don't want me to go in with you?"

"Thanks, but no, Ricky. I don't want to put you in danger. Besides, the Army trained me to do this stuff. I doubt any of those citified thugs are more dangerous than the German soldiers I fought."

"It's your funeral, *hombre.* Tell me how and when you want to do it."

"Tonight. Has to be now. I've scouted the place in daylight and found a place for you to drop me off and pick me up afterward."

Ricky whistled softly into the phone. "Okay, *amigo.* I'll be ready!" He agreed to pick him up at eight p.m.

***

"Come with me, Millie. Madam Trudy has arranged a nice brunch for the two of you" Miss Jennie held the door open and motioned for her to follow. She led her through the big quiet house to the far side and into Madam Trudy's private quarters. Millie had never been to this side of the house, much less inside Madam Trudy's quarters. She could only guess how long she had been there—it felt like at least two weeks, maybe more. They had only allowed her to spend a few brief times in the central area of the big house for brief walks around the room, always during the day, and always with Miss Jeannie or one of the scary guards at her side. The days and nights seemed endless; she had nothing to do. They gave her magazines to read, but they didn't relieve the boredom. Miss Jeannie had assured her that would change soon.

Madam Trudy was seated at a beautiful, blonde-colored dining table with intricately carved legs. Six chairs with similarly carved legs and deep seat cushions were arranged around it. It was the fanciest furniture Milly had ever seen. A large bouquet sat in the center of the table. Ornate silver serving trays held bacon, eggs, and assorted fruits, along with matching services for coffee, orange juice, and milk.

"Come in, my dear," Madam Trudy said. "I'm glad you could join me. Please have a seat."

Millie took the seat she indicated. She was still frightened and nervous; she didn't know what to expect from this woman. Miss Jeannie had been coaching her in some more feminine ways, teaching her the proper manners for the house. But she had never been told what was expected of her.

Madam Trudy said, "Enjoy breakfast while we chat, my dear. Help yourself to whatever you'd like."

Millie felt too nervous to eat. But she took a piece of toast and some orange slices and nibbled a few small bites. She noticed this room, unlike the rest of the building, was not decorated in orange colors. It had a subdued look about it: beige wallpaper with embossed floral designs, and plush light blue carpet. All of it complemented the color of the dining set. A large window cast cheerful morning light in the room.

"This is a big day for you, Lady Millicent," the woman continued. "Graduation day if you will. Everything we've taught you since you've been here was to prepare you for this day. A very special visitor we have been waiting for arrived today. We've been preparing you to meet him. He will be here to see you this evening. After our little chat, I want you to return to your room and relax. Take a nap if you want."

Millie said, "I don't understand. What is it I'm supposed to do?"

"Your special guest has gone out of his way to arrange a visit with you tonight. He may even stay with us for a while. You'll like him. He's a priest, sort of like your father. He has a special lesson just for you. Your only job is to do as he asks. I know you will because you are such a sweet girl."

"I've studied the bible all my life," the girl said. "I can't imagine what he might teach me I haven't already learned."

"Oh, there's much more, dear. But I don't want to spoil the surprise. I simply want you to enjoy and learn from what he has to teach you. I've told him all about you. He's excited to meet you and share your lesson."

They ate in silence. Millie managed to get down a few more bites of the toast, then pushed her plate away.

"Done so soon, my dear?" Millie nodded, and Trudy rang a small bell she had on the table. "Miss Jeannie will take you back to your room. Enjoy your evening. I'll be anxious to hear all about it in the morning.

She watched the girl as she left and chuckled to herself. *Yes, Father McGuire would be incredibly pleased.* Trudy had saved this girl for him, much longer than she usually held a girl back. She knew he would happily pay several times the Palace's regular rate to be with her for a night. *Hell—he might even reserve her for a whole week,* she thought. She was perfect: A plump young virgin from a deeply religious background. The priest's tastes were very erotic and specific. This girl would press all his buttons.

Millie was again locked in her room. Miss Jeannie said she would come back later in the evening with dinner and to help her dress and prepare for her "ceremony."

***

Sean came home from work and started laying out and checking his gear. He took the Colt 1911 apart, then cleaned and oiled it. The .45's action worked smoothly and almost silently. His Ka-Bar Marine combat knife slipped smoothly from its scabbard. He honed the seven-inch carbon steel blade to a razor-sharp edge, applied a thin coat of light oil, and wiped it down before putting it back. The M-2 paratrooper's switchblade knife also worked flawlessly, and Sean cleaned and sharpened it— every paratrooper carried a switchblade to cut himself loose if he became tangled up in the parachute cord after landing. It had been his constant companion during and since the war. The last items were an Army-issue monocular and flashlight with a belt clip he had used for surveillance in the war. He put the gear in a green canvas duffle.

He hoped he wouldn't need any of his weapons, but he was a believer in being prepared for anything. He dressed in a black long-sleeve t-shirt, dark denim jeans, and black boots. Then he carefully applied black grease paint to his face, neck, and ears. Lastly, he pulled a black watch cap onto his head and black leather gloves onto his hands.

Ricky pulled into his driveway at eight on the dot, and Sean went out to meet him. He tossed his duffle in the back seat of his Dodge sedan, then slid into the car's passenger side. Ricky whistled and said, "*Dios mio, hombre*! You look like some kind of haunt. I couldn't see anything but the whites of your eyes when you came out."

Sean laughed. "I hope the guards at this place don't have sharp eyes. Thanks for coming!"

They headed for the orange grove. Sean gave him directions as they got close to the drop-off point. It was about a quarter mile from the Orange Palace's driveway. Sean strapped on his combat belt with the.45 in its holster at his side. The Ka-Bar knife fit at the small of his back, the switchblade went into his pocket, the flashlight clipped to his belt, and the monocular went into a belt pouch.

"*Cuidado, amigo, y buena suerte*!" Ricky said.

"*Hasta luego, amigo*. I need all the luck I can get!" Then Sean disappeared into the night.

He quietly made his way through the trees. A sliver of the waning moon provided dim light, and the mottled pattern of the trees' shadows on the ground provided the perfect cover. The dim glow of lights shone through the trees ahead. He had only seen one guard at the gate as he slipped through the trees toward the lights.

He reached the edge of the Orange Palace's grounds and squatted in the shadow of the trees. The building was much larger than he had imagined, sprawling across the clearing in the trees. It had a massive covered front porch at the entry and a strange orange glow shone from several windows across its front. Sean was beginning to understand why it was called the Orange Palace.

Two men were hanging around a parking area where a new Chrysler and a Triumph Roadster were parked. They were smoking and laughing, not paying any attention to their surroundings. A few minutes later, Sean heard an engine approaching. A Cadillac sedan followed its headlights out of the grove's darkness and parked beside the other cars. Two men got out of the car; Sean studied them through his monocular. They looked to be in their forties or fifties, dressed casually in slacks and open-necked shirts. The two guards greeted them like old friends, and they shared a laugh. Then the two new arrivals went into the house.

Another car arrived shortly after the first. Another Cadillac. Obviously, the place's visitors were well off. The new arrival was only one man. He went through the same routine with the guards before going up the steps to the front door. Sean studied the man in the glow of light on the porch. He looked older than the others, at least sixty. He was dressed in a severe black suit, similar to a preacher's attire. Sean thought he looked out of place; maybe he was a mobster from Detroit.

He circled the rest of the buildings, keeping to the deep shadows. He saw what looked like four guest cottages. Two of them had soft lights in the windows. There were no other guards visible, and he went back to his shadowy hideout in front of the house. He was able to read the license plate numbers on the cars; they were all Arizona registries. He squinted in the dim light as he wrote them down in a small pocket memo book.

***

Miss Jeannie brought Millie's dinner at eight. She sat the tray on the room's two-person dining table and then took a seat. She motioned Millie to the other chair. Jeannie said, "I've brought your favorite for dinner: macaroni and cheese, sweet corn, buttered bread, and chocolate cake for dessert. Don't forget to take your vitamin first. You don't want your tummy to be upset." She smiled at Millie with a big Cheshire cat smile. She waited for Millie to begin her meal and watched her carefully with gold-flecked green eyes. Millie guessed she had once been a beautiful woman, but the stress lines on her face now made her look haggard and worn.

She had learned on her first two nights here that the so-called vitamin pill was anything but. They made her a little groggy, and it was hard to concentrate on anything. She learned to put the tablet in her mouth and push it up under her upper lip and gum, pretending to swallow with a sip of water. Tonight, as always, Miss Jeannie had her open her mouth to be sure she had swallowed the pill. Then she went to the little closet to pull out the clothes Millie was to wear. Millie spit out the pill and tucked it under the elastic band of her panties. She would flush it down the toilet shortly.

Miss Jeannie had taken out a flimsy negligee for her to wear. It was a sheer black lace teddy with tan trim. The neckline plunged provocatively and left little to the imagination. She had made her try it on when she first arrived, and Millie was beyond embarrassed when she saw herself in the mirror. She thought she looked like a racy girl she had once seen in a naughty magazine. Her mother would be shocked to see her dressed that way. Jeannie also set out a pair of black stiletto high heels for her.

Millie said, "I can't wear that! I'm supposed to meet a priest! What would he think, seeing me in something like that? And high heels? I've never worn shoes like that! I don't think I could walk in them."

"I can assure you he won't mind. It's part of his lesson on modesty. Besides, you'll be wearing a robe when you meet him. And you won't be doing much walking," the woman chuckled.

"Well, he will have to give me a good reason to take off the robe!"

"I'm sure he will, dear. Finish your dinner, and let's get you ready."

Millie used the bathroom after her dinner and flushed the pill. Jeannie had laid out the rest of her evening attire on the bed when she came out. It included a very brief pair of lace panties to match the teddy and a lacy robe. Miss Jeannie helped her change into the clothes. Millie put on the high heels and took a couple of unsteady steps.

"There!" Jeannie said. "Now you look like Lady Millicent. Your visitor will be pleased." She gathered up Millie's dinner tray and left. The door gave a distinct click when she locked it.

Millie put on the robe and waited. Minutes felt like hours as she sat on her bed, worried about what was coming. She was nervous and jumpy. She was never allowed to talk to other girls she had seen in the house, but she had a fairly good idea of what they did. If that's what this priest expected from her, she wouldn't cooperate. She didn't care what the consequences might be.

Miss Jeannie opened Millie's bedroom door at nine-thirty and motioned her guest inside. "Lady Millicent," she said, "this is Father McGuire, the man we've told you about. Please make him comfortable." She went out and closed the door. Millie noticed there was no telltale click of the lock turning this time.

The man looked more like an undertaker than a priest to Millie. The only color he wore besides black was a crisp white shirt under his jacket.

He was no longer a priest but always dressed in a dark suit. The church had excommunicated him many years earlier because of perverse sexual conduct with young girls and boys. It didn't report him to the police; as far as the church was concerned, he was dead to them. He still liked to be called "father" because it kept up his front of innocence. A large family inheritance allowed him to mingle in circles with many connections and live a lifestyle far beyond his time in the church. He had learned of Madam Trudy's operation shortly after it began and developed a relationship with her. She learned what he wanted and saved 'special' girls for him. She charged him at least four times her going rate, sometimes more. He was always happy to pay it.

He took off his suitcoat and laid it carefully over a dining chair. He said in a gravelly voice, "I'm delighted to meet you, my dear. I've heard a great deal about you. I'm sure we are going to be close friends!" The man looked ancient to Millie. She thought his face resembled the basset hound belonging to one of her neighbors at home. His droopy eyelids nearly obscured his eyes which were sunken far back under sagging, bushy eyebrows. Wrinkled cheek jowls hung below the corners of his mouth, and his ears sagged like the hounds. She might have laughed if she weren't so scared. His thin lips spread into an evil smile as he began taking off his necktie, shirt, and undershirt. The man was a bag of bones. His ribs were visible, and his wrinkled old breasts hung slack over the top of his rib cage. Millie thought he looked like a grotesque scarecrow—she was ready to run from the apparition standing before her.

Her eyes showed her fear as he sat down beside her. Now she understood why Jeannie had her wearing the sexy lingerie. He patted her shoulder and told her to relax. "I won't hurt you, my dear. I'm just trying to get comfortable. Why don't you take off this robe and get more comfortable, too?" She hesitated, and he reached across her and said, "Here, let me help you," as he slipped the robe off her shoulders. He rubbed her neck and looked at her firm, peach-shaped breasts under the sheer material. "My, aren't you a pretty young thing!" he exclaimed and gave a short, cackling laugh.

"You are supposed to be giving me a religious lesson!" she blurted in a loud voice.

"Oh, I am, I am. You know the story of Adam and Eve, I am sure. This lesson is simply a continuation of what you had learned." He stood and slipped off his slacks, then stood facing her in only his black hose and underwear. His body was repulsive to Millie— folds of skin with a grey, sallow look drooped all over his skinny frame. She looked away.

The man quickly sat down again on the bed and said, "Here, let me show you." He pushed her roughly down and lay across her body. Then his hand slipped below her waist and began to move under the thin band of her underwear. Her body instinctively convulsed, and she pushed him off, but he quickly rolled back on top of her. She had learned from her high school friends how to hurt a boy who got too fresh—she jerked her knee up into his crotch with all the force she could muster. He let out a weird high-pitched scream like a little girl, and she struck out at his face. Her nails peeled skin down his forehead and scratched one eye. He screamed again and rolled off her. He curled into a fetal position, holding his face, and whimpering like a child. She jumped off the bed, grabbed the robe and threw it on, kicked off the high-heeled shoes, and bolted barefoot for the door. The door opened easily, and she shoved it wide open—it seemed like a miracle to her that Jeannie had left the door unlocked. She ran down the hall toward the big main room, hoping and praying the main entrance door would not be locked.

Miss Jeannie had heard the priest's scream and was starting down the hall. Millie stuck her arm out and stiff-armed Jeannie like a running back in a football game dashing for the goal line with the ball. The woman staggered backward and fell over a chair. Millie didn't slow down; she ran as hard as she could for the front door. Madam Trudy sat with two men having drinks at a table near the bar. The men watched Millie streak across the room, frozen in inaction. Madam Trudy jumped up, knocking over her chair, and screamed, "STOP!" Millie ignored her, frantically turned the big front door's brass handle, and ran out into the night.

The two guards outside heard the commotion, unsure of what was happening. They were startled and even more confused when Millie burst out of the front door. Her robe billowed behind her as she flew down the steps and ran fast for the trees and shadows. She didn't know where she was; all she knew was that she had to get away from this place. The two guards had never seen such a sight and were frozen in inaction.

Madam Trudy burst onto the porch and yelled, "Stop, you little bitch! You can't escape!" But Millie had disappeared into the grove's deep shadows. "After her, you idiots!" she yelled at the guards. "Don't come back without her!" The men took off at a hard run toward where they had seen her go into the trees.

***

Sean heard a commotion from inside the house; then, a girl burst out of the big front door and ran down the steps. A flimsy robe was flying behind her, and she was barefoot. The girl ran toward him and down the aisle between the next rows of trees. An older woman dressed in an evening gown rushed out, yelling for her to stop. Then she yelled at the guards to catch her.

Sean knew in an instant that his instincts had been right. This was a brothel where they kidnapped and held young girls—this one was trying to escape! He was on his feet, running in the same direction as the girl. He could hear the two men pursuing her. The bright beams of their flashlights sliced back and forth through the trees' shadows as they searched for the runaway. He heard the girl utter a little scream and fall; she was just ahead and to his right. He knew the guards would be on her quickly.

She got up just as the first guard reached her. He reached out and grabbed her hair, jerking her backward. She screamed again as the man put an arm around her neck to hold her. Sean stepped into the next aisle, came up beside them, and expertly chopped the man in the throat below his left ear. The guard released the girl and collapsed onto the ground. Sean gripped the panicked girl's wrist to hold her and said, "I'm a police officer! I'm here to help. Run in the same direction you were and stop by the road until I get there!"

There was no time to say anything else. The second guard ran up and shined his flashlight on his fallen comrade, then at the retreating girl. A flicker like a shadow moved in his peripheral vision, and Sean stepped in front of him. He hit him at the base of his nose with the palm of his hand, followed by a stiff jab in his solar plexus. The guard exhaled all his air with a loud "whoof" and doubled over. Sean brought his knee up with all his force and caught the man under his chin. His head snapped back, and he fell backward onto the ground, unconscious, with blood running from his nose. Neither guard made a move or a sound. Sean took off running hard as he could in the direction the girl had gone.

He came out onto the road. The girl was nowhere to be seen. He yelled, "I'm a Maricopa County sheriff's deputy. I'm here to get you away from this place. My name is Sean O'Conner. Come with me, and I'll keep you safe!" He heard a slight rustling to his left, and the girl stepped out of the shadows. "Are you hurt?" Sean asked.

"I stepped on a dead tree branch thorn and fell. My foot is bleeding, but I'm all right," she answered.

"I'll help you with that soon. Right now, we need to get you out of here." He grabbed his Army-issue flashlight from his belt and stepped into the middle of the road. He pointed the light toward where Ricky was parked and flashed three short, three long, and three short flashes. He waited a few seconds and repeated the signal. Headlights came on down the road and blinked three times. Then he heard Ricky's car tires crunching on the gravel of the road as it neared.

Sean opened the passenger side door as soon as the car stopped. He helped the girl in, and then he got in beside her. "Turn around and get us out of here, Ricky! Fast! They'll be coming soon!" Ricky had to back up twice and maneuver around in the narrow lane to get the car headed back in the direction they had come. Sean looked out the back and saw a car's headlights emerge in the darkness behind them. "Step on it, Ricky! They're coming!"

They left the graveled farm road and continued back toward town on the main dirt road. Ricky drove faster than was safe and kicked up a massive cloud of dust behind him. Sean could feel Millie shivering beside him on the seat. He reached over and put the car's heater on high speed. "What's your name, miss?" he asked the girl.

"M M Millie," she said through chattering teeth.

Sean was stunned. "Millie? Are you pastor Billings' daughter?"

"Yes! How'd you know? Can you take me to him?"

"We'll get you back to your parents as soon as we can. Right now, we need to keep you safe. We'll take you to a hospital and call your parents. I'm sure they'll be with you soon."

"I want to go home!" Millie protested.

Sean said, "Millie, listen to me. Some terrible people are chasing you right now. They probably know where you and your parents live. It would be the first place they would look for you."

She studied him. "You look scary with that black stuff all over your face. I almost ran from you, too. But there was nowhere to go."

"It's just grease paint so I could blend into the shadows. I was watching the place when you escaped. Do you know if they call that place the Orange Palace?"

She shivered, even with the full blast of the car's heater blowing on her. "That's what they told me. It's a creepy place and full of awful people. They kept me locked in a room and only let me out once in a while to walk around a little bit—but only with a guard.”

 “You can tell us all about it later when you get some rest. Do you know who kidnapped you?”

 “I don’t know his name, but I had seen him before weighing cotton for people working in the fields by our place. I was waiting for my school bus, and he pulled up beside me in a shiny green car. He put a map on the hood and asked if I could find a place for him. I bent over to look, and he stuck me with a needle. I woke up a few hours later in a small shed. The next thing I knew, I was in another car with a hood over my head and my hands tied up. There were two strange men in the car; they took me to the Orange Palace. A woman named Madam Trudy took the hood off my head and talked to me for a minute. Then they took me off to a room and locked me in.” She started crying as the memories washed over her. “I just want my parents,” she sobbed.

 “We’ll get you with them as soon as it’s safe, okay? But we must be careful. We don’t want those people to find you first.”

 She nodded and was quiet.

 Sean said, “Ricky, let’s take her to St. Joseph’s hospital. I’ll call her parents and stay with her until I get more help from the department. Do you have any rags in the trunk I can use to wipe this grease paint off? I don’t want to scare the nurses at the hospital.”

Ricky chuckled. "Yeah, I think you could use a couple of old, sweaty, greasy rags back there. I'll get 'em out when we stop at the hospital." He laughed again and said, "You are a mighty scary-lookin' *hombre*!"

They hit the paved road to Phoenix. Ricky kicked up their speed, weaving around other cars on the street. They pulled into the emergency entrance of the hospital about twenty minutes later. Sean took the rags from Ricky's trunk and wiped off most of the paint. Then he helped Millie inside.

He identified himself as a deputy sheriff and showed the admitting nurse his official ID. "This girl is the victim of kidnapping and abuse. She needs medical assistance. She has a wound on her foot that needs treatment first thing."

The nurse picked up her phone and called for a wheelchair.

Sean said, "I will stay with her until I can get more help here. I need to use your phone to call her parents."

Pastor Billings answered the phone with a groggy and angry-sounding voice. "Who is this? Why are you calling in the middle of the night?"

Sean identified himself. "Pastor, we found your daughter. She is safe."

"You found her? Where is she?" The man had become instantly alert.

"She is at St. Joseph's hospital. I brought her here to be sure she had no injuries. Please come as soon as you can."

"Thank you, deputy. We will be there soon!"

Then Sean called the Sheriff's Department dispatch number. He explained the situation and told them they needed to get two deputies to the hospital as soon as possible.

He asked the nurse to inform him as soon as a doctor had examined Millie and she was taken to a room. There was a chance that her pursuers might figure he had brought her here; he couldn't leave her unguarded. He was prepared to stay as long as necessary until help arrived.

He made one more call, this time to his division commander. He answered with a slight slur, and Sean identified himself. The commander was instantly alert. "This better be good, Sean," he said. "It's almost one a.m."

Sean laid it all out for him. "Sir, I know I'm out on a thin limb with this. But I believe we need men at that place right now. They don't know I rescued the girl yet, but they'll work it out. Unless I miss my guess, they'll figure they have to shut down and get the other girls out of there immediately. They can't afford to be caught with more kidnapped girls, and I suspect there are several there."

The commander considered for a minute. "We will need an emergency warrant to go on the property or stop any vehicles coming out. I'll get a judge out of bed and give it my best shot. In the meantime, you lay low. No one should know you were on that property illegally, even if it was on your own time. You hot-foot it out of that hospital as soon as help arrives. Get some sleep. We'll deal with the rest of this in the morning." He hung up.

Ricky was waiting in the lobby. "Ricky, you need to get out of here. I don't want you involved with this. As far as anyone will know, I acted on my own. I put all my gear back in the duffel bag behind the front seat. I'll get a deputy to drive me to your place later." Sean put his hand on Ricky's shoulder. "Thanks, *amigo*. I couldn't have done this without you."

"*De nada, amigo*. Glad to help. Let me know how things turn out."

Sean thanked him and said he owed him a big one. They shook hands, and Ricky headed for home. Sean went back inside to Millie's room to wait on reinforcements.

CHAPTER 18

Pandemonium ensued at the Orange Palace. Madam Trudy had rousted out her customers and sent them on their way. They came out in various stages of dress: pants unzipped, shirts half buttoned and untucked, hair sticking out as if they had slept without combing it. Some carried suit coats; one man was carrying his lace-up dress shoes. She told them not to stop for anything until they were far away. The defrocked priest was the last one out; he was limping and carrying his shirt and coat in one hand and holding his eye with the other.

Miss Jeannie was running around like a frightened chicken who had just seen the fox, trying to figure out what to do. Obviously, the runaway had not taken the sedative with her dinner; it would have prevented her from escaping. No doubt Madam Trudy would have harsh words for her when things settled down. The guards were milling around, trying to figure out what had happened. They were all jumpy and on edge.

Madam Trudy knew something was seriously wrong when her men found the two guards in the citrus grove. They were out cold. Then the other guards she had sent to find the runaway came back empty-handed. One of them said, "We followed a trail of dust out of the groves but lost the car when it hit the pavement headed toward Phoenix. It's a sure thing somebody picked that girl up and hightailed it out of here."

The woman considered her options. She decided that whoever helped the girl was probably a cop who was in the

right place at the right time. The more she thought, the
more likely it seemed that it was that damn deputy sheriff
that had been a pain in the ass for so long. It had to be a
man with some serious capabilities to take out those two
men in the grove the way he had. One guard's nose was
broken and still gushing blood. He had been knocked out
by a man he said looked like a shadow within the shadows.
He couldn't describe anything about him. The other guard
said he had neither seen nor heard whoever hit him. Madam
Trudy figured those were the kind of capabilities a man
would learn as a commando in the Army. It also seemed
possible that the cops may have the operation under
surveillance. That raised all kinds of distasteful
possibilities.

To make matters worse, Billy Bones had not returned from
the assignment she had given him. *Could Kiefer have
somehow overpowered Billy*? She doubted that. Billy had
too much experience. Kiefer was nothing but a country
bumpkin. Still, she had a nagging feeling in the pit of her
stomach that something had gone horribly wrong. Right
now, she couldn't worry about it. She would have to get
one of the other men to help her with her next moves.

She had always had a plan for something like this.
Arrangements had been made a long time ago to evacuate
her girls and staff to a hotel in Phoenix that belonged to the
organization. It would accommodate her even if they had to
kick some customers out of their rooms. She could keep
them there until it was safe to move them out of state. She
would simply shut down the Orange Palace. Tell the police
it was a private lodge for travelers. She would have to

assign some men to act quickly to remove all evidence of the girls being there. It would be hit or miss whether they would be successful.

She had to move fast. If they moved quickly, they could have the evidence out before the cops showed up. She called everyone together and told them what she wanted them to do. Then she called the hotel and told them to be ready. The cops were likely to show up first thing in the morning. Hopefully, all they would find is a well-furnished but vacant building.

***

The commander had rousted out a grumpy judge at his home in Phoenix. He told him that one of his deputies on patrol had found one of the kidnapped girls and there were likely several more at the property she had escaped. He said they had to move quickly before the kidnappers could move them elsewhere. The judge said he understood the urgency and signed the search warrant.

The commander called dispatch and instructed that every available deputy in the county be sent to the location he provided. They were to stop any vehicle they found in the vicinity and wait for further instructions. He took the warrant and headed at top speed for the Orange Palace. He silently hoped Sean was right. This would be great on his record, maybe even a step up into headquarters. He hit the unpaved road and had to slow down. It was hard to see the edges of the road in the darkness outside his headlights' high beams—it wouldn't do for the district commander to wind up in a canal or irrigation ditch alongside the road.

The sun was just breaking through the early morning twilight as he pulled up to the gate across the lane to the Orange Palace. Tiny drops of dew on the treetops' leaves glistened like crystals caught in the first rays of sunlight. Deep shadows still hung stubbornly in the rows of trees.

The commander pulled the half dozen deputies already gathered there together and told them what to expect. He said, "Be prepared for heavy resistance, men. We think this outfit is connected to a big-time mob outfit in Detroit, and they may put up a fight. Remember, there are likely to be several innocent women here. We want everyone to come out of this alive. One of you stay here at the gate. The other patrol along the road. When more deputies get here, tell them to patrol the perimeter of this grove. I don't want anyone making a breakout from the trees. Don't let anyone leave. We'll stay in contact by radio." He got in his car and led the others down the lane to the big house.

Three sheriff's department vehicles came to a sliding stop in front of the main house. One car loaded with people roared out from behind the house before any of the deputies were out of their cars. It veered around the nearest deputy's vehicle and made a beeline for the road. The commander radioed to the deputy at the gate to be ready.

The police cars' high beam headlights lit up the front of the house. There were two more cars parked there, with several men scurrying around. One of them stopped, pulled out a pistol, and fired at the nearest police car. The deputies all took cover behind their cars.

The commander got out his trumpet shaped megaphone and called out, "Attention. This is the police. This place and the surrounding property are surrounded by sheriff's deputies. Come out peaceably with your hands above your heads!" No response. He tried again, "Come out now. We don't want anyone hurt here. Put down your weapons and come out now!"

Another shot ricocheted off his patrol car in answer. *Aw crap*, he thought. *It was going to be a standoff.* He needed to find a way to end it; the chance of a stray bullet striking an innocent person inside was too great.

Then the front door opened, and a woman came out on the porch. She had her hands above her head, and the commander told his men to hold their fire. She was visibly shaking, looked around, and then said loudly, "My name is Miss Jeannie. We don't want any more trouble. Let us leave, and you'll never see us again."

"You know we can't do that," the commander said into the bullhorn. "Send out the girls you are keeping in there! They are innocent. We don't want them hurt!" The woman turned on her heel and went back inside. *Damn it*, he thought. *Now it's a hostage situation.*

One of the deputies yelled, "Hey, there's movement in the trees behind the house! It looks like they are trying to make a break for it on foot!"

The lights went out, but it was apparent what was happening. The commander put out a radio alert to all cars to be alert for people coming out of the grove on foot. He told them to use extreme caution and to get back up if they spotted any of them —the escapees were armed.

***

The seven remaining girls were all huddled in the great room. They were in various stages of undress. Madam Trudy had left Miss Jeannie to deal with the girls and the police. She said, "Don't worry. Get the girls into their old clothes. Pretend you are one of them and keep your mouth shut. I'll make arrangements for you as soon as things die down. You can let the cops in as soon as I'm gone. You'll be fine." Then she slipped out a back door with one of the guards.

The rest of the guards followed behind them, and they all went in different directions into the orange grove. Madam Trudy had told them to stay hidden and watch for a chance to move out into the adjoining citrus fields. She promised to send someone for them soon.

Trudy had quickly dressed in jeans, a dark blouse, and low-heeled shoes. She had planned for this eventuality, too. She led Marvin 'the Mole' down a specific row of trees. He was Billy's second in command since Fast Eddie bought it. She knew the guard was competent with a gun and dependable, but he was dumb as a box of rocks. He would have to do until she found out what happened to Billy. They moved cautiously and slowly forward in the still, deep shadows. The couple covered an eighth of a mile through the trees to the farm road in about ten minutes. They crouched down in the rapidly disappearing shadow of the trees and watched carefully for any searching police. A patrol car came by a couple of minutes later, moving slowly, its searchlight stabbing through the trees. They huddled further back until it passed.

"Quick, now!" Madam Trudy said. "It's only a quarter mile to the next farm's headquarters. I have a car stored under cover there." It was the headquarters for all the organization's farming interests in this area. "We'll get out of this if we're careful," she said. They crossed the road and walked on, moving faster now. She needed to get far away as fast as they could without drawing notice.

***

Miss Jeannie stepped back onto the porch. She now had on jeans and a white blouse. She called out, "You can come in now," and waved the police toward the house.

The commander and his deputies moved forward cautiously, guns drawn, carefully watching windows and shadows around the house. Jeannie stood waiting for them. When the commander stepped onto the porch she said, "I'm called Miss Jeannie. There is no one here but me and seven other girls. Come in, and I'll introduce you."

He moved into the room, followed by two deputies. He motioned the others to guard the front. He told the deputies to search the house and keep their weapons drawn. Then he introduced himself to the huddled girls and asked their names and where they were from. They were all young, early teens, and seemed to be disoriented. They each gave their name and where they had last lived. All but one had been kidnapped from areas where their families were picking cotton; the clothes they were wearing now were what they wore when they were taken. They had no idea where their families were.

  He told them to relax and wait; he would get them all out and back to their parents soon. Then he went to his car and told dispatch to send the county prisoner bus to transport them. He would have them sent to the county hospital for examination and kept under guard until the department could figure out what to do with them.

  The deputies searched all the buildings and immediate grounds and reported that there was no one else there. The commander kept one deputy with him to help guard the girls and sent the others to patrol the area. He was sure the big fish of this operation had to be nearby. He called for more reinforcements and canine officers. They would find whoever was hiding among the orange trees.

CHAPTER 19

Miss Jeannie was booked into the county jail on suspicion of human trafficking and prostitution. She had refused to answer any of their questions and repeatedly asked for her lawyer. It was obvious she had been well briefed on what to do in this situation.

Deputies captured three of the guards in the citrus groves. One of them was wounded after exchanging shots with two deputies and was sent to the county hospital. The other two were booked into county jail under various charges: resisting arrest, carrying concealed weapons, and aiding and abetting human trafficking and prostitution. They all requested lawyers and refused to answer questions.

Information from the girls indicated there had been at least six guards at the Orange Palace. The whereabouts of the other three were unknown, and the search of the area continued. An alert was issued to all local police departments to be on the lookout for them.

Doctors examined the girls at the hospital; all were traumatized and suffering from disorientation, but otherwise in good health. It seemed they had been kept under the influence of some narcotic to keep them docile. After questioning, the girls were placed in a local facility run by the county's social services. Deputies were scheduled to be on guard duty twenty-four hours a day while social services workers tried to locate the girls' families. In the meantime, they were being provided intensive counseling after their ordeal. It would take several days to help them overcome the effects of the drugs they had been given at the Orange Palace.

The one piece of hard information the girls could provide was their kidnapper's identity. Several of them remembered his name when their heads cleared a little from the drugs. All but one described the same circumstances that led to their kidnapping: working in the cotton fields, a friendly man who weighed their cotton sacks and paid them at the end of the day, a chance meeting outside a little grocery store in Perryville, a promise of some nice clothes left by his deceased daughter, and the sharp prick of a needle in their neck. The other girl had been lured into the kidnapper's car off a street in Phoenix. After that, it was all a drug-hazed blur that continued after they arrived at the Orange Palace. Without exception, the six girls taken at Perryville identified their kidnapper as a man they knew only as Mr. Kiefer, the weighmaster.

Then there was the matter of the woman the girls called "Madam Trudy." She was the head of the operation. It was as if she had vanished into thin air. The deputies figured she must have had a car stashed somewhere else and an escape plan already in place. They would undoubtedly have found her if she were on foot.

There wasn't much else known about her. None of the girls had ever heard her called anything but Madam Trudy. Her real name was unknown, but they gave the police a good description of her. The sheriff's department put out an all-points bulletin for her arrest, but they weren't optimistic about finding her—she could have easily disguised herself after escaping the raid. The police figured that she was holed up somewhere locally, possibly in Phoenix, and she was waiting for her mob connections to get her out of state.

***

The weighmaster was up early, as usual. He switched his radio to KOY out of Phoenix for the local news and farm report, made his coffee, and smoked a couple of Chesterfields while he fried up a breakfast of fried eggs and sugar-cured ham with a slice of sourdough toast. It would be his last meal in his home—Jimmy the used furniture dealer was coming later that day to load up all the house furnishings; Jimmy had paid him for it earlier. Kiefer planned to hole up in a motel for a couple of days to wrap up his business before disappearing to Mexico. He was sipping hot coffee when a news bulletin caused him to spill it down his front. He cursed and turned up the radio. There had been a significant police action on the county's west side overnight. Details were sketchy. The announcer was excitedly talking about a police raid in some citrus groves and some rescued girls. It could mean only one thing— they raided the Orange Palace.

The police would come for him soon, he thought. *Maybe they were already on their way*. He left his breakfast sitting on the table and ran from his house to the barn, moved the bales of hay that concealed his hiding place, and grabbed the suitcase containing his money. Racing back to his truck, he tossed the bag on the seat, then ran into the house to get his big suitcase. He had packed it for this emergency—a 'go' bag with clothes and a few important documents. It

223

went into the bed of his pickup. His snub nose .38 Police Special lay in its holster on the table. He grabbed it and two boxes of ammunition and put them in a small duffel bag. Then he got his old Winchester .30-30 lever action rifle and a box of shells out of the closet. Both guns went into the cab of the truck. Finally, he tossed a cot, some blankets, and assorted camping gear into the pickup's bed.

He jumped in the Dodge's cab, fired up the six-cylinder engine, threw it into gear, and kicked dirt all over the side of his house as he spun around and took off out of his driveway. Then he drove to Litchfield Park and parked across the street from the Valley National Bank's office. As soon as it opened, he retrieved all his remaining money and his now useless "insurance" letter from his safe deposit box. Then he headed west, away from Perryville and, he hoped, away from any lawmen looking for him.

The weighmaster knew he needed a place to hole up for a few days—someplace the cops wouldn't look for him. Maybe, more importantly, someplace the Detroit bunch couldn't find him. If the Orange Palace operation was busted, his tenuous insurance policy with Madam Trudy would be worthless. They couldn't afford to let him live. He knew far too much.

He had a score to settle before he ran to Mexico. That deputy had brought him to this, and he would make him pay. He stopped at a gas station in Buckeye and used a payphone to call a number in Los Angeles. A gruff voice answered.

"This is Kiefer. I have a job for you in Phoenix. Name your price."

The line was silent for a long thirty seconds. Then, "What kind of job?"

"Cop," came the answer.

More silence. "I don't do that kind of work."

"Name your price. Do this for me, and you'll never hear from me again. We'll be even."

Finally, the man said, "Three grand cash plus expenses. You be my leg man to set it up. But it's going to be a couple of weeks before I can do it. I have a contract for a job on the east coast to take care of first."

It was double what Kiefer anticipated. But he had the money, and he wanted this. Wanted this more than anything he had ever wanted. Kiefer agreed, silently cursing the two-week delay under his breath.

He knew of an old, abandoned rock house a few miles off Highway 80 between Buckeye and Gila Bend. It was about a mile off the dirt road that led to a small settlement called Tonopah. An old prospector had told him that he stayed there years ago when he was in that area. It was out in a godforsaken stretch of desert about twenty miles west of Buckeye. A rough dirt track was the only way to get to it, and there wasn't much when you arrived—an old crumbling stone house, empty for many years. It was unlikely anyone would ever look for him there.

A little general store at the bridge over the Hassayampa River sat at the turnoff for the road to Tonopah. It had some basic supplies, and he bought enough to last two or three weeks. He didn't need much, figuring to only stay there until his business with his associate from Los Angeles was finished.

He drove to the deserted stone house and parked behind it. It would provide further protection by shielding his truck from the view of any traffic on the main road. He unfolded the cot inside the house and tossed a couple of blankets on it. The house had no window glass or doors, and the night breeze would cut right through it. He would need the blankets.

***

The district commander met with Sean, the two detectives, and two other deputies to decide on their next steps. Detective Johnson spoke up first.

"We're working with the Phoenix Police's intelligence section to find more information about the woman known as Madam Trudy. There are some leads related to real estate transactions with her. We believe her real name is Gertrude Coburn. Her last husband was a well-known attorney, and it appears his main client was the Detroit mob. He handled all their real estate transactions. She inherited the forty-acre parcel of orange trees when he died, then established the so-called Orange Palace. We're trying to identify any other connections she may have here or any other property she may own."

"That's good work, men," the commander said. "Tracking down that woman is your number one priority. I want you to coordinate with the police in Detroit, too. I will authorize travel for you as needed." He turned to Sean and said, "What do you have, deputy? Any new information about Kiefer? Anything on his whereabouts?"

"Nothing new, sir. We now have a warrant for his arrest—the two deputies who were dispatched to arrest him earlier this morning reported there was no sign of him at his house. With your permission, I would like to do another search of his property."

"Make it your priority, deputy."

"Yes, sir. Do I need another warrant to search the property again?"

"The arrest warrant is all we need," the commander replied. "I want daily reports on your progress." He turned to the other deputies in the room and said, "I want you two to stay on top of the Orange Palace. One of you keep any "looky-loos" out and help the forensics team who will be working there with anything they might need. The other can patrol the property and keep searching for the three missing guards. They may yet turn up if they've been hiding out in the groves."

The meeting adjourned, and Sean immediately headed for the weighmaster's house. The front door to the house was standing wide open when he arrived. Kiefer had clearly left in a hurry—what appeared to be the remains of a breakfast meal were moldering in the kitchen sink. Sean hoped that he might have left something important behind. All the furniture was gone; not even a stray fork or spoon remained. He carefully went through each room in the house, shining his flashlight into corners, cabinets, and closets. His light picked up something white back in the far corner of the closet shelf in the main bedroom. He had to stand on tiptoe and stretch to reach it. It was an envelope, and one corner of it was stuck in the crack between the shelf and the wall. Sean gently tugged it loose and moved into a better light to look at it. There was nothing printed on the outside, and it was not sealed. Inside, he found what appeared to be a bank statement from Mexico. The letterhead on the statement said Banco Nacional de Guaymas. It showed several entries over a period of about a year; each entry was a different amount. Sean hoped this might be a clue to where Kiefer had gone. He put it in an evidence bag and placed it in the glove box of his patrol car.

His detailed search of the rest of the property didn't yield any other clues. The farm equipment and tools he had seen before were still there. That seemed curious to him because everything else had been hurriedly cleaned out. Maybe Kiefer still had some business to transact with the property. He would alert the detectives to follow up on that.

Sean went back to Perryville. There were not many transient workers left since the cotton harvest wound down. Most had moved on. He pulled up to the Chevron gas station's pumps, where the department maintained an account.

Willie Jones, the attendant, said, "Fill 'er up, deputy?"

"Yep. Check under the hood for me, too. And I think that right rear tire's a little low."

"You got it, Sean!" Willie was like a whirlwind. He started the pump filling the tank with gas, cleaned all the car's windows, checked all the tires' air pressure, and added a little to the right rear. Then he popped the hood and checked the oil and radiator water, tested the belts, and closed it up. By then, the car's fuel tank was full. He wrote down the total gas sale and took it inside to the owner.

Sean had gone inside to talk to Herb, the owner. He was like rumor central in that part of the county. You could almost see the wheels turning in his mind when he picked up some juicy tidbit, thinking about how he could get the most mileage from it. He chain-smoked Pall Mall cigarettes, and the ashtray beside the cash register on the counter was always overflowing. The little station lobby was a favorite gathering place for locals. They could buy a soda, maybe a bag of peanuts, or a candy bar, and pass the time with their neighbors gossiping and talking about farm prices and the news of the day. Herb would soak up all the useful topics of conversation and continually add them to other conversations throughout his business day. He also owned the pool hall next door, which could be accessed through the station's lobby. There were two pool tables and a snooker table. A hand-painted sign on the wall said "POOL 10 CENTS A GAME, SNOOKER 15 CENTS A GAME. There were a couple of pinball machines against one wall, a nickel per game.

Herb was quite the real estate tycoon in Perryville. He owned the large, long red brick building, which constituted the entire business section on the south side of the village's only street. It contained not only his service station, garage, and pool hall but also included a grocery market on the far end of the gas station. He had a home behind the main building and owned other properties nearby.

Sean signed the chit to charge the gas to the department's account, and Herb said, "Been a lot of deputies running around this neck of the woods lately. What's going on?"

"Well, you probably heard there was a raid on a brothel up north of here. We're still looking for three men who were guards there. I doubt they would have come this far south, but we're checking all possibilities."

Herb whistled and said, "I hadn't heard that! Hope you catch 'em soon!"

"I'm looking for James Kiefer. Have you seen him around lately?"

The owner rubbed his chin and said, "Probably been three, maybe four days since I saw him pass through. Seems like he might have picked up stakes and followed the field hands to California. In fact, Buster Mason was in here the other day and said Kiefer had finally agreed to sell him his house and forty acres. Now I think about it, he mentioned him going to California, too."

Sean prepared to leave, and Herb said, "Oh, one more thing. Jimmy, that junk dealer from Buckeye, stopped by a couple of hours ago. He had a load of furniture and other stuff which filled his pickup truck's bed and a slat-sided trailer he towed behind it. He said Kiefer sold the whole house full of stuff to him because he was leaving the state."

Sean nodded and thanked him for the information. He asked him to contact the district office if he got any more information.

"Say," Herb said before Sean was out the door. "Why are you so interested in Kiefer? What's he done, anyway?"

"He's a person of interest in our investigation of the brothel we just closed down." He waved goodbye, got in his patrol car, and left.

Herb's eyes widened, and he rubbed his chin. *My, my,* he thought. *This will have tongues wagging for days. It's gonna be great for business.* He opened a fresh pack of Pall Malls and went about restocking his assortment of snacks on the counter and sodas in the cooler.

***

Sean called Ricky when he got back to the office and asked him to meet him for a beer at the Wishing Well bar after work. It was usually a quiet spot for beer and conversation. They got a booth away from any other customers.

Sean took the Mexican bank document from its envelope and slid it across the table to Ricky. "I can't read enough Spanish to understand this," he said. "What do you make of it?"

Ricky studied it for a couple of minutes. "Well, it's a statement from a bank in Guaymas. This account name seems strange. Robert Robertson. Sounds made up to me. And it's a post office box address in Phoenix. These numbers are in pesos, but it's some significant money. Probably from some kind of business. Where did you get it?" he asked as he slid it back to Sean.

"I found it stuck way back on a closet shelf inside the house of the guy we're investigating. Everything in the house had been cleared out, but they missed this. It was hard to see in a dark corner high up in the closet."

"So, you think your guy has some kind of business connection in Mexico and maybe skipped out to go there?"

"I don't know," Sean said. "Everything I've learned so far says he went to California. That seems likely, given the kind of work the guy did. But he's a slippery one. The California rumor could be a smoke screen."

"Yeah, with all the stuff you want him for, it might be too risky to go to California. He'd know it's the first place you'd look."

Sean agreed. "The more I think about it, the more I believe he would have gone to Mexico. This bank statement looks like he has connections there. It would be a lot safer for him than California!"

They talked about Guaymas for a while. Ricky said he was only there once, visiting family a long time ago.

"Do you still have family there?" Sean asked.

“I think they’re still there. They were my father’s first cousins. I could find out if you want me to.”

“If you don’t mind, I’d appreciate it. I don’t know where all this is headed. But it’s possible this Mexico connection could be important.”

“I’ll ask my father about it tonight.”

They finished their beers, talking and laughing about the old times they had together.

CHAPTER 20

Miss Jeannie called the attorney who represented Madam Trudy. She knew him from his many visits to the Orange Palace and had even entertained him a few times herself. He liked that she was more sophisticated than the other girls. He had long ago given her his business card. "Call me anytime," he said. "I'd be happy to help you." He was at the jail at nine a.m. the next day. He spent over an hour with her going over what had happened. He had not yet learned of the raid. He wondered why he hadn't heard from Madam Trudy and assumed she went into hiding somewhere.

He laid out the options for his client. "First, drop the nickname. From now on, use your given name. You want to present an innocent, lady-like presence. I'll have some suitable clothes brought in for you before you have a hearing. Second, the charges they have against you are very serious. It's likely that information from the girls they have in custody will implicate you deeply in what went on at the Palace. I recommend a plea deal. You can probably get the charges greatly reduced if you agree to provide them with the information they want."

"But what about the Detroit people? Won't they come after me if I do that?" she asked.

"I don't think so. There are too many corroborating witnesses with the girls. They wouldn't gain anything by coming for you. It would likely bring that much more heat down on them. Also, the police will no doubt offer you protection if you testify."

They talked a while longer. She took a deep breath and said, "Okay. See if they will do it. But only on the condition that they reduce my charges and guarantee to protect me after I testify."

The lawyer left the room to see what he could negotiate with the county attorney. He came back in an hour with a deal for her, which she readily accepted.

She was now known as Jean Hatcher, her given name. She had agreed to reduced charges which kept her out of prison, in return for helping them with the investigation. The police agreed to provide her with a new identity and place to live for her protection. She proved to be a deep well of information for them.

The sheriff's department brought in two members of the Phoenix Police's intelligence group to assist with the questioning. She told them she had been one of Madam Trudy's first attractions at the Orange Palace, but after a year or so, she became her assistant in grooming and managing new girls. She rarely provided any other services except for a couple of important men from Detroit who valued her experience over youth.

It seemed the questions might never end:

"This woman you call Madam Trudy – do you know her real name?"

"I have heard her called Gertrude, but nothing else."

"What do you know about connections in Detroit?

"I know they are very important business partners with Madam Trudy and that many of the girls were sent there to work for them after spending time at the Orange Palace."

"Do you know the names of the girls who were sent to Detroit?"

"I can make a list of those I can remember. There were quite a few over the years."

"Do you know the names of the men from Detroit?"

"I only know nicknames, like Johnny O, Billy Bones, and a few others."

"Do you know a man named Jim Kiefer?"

This last question opened the floodgates. Yes, she knew him well. Yes, he supplied all the girls. Yes, he kidnapped them. It went on for two hours as the detectives dug deeper into how the local operation worked. She told them Kiefer worked in the cotton fields with transient workers, where he found most of the girls he supplied to the Orange Palace. He used drugs to subdue them, and Madam Trudy arranged to have them brought to the Palace. They asked where the drugs came from—she readily identified Doctor Biggs and his location in Phoenix; she said she only saw him when he came to the Orange Palace for business.

The Phoenix Police quickly made connections between the information they had and the information the woman supplied. They contacted the Detroit police and began a coordinated effort to identify the players in the mob there. The FBI was brought in and began collaborating with them to develop a case for interstate kidnapping and human trafficking. Dr. Biggs' office was closed, and his whereabouts were unknown.

***

Madam Trudy, aka Gertrude Coburn, caught the first train out of Phoenix after the raid on the Orange Palace. She made her way to Detroit, where she had an apartment she had owned for many years. It was a far cry from the opulence of the Orange Palace, but it would have to do. At least for now. She still had connections here, and she would start over. Her bank accounts had grown fat over the years with tax-free income thanks to Johnny O allowing her to funnel money from the prostitution operation through a couple of his shell companies.

Johnny O had seemed sympathetic. He was sorry to lose the lucrative Arizona enterprise, but he had many others. But a couple of supportive phone calls were as far as it had gone since she had been back in the city. There was always some reason they hadn't been able to get together: travel, business meetings, and myriad other things seemed always to be in the way. She hoped it wasn't a bad sign.

Johnny called her one afternoon and asked if she was free for dinner that evening. She was thrilled and quickly accepted. He said he'd send a car to pick her up at six and bring her to his place. She smiled at her reflection in a mirror. *At last*, she thought. *Maybe things are turning around. Time to get busy*!

237

The knock on her door came at precisely six o'clock. Johnny had always prided himself on punctuality for himself and those who worked for him. She'd managed a last-minute appointment with her hairdresser and was dressed in her best evening gown and jewelry. One more check of her makeup and hair in her entry mirror and she thought, *Johnny O will be pleased with what he sees*! Then she opened the door.

A man she'd never seen before stood in the doorway. He certainly didn't look like Johnny's regular chauffeur, and she started to ask who he was, but he quickly gave her a hard shove back through the doorway before she could speak. She stumbled and caught herself against the wall. Her mouth opened for a scream that never came— the man raised a suppressed .22 caliber pistol and fired three shots point blank into her head. The shooter placed his first shot through her left eye. She died instantly. The other shots were insurance— the shooter's signature style. The woman once known as Madam Trudy lay in a tangled heap on the floor. The hitman quietly closed the door and left.

One more loose end Johnny O didn't have to worry about.

***

The detectives met at the district office with the commander, Sean, and the two other deputies who engaged in the search for the missing men from the Orange Palace. They huddled around the small table in the district office's conference room. Several of them smoked, and the air was quickly becoming hazy. Like most smokers, when someone nearby lit up, the others would too. Two big brown glass

238

ashtrays on the table rapidly filled with ashes and cigarette butts.

Detective Johnson opened the discussion. "A deputy caught one of the guards hitchhiking toward Phoenix yesterday. He didn't put up a fight and readily gave up his weapon to the deputy who arrested him. We have accounted for the other two men based on information from the woman arrested at the Orange Palace." He paused to light another cigarette. One of the men had finally opened the small high window in the room, and a puff of fresh air stirred the cloud of smoke slightly. Johnson continued, "One of them, another Detroit mobster and hitman named Billy, was presumed dead. Madam Trudy had sent him on a mission of some kind to Kiefer's place, and he never returned. The remaining guard helped Madam Trudy escape and was likely now back in Detroit."

Sean asked, "Are they sure the guy they sent to Kiefer's place didn't just hightail it back east?"

"We don't have any other information about him," Johnson replied.

"You know," Sean said, "the last time I was at Kiefer's house, I noticed some faint blood stains on the porch. Maybe, if he was sent to kill Kiefer, he had turned the tables on the guy." He paused a minute and added, "Another curious thing – we found an abandoned car parked outside the Perryville bar. It had stolen license plates and no registration documents. It might be worth a search for fingerprints. It's in the county impound lot right now."

"We'll do that," the detective replied. "But here's the most interesting news I have for you—The real name of the woman we knew as Madam Trudy was Gertrude Coburn." He had a sly grin and paused for effect. "The Detroit police department found her name as the registered owner of an apartment there. They went to investigate and found her dead just inside the apartment's door. She had three small caliber bullet holes in her head and had been dead for several days."

One of the deputies gave a low whistle. "Guess that settles that!" he exclaimed.

The commander asked, "What about the Orange Palace property? Are there any other owners or heirs?"

"Unknown at this time, sir." Detective Johnson replied. "There were no other owners of record on the deeds. We're working with Detroit to try and locate any next of kin."

"What's being done to find Kiefer?" Sean asked.

Johnson said, "The FBI has joined the investigation because of the interstate kidnapping charges. They will likely take over the main effort, with us supporting them as needed. They'll be contacting you shortly for a briefing."

"Aw, hell," one of the deputies said. "They'll never find that guy. He's long gone."

The commander looked at Sean. "You have some new information about him, Sean. Lay it out."

Sean described how the weighmaster's furniture had been cleaned out. "He sold it all to a second-hand dealer in Buckeye. Even the Pontiac was gone. He's probably driving that. It seemed to be his pride and joy, and I can't imagine him selling it. I also found out he made a deal to sell the place to a local farmer. He told the farmer and the furniture dealer he was moving to California, and no one has seen him around for several days."

"We'll alert the California State Police to be on the lookout for both the green Pontiac and his Dodge pickup truck," the commander said, but we may have been too late to catch him at the border. Tell us about the Mexico thing, Sean."

Sean laid the envelope on the table and took out the document. "I found this stuck in the back corner of a closet in his house after it was cleaned out." He passed it to the detectives. They looked at it and asked what he knew about it.

"I had a Spanish-speaking friend look at it. It is what it looks like—a statement from a bank in Guaymas, Mexico. There is an account number under the suspicious-sounding name of Robert Robertson showing regular deposits from a business in Guaymas. The numbers are in pesos; they are large dollar amounts if you calculate it from pesos."

The detectives studied it for a couple of minutes. Johnson asked, "Do you think Kiefer has a business there?"

"I have no way of knowing. But I suspect he must have. Otherwise, why would he have had this bank statement?"

The commander said, "It's one more unknown for the present. Right now, let's focus on the California angle. That seems the most likely place for him to have gone."

Sean wasn't so sure. But he kept it to himself. The rest of the meeting centered on dealing with the FBI and continuing clean-up work at the Orange Palace. Sean kept the mysterious Mexican bank statement.

CHAPTER 21

Sean moved back to his own house; there was no need to hide out any longer. He was of no importance to the Detroit mob now. The police had gotten all the information they needed from the girls they rescued at the Orange Palace. Miss Jeannie, aka Jean Hatch, was a wealth of information. The only wild card now was the weighmaster. Sean figured he was far away from Maricopa County. Probably gone from Arizona. Most likely in Mexico. He wouldn't risk a move against Sean now. Besides, what would he gain from it? The police knew all there was to know about his role as a kidnapper. He would spend the rest of his life in jail if they caught him, maybe even face the death penalty. *No,* Sean thought. *He's long gone and will probably stay that way.*

It felt good to be back at his place. Sarge was happy, too. He ran around the house like a kid on Christmas morning. Sean played with him, tossing a rubber bone for the dog to chase, and laughed at the dog sliding around on the slippery tile floor as he tried to stop. Annaleigh was coming later that day to help him 'put the house in order,' as she described it. Sean knew that meant a bunch of house cleaning was going to be the order of the weekend. It would be good to be out from under the strain and worry over the Orange Palace investigation. They could relax while they cleaned the house and talked about their wedding plans.

Starting Monday, Sean was going to cover a night shift for another deputy who was ill with pneumonia. It would be his first. He made another pot of coffee before he began his

243

shift that evening and hoped it would keep him alert through the night. As it turned out, that wasn't to be a big concern.

Working nights was an altogether different thing than day shifts. The nighttime brought out a different, edgier side of people and a lot more drunk drivers on the road late at night. Sean had to haul in two men who had been so drunk when he stopped them that they could barely stand when they got out of their cars. They had been weaving all over the road, a hazard to themselves and anyone else they met. Both men were argumentative, but they were too drunk to put up much resistance when he put them in the back of his car. They argued noisily with each other on the ride to the district office, where Sean booked them into the drunk tank. He was glad to unload the unruly passengers and called for a wrecker to impound their cars.

The second night he spotted one of the more affluent farmers in the area driving very slowly, his Cadillac weaving across the center line. Sean turned on his lights, but the man ignored him and kept going. The drunk barely missed the ditch running alongside the highway as he turned into the driveway to his farmhouse. He parked at an angle to his carport and was trying to make his way up the steps when Sean caught up to him. The porch light came on, and the man's wife came out and started screaming at Sean. He stayed calm and explained to the woman what had happened.

"Well, you ain't takin' him in," she yelled with a thick southern drawl. "He's on his own private propity right here, and I ain't lettin' you take him!"

Sean said, "Ma'am, I could take you in along with him, but I don't want to do that. How about this?" The woman stopped yelling and listened. "If you guarantee to keep him home till he sobers up, I'll let him stay, on condition I write him a citation for drunk driving. He'll have to appear in court and pay a fine. But it will keep him out of jail, and I won't impound his car."

"Y'all think you kin take me in, too?"

This woman is just being belligerent, Sean thought.

"Ma'am, I don't want to prove to you that I can. I'll call for reinforcements if you force me to. I will give you one chance to settle down, or we're going to find out."

"No jail?" she asked.

"If you do as I told you, I will only write a citation. He will have to sign it, and you will have to get him settled in the house while I wait outside to make sure you do."

She reluctantly agreed. "Wait here while I make out this citation." He finished it and told the drunk farmer to sign where he showed him. His wife was supporting him to keep him from falling off their porch, and she steadied him so he could scrawl a barely legible signature using Sean's pen. Sean gave his copy to the wife and showed her the date he needed to be in court. Then he said, "One more thing—If I or another deputy catch your husband driving drunk again, he will go to jail, no questions asked. I will see to it that he stays for the maximum time for the offense. And if you interfere with a deputy enforcing the law again, you will be in jail with him." She glared at him and took her husband by the arm and guided him into the house. Sean waited in his patrol car until he was satisfied that everything had quieted down.

On the third night, he got an urgent call from dispatch at about ten p.m. There was an altercation at the Oasis Bar with a report of shots fired. He put on his red lights, turned on the siren, and headed for the bar.

The place was about three miles west of Avondale. There was a modest market beside the bar and a small labor camp behind the buildings. A couple of bright neon beer signs cast a reddish glow over a cluster of men outside the front of the bar. Sean got out, released the scabbard strap for his pistol, then tucked a nightstick under his gun belt. The men were so busy yelling and waving fists that they hadn't seemed to notice Sean's arrival and the red lights blinking on top of his patrol car. He walked up to the circle of men and blew his police whistle three times in succession. It was enough to stop the yelling, and all the men's eyes focused on Sean. There was a man on the ground, bleeding. Another man stood to the side, brandishing what appeared to be a long switchblade knife. A third man was waving a small caliber handgun in the air.

Sean pointed his nightstick at the man with the pistol and yelled, "Sir, put down the pistol. Do it now!" The barked command seemed to quiet the group even more. The man turned toward Sean, the pistol leveling toward him as he turned. Sean reached out with the nightstick and whacked the man's wrist on the arm holding the gun. There was a sickening crunch of bone. The man dropped the pistol and started screaming, holding his wrist. "You bastard! You broke my wrist!" the man yelled in between screaming and moaning.

Another man standing beside the gun wielder lunged for the pistol on the ground. Sean caught him across the side of his skull with the nightstick, and the man collapsed. Sean reached and picked up the firearm and stuck it in his belt. The crowd was still angrily milling around, but they backed some distance away. They were leery of Sean's nightstick.

He approached the man with the knife and calmly said, "Sir, please hand over that knife, handle first."

"I ain't gonna!" he exclaimed. "These sonsabitches will kill me if I do."

"I won't let that happen. Give me the knife. Now!" Sean waved the other men back with his nightstick and told them to keep back. "This man on the ground needs medical attention. Stay back!"

He turned to the man with the knife and held out his hand. The man reluctantly placed the knife in Sean's palm. "You go wait by my patrol car while I see to this man," he said. The man did as he was told, carefully watching the others in the crowd. "Hope the sumbitch dies," Sean heard him mumble as he walked away..

The situation seemed to have been defused by Sean's actions. He knelt and checked the wounds of the man on the ground—he was alive but bleeding profusely from a knife wound in his belly. Sean asked for someone to bring a couple of clean towels from the bar. One of the younger men in the crowd ran into the bar and brought out some towels. Sean looked at him and said, "Kneel here on the other side of this man." The young man did so, and Sean showed him how to place the towels and keep pressure on the wound to slow the bleeding. "Hold those towels in place until an ambulance arrives," he said. Then he went to his patrol car and called dispatch to send an ambulance. He put the man who had done the stabbing in the back of the car so he could deal with him later.

The man with the gun had disappeared, but the man who had tried to grab the gun on the ground was still lying where he fell, unconscious. The rest of the men saw it was all over, and nobody wanted to confront the deputy. They all drifted away, going for their cars or into the labor camp to get away before the deputy questioned them. Sean didn't care, he had his hands full with a wounded man, an unconscious man, and a prisoner.

The ambulance arrived and bandaged the wounded man's knife wound, then loaded him in the ambulance. They were able to revive the unconscious man. They put a bandage on his head and checked his eye movements. The head medic said, "You have a mild concussion. Go home and stay in bed. See a doctor tomorrow." Then they switched on lights and siren and headed for the hospital.

Sean went into the bar to speak to the bartender. "That was pretty damn gutsy, what you did out there," the bartender said. "Don't believe I ever saw anything like it."

Sean said, "Tell me what that was all about."

Well," the bartender said, "most of those guys were friends or relatives of the guy who got stabbed. The man doin' the cuttin' was pissed because the guy had beat up on his sister. They argued, and I told 'em to take it outside. The guy with the gun and the one with him was friends of the wounded guy. He fired off a shot with that little pea shooter when they got outside, or else that man would likely have been dead. Somebody had called for the cops, and it was pretty much as you found it when you arrived. What we call a Mexican stand-off. Guy with a gun, guy with a knife eyeballing each other. Thanks for breakin' it up!"

Sean took down any names and other information the bartender could supply and then left to book his prisoner into the county jail on a charge of assault with a deadly weapon. The rest of his shift was thankfully quiet the rest of the night.

The fourth night was burned indelibly into Sean's memory like a vivid nightmare. It had started peacefully with only a couple of traffic citations for speeding. He was on Yuma Road a couple of miles east of Perryville when a car passed him, a late model Hudson sedan, traveling extremely fast. Sean gave chase with lights and siren, but the driver ignored him. They roared into the village, and the other driver cut through the entrance to the now-closed Chevron station, made a sliding turn to the south spewing gravel over the gas pumps, then raced south on Perryville Road. Sean lost ground by slowing to a near stop before turning to follow the other car.

It was exceptionally dark; the road dissolved into inky blackness ahead of Sean's headlights. There was no moon, no lights of any kind along the road. Even the scattered farmhouses were dark at this late hour. Lights came on in some as Sean roared past with his siren blaring. Sean concentrated on following the light from his high beams. Running off the narrow two-lane road at this speed could be disastrous.

The other car's taillights were a dim glow ahead on the road. Sean's speedometer showed over eighty miles per hour, and the Hudson still pulled away from him. These speeds were extremely dangerous on the rough and narrow pavement with irrigation ditches along both sides of the road. They would soon go over a bridged crossing on the Buckeye Canal. It was not a straight alignment with the road and was hazardous at these speeds. The other car was likely to lose control if the driver didn't slow down before he reached it.

Sean was momentarily blinded by the sudden flash of an explosion ahead, followed by bright flames. He began slowing, easing closer to the flames, and could see the Hudson he had been pursuing completely engulfed in flames, its front end crumbled like an accordion's bellows. The Hudson's fuel tank had exploded after impact with a freight train's car—Sean could see the outline of moving railroad cars in the fire's flickering light. He stopped as near the burning car as he could, grabbed the fire extinguisher from its floor holder, and ran to try and pull the driver out. The stream from the fire extinguisher was no match for the gasoline-fueled flames; they were too intense to get closer than ten feet or so. Sean could see the man inside was already dead, and flames were consuming him too.

This man died in front of my eyes, Sean thought, *and there was nothing I could do to save him. It was worse than one of my war-time nightmares; this was real and in the present.*

The train had come to a complete stop, and the engineer and brakeman came running up to see if they could help. There was nothing any of them could do until the flames burned themselves out.

It was a typical train crossing in the country. There were no lights, no crossing arm, nothing. There were warning signs on the road approaching the tracks, but nothing else. A car driving the forty miles per hour speed limit would have likely seen the train in the dark in time to stop. But this car was probably going ninety miles per hour. From a distance on a dark night such as that one, the rail cars would have simply looked like a darker place on the road ahead. The driver would have only had a fraction of a second to react at that speed when he saw them ahead.

Sean radioed for a fire truck and ambulance, knowing it was a futile gesture. But operating policies required him to do so. Two more deputies showed up to block traffic on either side of the crossing. It was getting light when it was all wrapped up. The body, burned beyond recognition, was removed by medics, placed in the ambulance, and taken to the county morgue to await identification. A wrecker showed up and hauled off the charred wreckage of the car. It was barely identifiable as a Hudson Hornet with a big V-8 engine—the cars were known for speed.

The tracks were cleared of debris, and the freight train had moved on. Sean lingered at the scene, writing his report on the hood of his patrol car in the early morning light. He marveled at how quickly a life could be accidentally snuffed out in peacetime. He hoped he would learn why the driver was speeding and why he wouldn't stop. *Such a senseless waste of a life*, he thought. It was nearing the end of his shift, and he went back to the district office to finish the paperwork.

The commander met Sean before he left on patrol that Friday night. He said, "Sean, I want you back on day shifts starting next Monday. I have a hunch your friend Kiefer may yet show up in the area. There's been no sign of him in California, and he may still be hiding out here. I want you to put out feelers to everyone you know who might come in contact with him. Let's keep maximum pressure on that SOB until we catch him."

"I need the weekend off for personal business, commander. I've made plans with Annaleigh to work out details for our wedding."

"No problem, Sean. Get back on your regular schedule Monday."

CHAPTER 22

The weighmaster arranged to meet his old associate at Stout's hotel in the little town of Gila Bend. It was situated on the highway between Phoenix, Tucson, and San Diego; motels and service stations were the town's lifeblood. It had the well-deserved title of 'The Fan Belt Capital of the U.S. Crossing the long stretches of the desert was particularly hard on car's fan belts and radiators.

Kiefer chose the town because it was far away from the Orange Palace and the ongoing investigation. The hotel had been in business since 1914, withstood a fire in 1916, and undergone several additions to reach its present form. It had sixty-five rooms, a café/restaurant, a couple of travel-related stores, and a pool hall in the basement.

They chose a table in the far corner of the room; there were no other customers in the café. Kiefer chose a seat with his back to the wall and a clear view of the place.

"Long time no see, Bobby," he said.

"Yeah. Like ten years, no see. That's the way I like it," the man replied.

He looked the same as he had the last time Kiefer had seen him. His face and head were perfectly round and hairless. No eyebrows, nothing. He said it was some sort of genetic disorder. His skin was a bright shade of pink as if he'd spent hours under a blistering sun. His eyes were pale grey, nearly colorless. Most people instinctively looked away when they saw him for the first time—women, especially.

Bobby knew they found him creepy looking. It was easy to underestimate someone who looked like that— Bobby Riggs preferred it that way.

Kiefer said, "You ever hear anything about the old gang?"

The man gave a derisive snort and said, "Hell no! And after that last job, I never want to. They're probably still in jail, for all I know. I didn't want to see you, either. But I owe you. So, let's get to it. What's the job?"

The men had met ten years earlier when Kiefer's cousin recruited him to drive the getaway car for a bank heist. "All you gotta do is show up and drive," the cousin told him. "It will be a piece of cake. It's all planned out. And we'll cut you in on twenty-five percent of the haul." Kiefer had been reluctant, but the cousin kept nagging him, telling him what a sweet deal it was. He finally agreed.

The job was at a bank in downtown San Diego. Kiefer lived in Bakersfield at the time; it was where he had begun his business in the cotton fields after leaving Kansas. He had previously lived in San Diego for six months and knew the streets well.

The men were a gang of four. They met and went over the plan and then made two dry runs with Kiefer driving. The plan was to hit the bank at closing time. Bobby was an explosives expert whose job was to blow the vault door open if the manager wouldn't cooperate.

But the plan went south. One of the other men had gotten drunk in a bar and bragged about their plan, and the police were waiting for them. They ambushed the robbers as soon as they entered the bank. Bobby was the only one with a backup plan – he detonated a smoke bomb and ran out the door before anyone knew what was happening. The other two men didn't make it out, but Bobby made it to the getaway car with Kiefer waiting. He jumped in and yelled, "DRIVE!" Shots rang out, and bullets ricocheted off the front of the car.

 Kiefer spun the wheel as he hit the gas. The car made a 180-degree turn in the street with tires squealing and smoking. The police weren't ready for that, and the would-be bank robbers made their escape running fast through the downtown streets and alleys. Then they ran up the coast, ducking through the small beach towns. Eventually, they cut across Los Angeles and made it to Bakersfield, where Kiefer had a small house. He hid the getaway car in his garage; it would need major cosmetic work to cover the bullet holes. The two men stayed put for two weeks until they were sure the police hadn't somehow tracked them there. They saw in the newspapers that the other two men had been captured and were awaiting trial. Kiefer and Riggs sweated out the following month, hoping they hadn't been ratted out by their fellow robbers.

 That was the beginning and end of Kiefer's career as a bank robber. There were much better and safer ways to make his fortune, he decided. He drove the bullet-riddled getaway car out into the desert, poured five gallons of gas over the inside and exterior, and torched it. Then he hitchhiked back to San Diego and retrieved his own car he had left in a public lot.

When Bobby prepared to catch a bus for Los Angeles he said, "I owe you, Kiefer. Let me know if I can ever do anything for you." The men shook hands, and it was the last they had seen each other until this meeting in Gila Bend.

Kiefer laid out all that had happened with the Orange Palace. He said the deputy was the remaining loose end he had to tie off before he would feel safe.

"So why don't you just take care of him yourself?" Bobby asked.

"The mob sent two professional hitmen to take this guy out, and they failed. He's some sort of badass with Army commando training. Not only did those guys fail, but he killed one and nearly killed the other. I don't have the ability to take on someone like that. It needs a less direct approach."

"What do you have in mind?"

Kiefer had heard through the grapevine that Bobby had made a career of eliminating people who were crossways with the L.A. mobsters. He had a remarkably effective skill set as a bomber.

"I want you to plant a bomb on his truck and take him out. It's the only way I can think of to get to him."

"You got the cash?"

Kiefer nodded and said, "Look, there's still a lot of heat on me, and this needs to happen quickly."

"Yeah, yeah. Ain't it always the case? Get to it. I need to get this done so I can get back to L.A. What have you got?"

"I want to hit the guy where he works. Send a message to the rest of that bunch of hillbilly cops that they shouldn't mess with me. It's going to mean planting the package in daylight, first thing in the morning after my guy arrives at the sheriff's station and after he leaves for patrol. You'll have to set up and watch him for a couple of days to get the timing right."

"You were supposed to be the leg man on this job. I ain't got time to sit and watch a cop come and go."

"You know I can't stake him out. I'd have to be too close and run the risk of being seen. You're unknown here. Nobody should give you a second look."

"I don't like it. And I don't like the idea of doing it in front of a cop's office. Too many variables, too much risk. Maybe we should just forget the whole thing. You pay my expenses so far, and I'm gone."

The two men sat staring at each other for a few minutes. Finally, Kiefer said, "All right. I'll do the stakeout. But I'll need to use your car. My truck is too recognizable to be seen in that neighborhood."

"I still don't like the setup. Why don't we just do it at his house?"

"Look," Kiefer said. "This is personal for me. I need it done this way to send a message."

"What message? Your little house of cards already fell down around you."

"The message is payback for what they did to me and my operation," Kiefer said.

"Well, it's your money, ace. I'll get the stuff together, and you do the stakeout. I'll do the job as soon as you give me the green light on the plan. And take care of my car, too. I want it back in the same shape as it left me!"

Kiefer said, "Today's Friday. I'll start the stakeout on Monday morning. We should be able to move by Wednesday or Thursday."

Bobby grumbled as he climbed into Kiefer's pickup truck. He watched as Kiefer drove away in his 1944 Chrysler Royal. *What a screwed-up deal this is*, he thought. *He better not put a scratch on my car*!

Sean was returning from an uneventful patrol that afternoon. He passed a pickup truck a few miles out of town and did a double take—something about the truck seemed vaguely familiar. A bald, ruddy-complexioned man was driving—no one he recognized. But something about the truck reminded him of Kiefer. He couldn't put his finger on it, though. *I'm just getting jumpy*, he told himself. It would do him good to spend the weekend with Annaleigh.

***

The weighmaster parked down the street from the sheriff's department's district office on Monday morning. He was situated down the street so he could see the building in his rearview mirror. Bobby's Chrysler made him feel conspicuous. It was shiny black, new, and expensive, and it stood out like a sore thumb in that neighborhood. Most of the people around the area could barely afford a beat-up old used car. He would have to be cautious not to raise suspicions of anyone seeing the car too often.

It was a little before seven a.m. Kiefer knew in the past that the deputy usually arrived around that time. This day was no different. He watched in his rearview mirror as a pickup turned in at the police station, parked in front, and the deputy got out and went into the office. When Sean left on patrol he'd get a closer look at the truck parked in front of the building. Bobby would need a clear description to carry out his job.

Kiefer watched as three different patrol cars left the fenced yard behind the office. His hat was pulled low on his forehead, and he slumped down behind the wheel of the Chrysler as they passed. He had his back to the street, and no one would recognize him in this car. He saw that Sean was in the third car that came out.

A few minutes passed before Kiefer pulled onto the street and circled back toward the police station. He drove as slowly as he could so he could get a good look at Sean's Ford pickup truck. It was a late step-side model, light green, no more than two or three years old. He made note of the license plate so there would be no mistake, then drove into Phoenix and checked into a motel on Van Buren Street. A diner next door was open twenty-four hours, and he decided he could risk a decent meal. No one would connect him to the car he was driving. He checked in under a false name; he should be safe.

He made another reconnaissance trip the next morning to confirm the deputy's schedule. All appeared normal. Now it would be up to Bobby. The two men met that night at Bobby's hotel room to go over the details. Bobby said he would do it the next morning; he planned to be back in Los Angeles before nightfall tomorrow. They again swapped cars, and Kiefer left in his pickup truck.

The weighmaster was up at five a.m. He skirted around Tolleson, Avondale, and Buckeye. There was a chance of some random cop spotting him passing through a town in his pickup—he was certain there was a police alert to watch for it. He stopped at the little store at the Hassayampa River bridge on his way back to the remote stone house where he had been hiding. The place was closed at that early hour, but he only needed the payphone outside the building. At precisely ten minutes after seven, he dialed the operator and asked to be connected to the sheriff's department's district office in Avondale.

The clerk answered the phone, and he said, "I need to speak to Deputy O'Conner. I have important information for him."

"Just a minute," the clerk said, "he's ready to leave on patrol. I think I can catch him." Sean was almost out the door into the vehicle compound when she caught him and said he had a call. He came in and picked up the phone on one of the desks the deputies shared in the office.

"This is O'Conner."

The line was silent for a few seconds. Sean was about to hang up when a voice said, "This is Jim Kiefer.' More silence. "Bet you never thought you'd hear from me, did you, deputy?"

Sean said, "What do you want, Kiefer? Where are you?"

Kiefer laughed into the phone. "You surely don't think I'll tell you where I am. That don't matter. What does matter is that I want you to know I'm gonna square things with you.

"How do you plan to do that?"

Kiefer continued, "You ruined my life, deputy. Your snoopin' and pryin' started all the stuff that led to shutting down the Orange Palace. That was my bread and butter, as I expect you know. Now there's nothin' left for me except to get even with you. You won't know when or where it will come from, but you will get what you deserve."

"You're crazy, Kiefer. I was only doing my job. Come in, and let's talk about it."

The weighmaster laughed into the phone again. "You played me for a fool for the last time, O'Conner. I'm makin' new rules, and the game is on. Be ready." Then he hung up abruptly.

Sean stood looking into space for a minute. He thought: *The man has gone crazy. What is he planning? An ambush of some kind? I have to be ready for anything.*

He walked into the commander's office and recounted the phone discussion. They talked about various scenarios for an ambush.

The commander said, "My rental house is vacant. You can go there if you want."

Sean said, "Thank you, sir, but I don't think he would try anything at my house. That didn't work out so well for the last guy who tried it. My guess is that the Detroit bunch has probably cut him loose as a liability. It's doubtful he'd have access to any more of their hitmen. He's a slippery guy, and he's been stewing on this for some time. I think he will try to set me up somehow."

"Watch your back, Sean. Be careful on any calls you respond to. Don't rush into anything. And don't be afraid to call for backup if something smells wrong."

"Yes, sir. I will be careful."

Sean double-checked his .45 pistol and ammunition before he got into his patrol cruiser. He took the short-barreled Remington 12-gauge pump action shotgun from its holder on the dash and checked its load, then double-checked the extra box of shells in the glove box. He had his trusty paratrooper's switchblade knife in his pocket and a nightstick lying on the seat beside him. He was as prepared as he could be. Now it was up to Kiefer to make his move.

***

Bobby had wasted no time in procuring the items he would need. A stop at a hardware store provided him with wiring, alligator clips, and duct tape. Then he went to a construction supply business one of his L.A. associates had told him about. Normally he would use two sticks of dynamite and a detonator for a job like this. But Kiefer wanted to make a big statement, so he bought four. The store's owner asked no questions and made no record of the sale.

Tuesday night, after meeting Kiefer, Bobby carefully assembled the final package, wrapping the sticks of dynamite into a tight package held together with duct tape, and connecting the detonator. He put the bomb, along with the tape and wire, into a small rucksack he had brought for the purpose. He considered the rucksack a kind of good luck charm—It had served him well on numerous prior jobs of this type.

He couldn't show up in his typical L.A. duds; he'd be made for sure. A second-hand store had supplied him with old denim jeans, a faded red plaid shirt, a pair of brown work boots, and a green cap with John Deere spelled out in white letters on the front. It would cover his shiny bald head. He carefully placed the bag containing the bomb solidly on the passenger side seat of the Chrysler and stuffed some blankets around it to keep it from sliding off if he should have to brake hard. Then he drove exactly five miles per hour under the speed limit back toward Avondale. If all went according to plan, he would arrive at his target around eight a.m., well after the deputy had left on patrol.

The patrol cars were gone from the district office's fenced compound, as planned. Bobby drove past it and pulled into the same alley that Lucky Lenny had used previously. He grabbed the rucksack and slung it over his shoulder, pulled the cap down over his eyes, and sauntered casually back toward the police station. No one was in sight. The deputy had parked the truck toward the side of the building, just as Kiefer said he would. It was well out of view from the single window in front. The other deputies' cars were parked in a row alongside his target.

He stopped as if to tie a bootlace, then quickly slipped beside the truck and onto his back. Working his way under the truck, he easily found the connection he wanted. Three strips of tape around his package secured it to the frame, and a simple alligator clip connected the wire from the detonator to the wire leading to the brake lights. The wire would become hot when someone in the cab stepped on the brake pedal.

He grabbed the empty rucksack and quickly slid out from under the truck. He stood up slowly and looked around. The street was empty except for a couple of cars that had just passed. He continued walking away from the station, crossed a side street, and walked back to his car. Eight or nine hours from now, he would be back in his hometown. He could read about the results of his work in tomorrow's paper.

CHAPTER 23

The water pump had started leaking on Annaleigh's old Chevy step-side pickup. She planned to trade in the old Dodge for a new car when she and Sean were married. He had a pickup, too. *Maybe they wouldn't need two of them*, she told herself. She imagined herself in a new Chevrolet convertible coupe, cruising down the back roads with her ponytail blowing in the breeze. There was plenty of time to talk to Sean about that. Right now, her old truck needed a new water pump before it went out and left her stranded.

She called Ignacio's garage in Avondale and made an appointment to take it in on Wednesday morning. Ignacio assured her he had a replacement pump available. She checked that the radiator was full of water and put a five-gallon jerry can with extra water in the back, just in case. Her mom kissed her on the cheek and told her to drive safely. They both chuckled at the subtle joke —Annaleigh was notorious for a lead foot and driving as fast as she could. She said she should be back by mid-afternoon. Then she gunned the old truck out of the driveway onto the dirt road. Her mom watched her truck grow smaller at the head of a cloud of dust. She smiled to herself and shook her head.

Annaleigh pulled up to the open bay at Ignacio's garage— "Used Parts and Fair Rates" were hand painted in bright red letters on the sign over the building's front door. Ignacio came out to greet her. "*Buenos Dias, señorita.* You look beautiful as always. And you are right on time!"

"*Buenos Dias*, Ignacio, you old flirt," she replied. "How is your family?"

"Very well, thank you, *señorita*. My wife grows fat, and my children grow tall. What more could a man want?"

Annaleigh laughed. "You scoundrel. I know your wife is a beautiful woman."

Ignacio's round brown face wrinkled up in a wide smile. He had one gold tooth in front he liked to show off. "I never argue with a lady, *señorita*!" he said and laughed a deep belly laugh. "I have a water pump for your truck. It will take me two or three hours to do the work."

"That's fine, Ignacio." Can you give me a lift to the sheriff's department office? I'm going to use Sean's truck while you work on mine."

"Of course, *señorita*. One moment while I wipe the grease off my hands."

He dropped her off in front of the sheriff's department building. "*Adios*. Come by my shop when you are ready, and I will help you change trucks."

She waved to him as he turned around and headed back to the shop. Then she went inside to visit Rachel, the office clerk. Rachel said, "Everyone is thrilled that you and Sean are to be married. I am beyond happy for both of you!"

"Thank you, Rachel. I'm excited to go shopping for a wedding dress this morning. I'm going to use Sean's pickup today while mine's in the shop."

They spent a few minutes giggling and talking about wedding plans. Then Annaleigh went out the front door and waved to Rachel through the front window as she walked past; the clerk's desk sat beside it and gave her a view of the street. As usual, Sean's truck was parked a little to the side of the building's front. She tossed her purse on the seat, fished around under the floormat for the key Sean had left there, then slid onto the seat. The key was a little sticky to fit into the ignition switch. She jiggled it a couple of times and it slipped into the key slot. A brief premonition of something not right swept over her, but she shrugged her shoulders, pushed in the clutch, and turned the key to the on position. The truck started when she pressed the starter button; she put it in reverse and backed away from the building a short way.

She touched the brake pedal and Sean's truck erupted in a blinding flash of light, nearly vaporizing her in the blast. The truck's full tank of gas added to the power of the explosion. The concussion from the blast shattered the front window of the district office, and Rachel died instantly, cut to pieces by a thousand pieces of glass. The outside wall collapsed and partially covered her body with broken cinder block. The interior wall that separated the commander's office blew inward, burying him under flying debris.

Shrapnel from the pickup's explosion radiated in all directions. A man walking across the street was hit by a flying chunk of steel and nearly decapitated. The force of the blast slung the nearest car into the next one beside it. The first car's fuel tank ruptured, and the leaking gas was ignited by the nearby blaze. Then the tank exploded, engulfing both cars in flames. Two other cars parked nearby in front of the building were heavily damaged: their paint was stripped off, and their windows shattered. The blast had blown out the windows of several buildings nearby on the street, including a couple of homes behind the office. Several people were injured by flying glass shards.

Ignacio had just arrived back at his shop when he heard and felt the blast. He looked in the direction of the explosion and could see a cloud of black smoke swirling upward. "*Dios mia!*" he exclaimed and crossed himself. He got in Annaleigh's truck and drove back in the direction of the smoke. "*Dios mia!*" he exclaimed again and crossed himself. Sean's truck was reduced to a twisted, flaming, and smoking pile of metal. It sat lopsided in a crater blasted out in the parking lot. Ignacio got out and ran to Sean's truck, but the heat kept him from getting close enough to see if anyone was in the wreckage. He couldn't imagine anyone could have survived an explosion like that. By then, people were running up from all directions, and the volunteer fire department truck arrived to begin trying to put out the inferno of the three blazing wrecks.

The commander staggered out of the office wreckage; he was obviously in shock and dazed. An ambulance arrived, and a medic bandaged his bleeding wounds and had him wait inside the ambulance while they checked for any other survivors. They confirmed that a person had been in the vehicle when it exploded: there were bits and fragments of bone and skin visible. Rachel was sprawled in a bloody heap across the room from her desk in the sheriff's office. The medic checked her pulse, even though he knew there was no hope. He quickly checked the rest of the building and found no one else inside. Then he got a blanket from the ambulance to cover Rachel's body. The medics moved the man who had been killed across the street off to the side of the road and covered him with a blanket.

Another ambulance arrived. The medics and a couple of the firemen went door to door checking for victims of the blast. They treated several people who had severe bleeding from glass cuts. Many people were in stunned shock, not sure of what had happened. The medics took a couple of the people with the worst injuries to the hospital. By then, sheriff's department deputies were beginning to converge on the scene.

***

Sean was investigating a break-in at a farmhouse near Buckeye when his patrol car's radio erupted in excited and confusing chatter. Something had happened at the district office. He caught radio chatter about an explosion, unknown injuries, and unknown dead. He jumped in his car, turned on lights and siren, and sped back toward his office.

He arrived at a scene in complete chaos. There were several patrol cars and ambulances parked haphazardly around the building. People were milling around in dazed states, and a firetruck was putting water on the still-blazing vehicles. Sean realized with shock that one of the vehicles they were working on was his.

He jumped out of his car and ran toward his wrecked truck. "Annaleigh! Annaleigh!" he shouted. Another deputy grabbed him by the arm, but Sean pulled away and continued calling his fiancé's name. It took two deputies to restrain him. One of them was his friend Brad Jones who said, "Sean, it's too late. There's nothing you or anyone else can do." Sean struggled against the two men holding him. "No! It can't be! Let me go! I have to find her!"

The deputies kept a grip on him but led him a little closer to the still-smoldering wreckage. "Sean," one of them said, "no one could have survived that. We don't know who was in the truck, but there was no chance of surviving that blast."

Sean had gone silent and quit struggling against his friends. After a minute, he said, "Annaleigh was in the truck. She was going to use it while hers is in the shop. It was her." Then he started sobbing, and the deputies led him to an ambulance.

"This man's in shock," they told the medic. "It was his truck, and we think his fiancé was in it. Give him something to help him."

The medic gave him a sedative and said, "Stay with him. Get him home if you can. Let him cry it out." Deputy Jones nodded. "I'll stay with him," he said and took Sean to his patrol car. "Let's get you home, Sean. Let others do what has to be done here."

Sean had stopped sobbing. "Kiefer!" he said. "It had to be Kiefer!" He could feel the beginning of his shock and grief

beginning to morph into a deadly, cold rage. His friend
took him home, helped him into his house, and told him to
lie down. The sedative finally dragged him down into a
fitful, dream-filled sleep.

***

The weighmaster had hung up the phone after calling the
deputy, then driven as fast as possible to the old stone
house he was using as a hideout. He gathered his camping
gear and suitcases and put them in the bed of his pickup.
He had one major chore to do before he headed for Mexico.

He retrieved his carefully hidden suitcase full of money
from an outcropping of rock a short way from the house. It
was easy to remove the bolts holding the pickup's seat and
take it out of the cab. Then, placing it on the floor of the
old house, he used a straight razor to slice an opening along
the back and two sides of the seat covering. He folded it
back and removed the latex foam padding between the
springs. The wads of large denomination bills in his
suitcase fit nicely as he stuffed them between the springs.
Then, with a large sewing needle and fishing line, he
stitched the covering back down onto the seat. The fishing
line roughly matched the color of the upholstery; it should
pass any but a very detailed examination. He bolted the seat
back into position. His money should be safe—now, he was
ready to go.

His route led down the US 80 highway to Gila Bend
where he stopped to gas up at a Texaco station. The
attendant cleaned his windows, checked under the hood,

and gauged all his tires' air pressure. Kiefer stepped inside the little lobby of the station to pay for the gas.

"Quite a to-do in Avondale this morning. Did you hear about it?" the manager asked. Kiefer said no, and the man continued, "The news on the radio said some kind of bomb went off at the sheriff's station there. Killed two women and a man, did a lot of damage."

Kiefer asked as calmly as he could, "Is that all they said? Were any sheriff's deputies injured?"

"They didn't say on the news. But they said several cars and buildings were damaged. Musta been a helluva blast, is all I can say."

"Sounds like it," Kiefer said as he walked out of the lobby.

"Come again, mister," the manager waved.

Kiefer pondered the news. Two women? What could that mean? It had happened too early for the deputy to have finished his patrol and gone back to the station. Did something else set off the bomb? It had been known to happen.

He picked up some news on his truck's radio and learned that one of the women killed was the fiancé of a sheriff's deputy; the other was the clerk who worked in the sheriff's office. Flying debris had killed a man walking across the street.

He was stunned. O'Conner's fiancé! How the hell had that happened? It sounded like Bobby's bomb had the desired effect, all right. Now it would bring tremendous heat down on him. His little revenge call that morning would remove any doubt of who was responsible. He had planned to be well down into Mexico by the time the deputy finished his shift and triggered the bomb. Now he hoped he could get across the border before they put out an alert for him there. It was only a couple of hours to the crossing. He couldn't afford a traffic stop and resisted the urge to speed. He passed through the mining town of Ajo, where he stopped and bought Mexican auto insurance from a local dealer. Back on the highway, he passed the wide spot in the road called Why and then passed through the little Arizona border town of Lukeville at the border crossing.

The border guard knew him from his previous trips. "*Hola, señor*. More fishing this time?"

"*Si*, Carlos. Maybe I'll catch the big one this time," Kiefer laughed. "For your family," he said, passing the guard a ten-dollar bill.

The guard's face lit up with a big smile. "*Muchas gracias, señor! Muchas gracias!*" he said, waving him through the gate. He didn't bother with any inspection.

The weighmaster had learned long ago that a few dollars went a long way in Mexico. He heaved a big sigh of relief. No alert had been put out for him yet—at least none had reached this place. But he had to put miles between himself and the border. He passed through the sleepy Mexican border town of Sonoyta and drove fast for the next town of Caborca, where he again bought gas. He would gas up again in Hermosillo, then push on to Guaymas. Relaxation in a good bed with the sound of the surf outside his bedroom window was only a few hours away.

***

The bomber was back in his LA apartment on Thursday morning, enjoying a leisurely breakfast of coffee, toast, hard-boiled egg, and fresh orange juice. He was relaxed, lounging in his favorite blue silk robe, happy to be home after a good night's sleep. Maybe he'd go to the race track this afternoon and hang out with some of his buddies, see if he could double some of the money Kiefer paid him. The morning LA Times newspaper slapped up against his door. He brought it in to read while he finished breakfast.

It was the same old stuff on the front page. The mayor was in trouble again, the war was still raging against Japan in the Pacific. He flipped past the first page, and a headline caught his eye:

THREE KILLED BY BOMB BLAST AT COP STATION IN ARIZONA. The smaller headline said ORGANIZED CRIME SUSPECTED.

He read on. The article said two women and a man were killed in the blast. What the hell? Two women? What went wrong? They weren't the target. Besides, he didn't like the idea of killing women. It sounded like the blast made the impression that Kiefer was wanting, all right. The blast damaged the cop station, a few buildings in the neighborhood, and some nearby cars. The name of the woman killed in the vehicle was not disclosed. But it said a woman who worked inside the police building was killed by flying glass. The man killed was a random passerby on the street.

He lost interest in the rest of his breakfast. What could this mean? It might be good news if they think it's connected to the Detroit mob Kiefer had told him about. That would point them away from him. But if they find Kiefer, then all bets are off. He'd sing like a canary to save his own skin. He had no way to contact him now. Hopefully, he would hear from him sometime soon. He needed to know why the job had gone south.

CHAPTER 24

The dream seemed endless, like a scene repeating continuously on a movie theatre screen. It was D-Day all over again. Sean and his team were sheltering behind the wrecked truck for protection from enemy fire. Suddenly, seemingly from nowhere, a German soldier appeared with a flame thrower mounted on his back. He swept the car with its volatile flaming mixture, and the vehicle burst into flames. Enemy fire pinned the men, and they had no way to escape. The truck's gas tank exploded, instantly covering the other men in flaming gasoline. Sean could do nothing but watch and try to blot out the sounds of their agonizing screams for help. He was paralyzed by the instant hell before him.

Then, through the flames and carnage, Annaleigh appeared in a wedding gown. She was motioning him toward her when her gown was suddenly enveloped in flames and her beautiful hair turned into a torch on her head. The flesh melted off her face; she tried to scream, but no sound came from her mouth. Sean watched her fall to the ground writhing in agony as she died.

The dream repeated over and over. He felt himself screaming, but he couldn't force himself awake. Finally, he came out of it enough to feel the familiar warm tongue slide across his cheek. He opened his eyes and was momentarily blinded by the bright light streaming in his east-facing window. Then he focused on Sarge's face beside his, and the dog licked his cheek again. Sean came fully awake, reached out, and stroked the dog's head.

"Good dog," he said. The dog's tail thumped happily on the bed. "You're a real good dog, Sarge." The dog jumped off the bed and watched him expectantly.

His bedroom door opened, and Annaleigh's mother came in. "I thought I heard your voice. I'm glad you're awake."

Sean looked at her, trying to understand why she was there. Then it all came flooding back. He started sobbing. "I'm so sorry, Mrs. Childs," he got out between sobs. "It should have been me," he sobbed again. "It should have been me." He repeated it until it was only a whisper.

She sat beside him on the bed, leaned down, and hugged him for several minutes. Her eyes were filled with tears when she sat up. "Sean, we know it was meant for you. But fate intervened. For whatever reason, it was God's will that Annaleigh be taken from us. You are not to blame. The evil people who did this are to blame. You can't go through life blaming yourself."

Sean sat up, shaking his head. "I'm so sorry," was all he could get out. Someone had undressed him the day before, put him in bed, and left his uniform folded neatly on a chair. He recalled he had been given some kind of drug and slept a troubled sleep through the evening and night. Now he felt like he had a tequila hangover—his head hurt like hell and felt like it was stuffed with cotton.

Mrs. Childs said, "When you're ready, get dressed and come into the kitchen. There's fresh coffee, and I'll fix you something to eat.

"I don't think I can eat but thank you for making coffee."

He was surprised to find Annaleigh's father sitting at the dining table. He stood when Sean came in, walked up to him, gathered him in his arms, and hugged him for a long time. Sean started sobbing again. "Let it out, son," Mr. Childs said. "It's the only way. We know how much you loved her and what she meant to you. There are no words for how we all feel. Have some coffee, and we'll talk."

They sat at the table in silence and sipped coffee. Sean was finally able to eat a piece of toast. He said, "Thank you both for being here. I can't tell you how much it means to me."

Mr. Childs' face was deeply creased with stress lines, and his eyes were sunken and bloodshot. He had had no sleep since the explosion. He said, "Sean, you're like a son to us. We'll always welcome you as one of our family." He nodded to his wife and continued, "Mary will stay here with you as long as you need."

Sean thought Mrs. Childs looked even worse than her husband. "Thank you, sir. But I know you have much to do. I'll be okay. I'm going to take some time away from work to try and clear my head." Sean looked at them, amazed that they were here to take care of him, even in their grief. He said, "I can't imagine how awful this is for you. I want to help in any way I can. Please let me know what I can do."

"We'll do that, Sean," Mr. Childs replied. "We'll talk more when we're all over the shock. For now, take care of yourself. We must see to some arrangements. But first, we're going to get Annaleigh's truck from the shop and bring it here. You will need something to drive until you sort things out." They were gone for about half an hour and returned with the pickup. Mr. Childs said, "Ignacio wouldn't let us pay for the work he had done. He's a good man." He handed Sean the truck's keys. "Keep it as long as you want, Sean. We don't need it."

Mrs. Childs said, "I can stay with you if you need me. I worry about you here alone."

"I'll be fine," he said. "Thank you for helping me, but I know you have much to do. Let me know how I can help with anything you need. I want to do whatever I can with arrangements for Annaleigh." Both Annaleigh's parents gave him another hug, then they said a tearful goodbye.

The first thing he did was to call his office. There was no answer. He dialed the operator and asked if there was a problem with the phone line there. She checked and came back on the phone. "I'm sorry, sir, that phone line appears to be out of service temporarily."

"Please connect me with the Maricopa County Sheriff's Office," he asked. There were a few clicks and pops on the line before the phone rang. "Maricopa County Sheriff's Office," the receptionist said.

"Hi, Kathy. This is Sean O'Conner. There's no phone service at my district office. I need to speak to the district commander."

"Oh, Sean. I am so sorry. Everyone here is devastated by what happened. Are you all right?"

"I'm fine, Kathy. I need to speak to someone in charge."

"Sure, Sean. Wait a moment."

More clicks and the line connected. "Sean, this is Sheriff Roach. How are you, son?"

"I'm okay, sir. Thanks for asking. I'm trying to find out what happened to our district office. The phone line there is dead."

The sheriff was quiet for a moment. "You haven't heard any news, son?"

"No, sir. I just woke up a little bit ago. What happened?"

"First, let me say how sorry I am for your personal loss. I know you were engaged to be married soon. I want you to take all the time off you need to deal with your grief and make whatever arrangements for your fiancé are necessary."

"Thank you, sir. I appreciate it. I'm still in shock. Is everyone else okay?"

Sheriff Roach said, "The front of the building was severely damaged. Rachel, the clerk, was killed when the front window exploded into a storm of shattered glass. The concussion knocked down the wall to the commander's office, and he received some serious head wounds and a concussion. He's in St. Joseph's Hospital. There was no one else in the office at the time, thank God, but a man walking across the street was killed by shrapnel from the blast. He was just passing through and we haven't been able to find out anything about him."

Sean was speechless for a moment. "Sheriff, I am very sorry for all this. I feel like it was my fault. That bomb was meant for me. Jim Kiefer called me yesterday morning and threatened me with revenge for his loss of business. I figured it was probably hot air; I didn't dream he'd do something like this."

"I didn't know that Sean. There's no accounting for the craziness that can be brought on by lust for revenge. You did a great job with this investigation and deserve the credit for bringing down that awful business. There is no fault in doing your job and doing it well. There are always risks to those of us in this profession, and sometimes those risks spill over to our families and loved ones. You can take pride in your work. Don't blame yourself for doing what is expected of you."

"Thank you, sir. But it's a hard thing to wrap my brain around. I keep second-guessing what I did and didn't do."

"I understand," the sheriff said. "We need you back on the job when you feel like you are able. Feel free to contact me any time you want to talk."

"Thank you, sheriff," Sean said.

"And Sean… we will get the bastards responsible for this." Then the line went dead.

There was a knock on the door. Sean opened it to Brad Jones and Steve Riggs, fellow deputies from the district office. Brad said, "How you doin', buddy? You looked awful rough when I got you home yesterday."

"Thanks for doing that, Brad. I appreciate it. Whatever that medic shot me with would have left me wandering around like a lost drunk if you hadn't helped me. Did you help me to bed, too?"

"Yep. Got you undressed and convinced you to take another sedative pill before I tucked you in. Your dog was growling and uneasy at first, but I reckon he decided I wasn't hurting you." He chuckled and said, "I wouldn't want that dog thinking I was not a friend!"

Sean finally smiled and laughed a little. "Yeah, Sarge is very protective. He stayed in bed beside me all night and woke me up from a bad dream this morning."

Steve said, "We're sorry for your loss, Sean. That was a helluva thing. What can we do for you?"

"I just appreciate you stopping by. It helps more than you can know. How is the commander doing?"

Brad said, "We checked with the hospital a little while ago. They're releasing him today. He's supposed to stay home for at least a week's bed rest, but you know how that will go— I'll believe it when I see it. His wife's a nervous wreck."

"What's being done for Rachel's family?" Sean asked.

Steve replied, "We've started a collection to help her husband with expenses. One of the other deputies stayed with him overnight and said he seemed okay this morning."

"What's being done for Annaleigh in the wreckage?

"The coroner's office was there most of the day yesterday," Brad said. "It was bad. Real bad, Sean. They did the best they could. They are holding her remains in the morgue."

Sean sat for a moment, nodding his head, staring into space.

Brad continued, "When the coroner was done, a wrecker picked up your truck and took it to the county's impound lot. There wasn't much of it left that's recognizable. The department is holding it for investigation; there's a team working on it now, trying to gather information about the bomb."

Mrs. Childs had made a fresh pot of coffee before she left, and the men poured cups for themselves. They sat around the kitchen table and talked for a while about the damage to their office. Steve said it wouldn't be usable for some time. "The whole front part of the building was pretty much demolished. It was a tremendous blast. It also damaged several other cars and about a dozen homes and businesses. The medics treated a bunch of people for cuts and puncture wounds from the broken glass. We're working from the headquarters office until other arrangements are made."

Brad said, "We've got to get back on patrol. I'm glad to see you looking better. Let us know If there's anything we can do for you, Sean. We are deeply sorry for your loss."

Sean saw them out the door, and Brad turned to him and said in a low voice, "We'll get whoever did this, Sean. We're ready to do whatever it takes." The men shook hands, and the deputies left.

CHAPTER 25

Ricky showed up at five o'clock with dinner and two six-packs of Coors. His mother had made up a batch of green chili, pork tamales, cheese enchiladas, and some fresh flan she packed on ice to keep it firm. The two men embraced for a moment, sharing their anguish.

Ricky said, "*Que tal, amigo*! How you doin'?"

"I'm better, Ricky. Last night was rough, but my head's clearer now. Thanks for coming. And thank your mother for the food. Tell her I love and appreciate her."

Sean was ravenous. He had only eaten part of a slice of toast at breakfast and forgot about lunch. The food was delicious and filling, and Sean felt better immediately. The green chilis had just enough bite to linger in his memory and leave a pleasant warmth in his stomach. Nobody did it better than Mrs. Martinez. The men each cracked a can of beer and sat on the living room couch with full bellies, sipping and thinking.

"What now, Sean? What can I do for you?"

"Everybody has the wrong idea about all this. I don't believe the Detroit bunch had anything to do with it. This was personal, some kind of vendetta with that Kiefer guy." He told Ricky about Kiefer's phone call to him that morning before the bombing. "I think he's obsessed with me as the reason his life's gone to hell. He wasn't man enough to face me, so he took the coward's way. And it would have worked, too, if not for Annaleigh."

He sat quietly for a minute. Ricky knew he wasn't done.

"Ricky, I'm going to find that miserable son of a bitch if it's the last thing I do. He doesn't deserve to live."

Ricky nodded. "I hear you, *amigo*."

"Kiefer set this up to make us think he ran to California. I think that's just a smoke screen. I believe he's in Mexico, and I need your help to find him."

Ricky sipped his beer. "What do you want me to do?"

"Remember that Mexican bank statement I showed you? It's the key. We find the connection with that, we find Kiefer. What do you know about Mexican banks?"

Ricky considered. "I've never done any business with one of them. But my parents have, and our relatives in Mexico use them. I'll find out what I can."

"That will be a big help. I'm going down there, Ricky, as soon as I get things settled here. The sheriff told me to take whatever time off I need, and I'm going to use it to chase that bastard down. I could use your help when I go if you're up for it."

"I wouldn't miss it. I and my family loved Annaleigh, too. You are like a brother to me, one of our family. We will find this man and do what needs to be done."

They finished one six-pack. Ricky said he still had to drive home, and he'd had enough. "My father found a phone number for his cousin in Guaymas. I'll try to contact him tomorrow. I'll let you know when I have something to go on." He gave Sean another quick hug before he left. "Take care of yourself, *amigo*. You're gonna need all your strength and wits for what's coming."

Sean drank one more can of Coors and made plans for the next day. Thankfully, he slept through the night without any more wartime nightmares.

CHAPTER 26

Sean called the Sheriff's office first thing the next morning and asked for Detective Johnson. Kathy, the receptionist, said she'd find him and have him call back. He broke up two of Mrs. Martinez's tamales in a skillet and scrambled them with a couple of eggs for breakfast. Ricky had taught him the trick years ago, the first time he stayed overnight at his house. It was a meal that would stick with you all day.

The phone rang as he was finishing. Detective Johnson said, "Hello, Sean. I was surprised to hear from you so soon. I am sorry for your loss. Are you back to work already?"

"Thank you, detective. No, I'm taking some time off. But I want to keep up with the case and help if I can. Is there anything new?"

"Well, we don't think that Kiefer made the bomb. The experts have looked at a few pieces and concluded it was a fairly sophisticated device. Not the kind of thing just anyone could have made. The working theory is it was done by a Detroit specialist." He paused for a couple of seconds and continued, "And Sean—the bomb guys say it was a far stronger explosive charge than what would have been needed just to take out the truck. The mob was sending a message to the entire department, too."

"Wow! I'm so sorry for all of this."

"Nothing to be sorry for, Sean. You were just doing your job."

"Why do you think the mob would still be after me? There's nothing else I could do that would be a danger to them."

"Revenge seems the most likely motive. You made a big dent in their operation."

Sean recounted the phone call from Kiefer just before the bombing. "Seems like it was a very personal thing for him. Would he still be connected to the Detroit bunch after all that's happened?"

"I hadn't heard about that call, Sean. You're right. That puts a different light on it. Might just be Kiefer after revenge. Maybe we should expand the search for potential bombers that Kiefer could have connected with to do the job. Thanks for sharing that."

"Do you know anything about Kiefer's property? I was told a local farmer was buying it," Sean said.

"We're looking into that. We've identified an attorney who did work for him in the past. It's possible he could be representing him on the sale."

"What's his name? I might have heard something about him."

"Name's James Harrison. He has a small practice in west Phoenix."

"Thanks, detective. Haven't heard of him. Please keep me posted on anything significant."

The detective said he would and ended the call.

Sean immediately looked up the attorney's address in the phone book. He dialed the number listed. A woman with a candy-sweet voice answered.

"James Harrison, Attorney at Law. How can I help you?"

"I'd like to make an appointment with Mr. Harrison as soon as possible."

"Of course. He has a cancellation this afternoon at two. Would that work for you?"

"That's perfect," Sean said. He gave her his name and told her he needed help with a personal matter.

***

Sean felt oddly out of place in the cab of Annaleigh's pickup truck. It had the subtle odor of her perfume embedded in the fabric of the seat, her lucky four-leaf clover charm on a chain dangling from the rearview mirror, and her blue windbreaker folded neatly on the seat. He simply sat in the cab for a few minutes, memories and visions of her flashing through his mind. The old six-cylinder engine started on the first turnover, and he set off toward Phoenix.

Sean pulled up to the house that served as the attorney's office at precisely two p.m. The most prosperous-looking thing about the place was a sign over the door with fancy lettering that said 'James Harrison, Attorney at Law.' It was in an older west Phoenix neighborhood that had seen better days. He walked through the door and told the receptionist who he was. The woman's voice had sounded like a sixteen-year-old girl on the phone; Sean now guessed her age at well over fifty and showing every year. She was overweight and had too much makeup. It made her look like a chubby child's doll. The reception area was nothing fancy: a couple of wooden office chairs against one wall, a sickly dieffenbachia plant in a cheap pot, and a well-worn rug with a metal receptionist's desk sitting on it. She asked if he'd like coffee or water; he declined, and she showed him into the attorney's private office. It didn't look much more affluent than the front office. This room was carpeted, however, and a large wooden desk sat in the middle of the room with a couple of worn leather chairs in front of it. The attorney's school and law diplomas hung on one wall beside a painting of the Lincoln/Douglas debate. A small statue of blind justice sat on a small table under the room's single window with a view of the yard where a date palm's fronds swayed gently in the afternoon breeze.

The attorney rose, offered his hand, and said, "Welcome, Mr. O'Conner. Have a seat."

Sean took the chair indicated and sat facing the lawyer.

"Tell me how I may help you today," Harrison said.

"You can help me find someone. A client of yours, I believe."

The attorney's eyes shifted around the room. "I'm not in the habit of divulging information about my clients, Mr. O'Conner. Who is it you are looking for?"

"Jim Kiefer. I believe you have represented him."

The man's eyes narrowed. "Well, sir, even if I had, I would not be at liberty to tell you anything about him." The lawyer shuffled uneasily in his seat and said, "I'm sorry, but I must ask you to leave. I can't help you."

Sean didn't move. "Mr. Harrison, all I need is for you to confirm his location."

The attorney stood up and said, "I'm sorry, sir. I can't help you. Please leave."

Sean stayed seated. "Mr. Harrison, let me explain a few things about your client. You should know that I am a Maricopa County sheriff's deputy, and what I'm going to tell you is true. First, he is a fugitive wanted for multiple cases of kidnapping underage girls and human trafficking for sex."

The lawyer's eyes got wide, and he sucked in a breath. Sean could see the color drain from the man's face and continued, "In addition, he is wanted for murder. I'm sure you heard about the car bombing day before yesterday that killed three people. One of those people was my fiancé. That bomb was meant for me, Mr. Harrison, but it killed her instead. I know beyond any doubt that Kiefer is responsible for her death."

Sean paused and looked the attorney square in the eye. He shifted nervously in his chair. Sean said, "I know you are associated with this man. I believe you are handling a real estate transaction for him to sell his farm near Perryville." He paused, and the lawyer said nothing. He continued, "I also believe I know where Kiefer has gone into hiding. The only thing I want from you is to confirm the location."

Harrison was rattled and spluttered out, "I can't reveal confidential information about my client. Please leave now, or I will call the police and have you escorted out!"

"I don't think you will do that, Mr. Harrison. If you don't help me, my next stop will be at the Arizona Republic and Gazette Newspapers office. I will share what I know about you helping a vicious human predator wanted by the police."

A genuine look of terror crossed the lawyer's face, and he stared at Sean for a long minute. "Mexico," he said, finally. "That's all I can tell you."

Sean took out the statement from the bank in Guaymas and laid it on the desk in front of Harrison. "Is this where he is? Is this where he told you to wire the money from his farm sales?"

"Where did you get that?" The lawyer nearly came out of his chair again.

"I found it in his house during a legal search. Is this where he is, Mr. Harrison?"

He said nothing.

"Do you want to be associated with a kidnapper and murderer?" Sean pressed.

The attorney slowly nodded and said, "Yeah, that's where he told me to send the money." He shoved the bank statement back across the table to Sean. Now please get out. I gave you want you wanted."

Sean stood and said, "One more thing, Mr. Harrison—If Kiefer is warned and escapes the net we'll throw around him, we will know who tipped him off. And you, Mr. Harrison, will be charged as an accessory to enough crimes to put you away for a very long time."

Sean thanked him for his cooperation and walked out of his office. Now, he knew what he had to do. The receptionist smiled sweetly and said, "Nice to meet you, Mr. O'Conner," as he went out the front door.

***

The commander lived in a well-kept house on the outskirts of Goodyear. Sean knocked on the door, and Laura, his wife, answered. "Sean! This is a surprise! Come in."

He said, "Thank you, ma'am. I don't want to intrude if this is a bad time. I just wanted to say hello to the commander."

"He's under doctor's orders to stay in bed, but I'm sure he will be glad to see you. Just a minute while I tell him you're here."

She disappeared down the hallway and into a bedroom. She was back in a couple of minutes and waved him into the room. Sean was taken aback by the commander's appearance—his head was heavily bandaged, he had several bandages on his face and arms, and his skin had an ashen appearance.

"Come in, Sean," he said. "It's good of you to stop by."

"Hello, sir. I won't keep you. I just want you to know how sorry I am for all this. I feel like I should have seen it coming."

"That's crazy talk, Sean," the man replied. "No one, and I mean no one, could have seen this coming." He reached out for Sean's hand and said, "I am so sorry for your loss, son. She was a sweet girl, and we all thought a lot of her."

"Thank you, sir. I loved her very much." He looked at his boots and said, "The sheriff told me to take some time off. I hope that's okay with you." The commander nodded, and Sean continued, "I have some personal things to take care of for Annaleigh. Then I'm going to devote all my energy to finding Jim Kiefer and bringing him to justice."

"Sean, you should just get some rest and try to get over your grief. Let the department deal with Kiefer. When you go through something like this, you may not be thinking clearly. You don't want to get yourself in trouble or, worse, get yourself hurt or killed because of a bad decision. Let us chase this SOB. We'll find him. Go home. Drink some beers with friends. Give yourself some time to heal."

"Thank you, sir. I'll try. But I don't know if I can sit on my hands while that animal is out there. I want to help."

"We'll let you know how it's going, Sean. I appreciate you coming by. Now go home and get some rest. You look like hell."

They shook hands, and the commander's wife walked Sean out of the room. He said, "Thank you, ma'am. Take good care of him."

She smiled and patted him on the back as he went out the door.

***

Sean and Ricky met at the Wishing Well bar, their usual watering hole. It was Friday night, and the place was busy and noisy. They got a couple of greasy cheeseburgers and ate while they talked.

Ricky said, "I was able to contact my Dad's cousin in Guaymas. He's a fisherman and said he knew of a man from Arizona who was part owner of a fishing boat there. He knows the local partner, but not well. He also said there were rumors that the man made a lot of money in Arizona and had bought a beach house a little way out of town. He couldn't tell me anything else."

"That fits with what I learned today," Sean replied. "I paid a visit to the attorney Kiefer uses. He's currently handling the sale of Kiefer's property by Perryville. I persuaded him to verify that the account on the Mexican bank statement was the one Kiefer used. He said Kiefer instructed him to wire the money from the sale to that account."

"Persuaded him?"

296

Sean smiled and said, "I offered to give him a lot of free publicity. I said the newspapers would be extremely interested in all the background on his relationship with a vile wanted criminal. He seemed willing to cooperate to avoid that."

Ricky burst out laughing. "That's maybe the best persuasion technique I've ever heard of." Sean laughed too, and the men ate in silence for a little while. Then Ricky said, "What now?"

Sean washed down the last of his cheeseburger with a swallow of beer. "I need your help, Ricky. I don't know much about Mexico, even less about Guaymas. What I do know is I have to go down there and find that bastard. You can help me find him, maybe help me avoid trouble with the local police."

"When do we leave, *amigo*?"

Sean smiled again. "I hoped you say that. We can leave as soon as funeral services are finished for Annaleigh and Rachel. I'll have to buy something else to drive. I doubt Annaleigh's old rig is up for a trip like that. And besides, it's not mine. Her parents were kind enough to let me use it temporarily."

They spent another hour talking about how to plan the trip, what to take, and possible scenarios when they get to Guaymas. Sean said he'd let Ricky know when the funeral services were scheduled, and they could firm up details.

Sean arrived back at his home. It remained hard for him to think of it as his home—it was still his parents' home in his mind. He was haunted by the last time he spent here with Annaleigh. Her presence lingered in the room, like a beautiful ghost keeping him company. He cracked open a can of Coors and sat on his couch, pondering all that had happened: The call to investigate the first girl's disappearance, consoling her distraught parents, running down information about other missing girls, the preacher's daughter going missing, and the first real clue—a shiny new green Pontiac. The rest was like a string of scenes in a bad movie: the disappointment of finding hard evidence and not being able to act on it, the cat-and-mouse game of searches at Kiefer's property, making the decision to go to the Orange Palace on his own, and finding the Mexican bank statement.

He had brought the whole human trafficking operation down and likely saved a girl's life in the process. But it had cost him the love of his life. Kiefer had slipped through his fingers. He was the thing Sean had wanted most. And now, his failure to catch him would haunt him for the rest of his life.

Sean's father had once told him that there was never a wrong time to do the right thing. He believed that what he was planning to do was the right thing, despite its legality.

His mind was an emotional roller coaster, dipping into deep grief, then rising to anger, and topping the track in a searing rage. The rage was consuming him, driving him to act. He wanted to leave immediately, drive non-stop to

Guaymas, and wrap his hands around Jim Kiefer's neck. But he had other responsibilities first—two funerals to attend. His more rational mind brought him back to reality. He had to plan his next actions carefully lest he fail to take his revenge on his quarry. Two more beers made him sleepy, and he went to bed. Maybe, he hoped, the alcohol would hold off the nightmares.

CHAPTER 27

Sean showered and shaved, put on some freshly pressed clothes, and tried to wash away his hangover with copious cups of coffee. It was Saturday morning, and he hoped the bloodshot streaks in his eyes would pass before he got to Annaleigh's parents' house.

They invited him to help plan a service for Annaleigh. He steeled himself for the emotional task he knew it would be. It would be much tougher for her parents.

He was nervous when he arrived and knocked on the door. Mrs. Childs greeted him and embraced him for a long minute. "It's nice to see you, Sean. Thank you for coming. Please come in."

"Thank you, ma'am. I appreciate you inviting me."

Mr. Childs warmly shook Sean's hand and embraced him, then they all sat at the dining table. Mrs. Childs poured coffee and put some fresh cookies on the table.

Annaleigh's father began. "We have arranged a funeral service through the mortuary in Buckeye. The Baptist church has volunteered its chapel for a service next Thursday morning at ten a.m. We expect a lot of folks will want to come."

Sean nodded, and Mr. Childs continued, "There will be a casket for the burial. The county coroner graciously volunteered to provide her remains in a dignified and sealed box to be placed in the coffin." He paused, trying to restrain his tears. "Please convey our thanks to him and the sheriff for being so kind and considerate to us."

"I will do that, sir," Sean replied.

Mrs. Childs said, "We want to talk to you about the service. It would be wonderful if you would be willing to say a few words. You are like family, and I hope you can do this for her."

Sean teared up and sat for a moment to regain his composure. He knew this was coming, but that didn't make it any easier. He said, "I would be honored. I'm not much of a speaker, but I would do anything for her."

"Just say what's in your heart, Sean," Mrs. Childs said. "It doesn't have to be a long flowery speech. Say what you feel, whatever you want people to know about her."

Sean nodded. "I'll do my best. Thank you for giving me the opportunity."

Mrs. Childs said, "Thank you, Sean. Please stay for lunch. We have more to discuss."

They spent the time reminiscing about Annaleigh. It made Sean feel better, expressing a lot of the feelings he had been keeping inside. They had a nice lunch of sandwiches and fresh salad from the Childs' garden. Sean said he had a lot to do, and after hugs all around, he headed back to town.

Time to prepare, he thought as he drove. He would leave the day following Annaleigh's service.

When he returned, he called the commander's home and asked his wife how he was doing. She said he was getting stronger and able to be up for short periods. She also told him that arrangements had been made for Rachel's service at a Methodist church in Phoenix the following Tuesday. He thanked her, told her about the funeral for Annaleigh on Thursday, and asked her to convey his good wishes to her husband.

Sean found Ricky at the Martinez market in Avondale. He was stocking shelves and straightening up after the store's busy rush of shoppers on Saturday morning. He hadn't yet found a full-time job, so he helped his parents with the store when they needed it.

Sean bought a bottle of Barq's root beer from the cooler, and the two men sat on red metal chairs in front of the store. Sean said, "Annaleigh's service is next Thursday at 10 a.m. in the Baptist church in Buckeye. I plan to leave the next day."

Ricky nodded. "What are we going to do about transportation? My car's in worse shape than her truck," Ricky said. "The tires would never make it, and it's leaking oil about as fast as I can replace it. I don't have money for that stuff right now. I won't until I find a decent-paying job."

"Don't worry about it. We'll make it work somehow. I haven't heard from the insurance company on Dad's truck, but I finally got a settlement of four hundred fifty dollars from the company for the Chevy my parents were driving in the accident. I know it was worth more than that, but the insurance company wouldn't budge. I have some money from my folks' life insurance, too. I'm going to the Chevy dealer in Buckeye to see what kind of deal they will make me. The owner knows me and my family, and Dad bought his Chevy there. Just be ready to go early next Friday morning."

They talked some more about their plans and what they would do when they got to Guaymas. "My cousin said we could stay at their place if we want to."

"That's great, Ricky. It will help a lot." Sean put his empty soda bottle in the wooden crate beside the cooler. "I'll see you next Thursday at the funeral," he said. Annaleigh's truck started up, and he waved goodbye as he pulled into the street.

His mission for the rest of the day was to go shopping for a suit he could wear to the upcoming funerals. He had never owned a real suit; he rented a tuxedo when he went to his high school proms.

He parked at a meter outside the big Korricks' department store in downtown Phoenix. He remembered it from shopping with his mother years ago when he had marveled at all the fancy men's clothes on display. He figured it was as good a place as any to find a suit. He told a salesman what he needed and that he had a limited budget. The man did some quick measurements and came back with two suits for Sean to try. The first was a little big; the second seemed to be a good fit. It was black, as he had requested. The salesman had him stand in a three-way mirror and turn side to side. "Well, sir, this is your lucky day. That's an excellent fit and we only need to hem the cuff. We can do that while you wait." Sean agreed and said he would return in an hour.

He went outside and put more money in the parking meter. Then he went back to the Woolworth Five and Dime store for coffee and a piece of apple pie a la mode while he waited. The place brought back more fond memories of being there as a child with his mother.

The clerk at the department store greeted him when he came back and helped him pick out a white shirt, black necktie, black belt, a pair of black dress shoes, and black dress socks to go with his new suit. Sean spent more than he could afford, but he wanted to look his best for Annaleigh.

There was a sporting goods store nearby, and he bought a fishing vest with many pockets and a red cap that said FISHING IS LIFE in white letters on the front. Then he headed for home.

That night he didn't have any nightmares for a change. He woke up refreshed and clear-headed. He spent that Sunday working on his preparations for the trip to Mexico. He had a deeply ingrained habit of maintaining his equipment to keep it in top condition. His father had taught him that success or failure in hunting could depend on his firearm working properly. He had carried that philosophy with him into the Army—his life would depend on it. The mission he was preparing for was no less dangerous.

It was only a few days since he had last checked his gear, but he went through the process again. He disassembled his Colt 1911 .45 pistol, cleaned it thoroughly, gave it a thin sheen of gun oil, and reassembled the weapon. It had been with him since his first training as a paratrooper; it was like an old friend. Going through the pistol's maintenance procedure was a comfort to him; he could do it in his sleep. Then he took out his Dad's Remington 12-gauge pump action shotgun. His father had taught him how to handle the gun when he was twelve years old. They had gone duck hunting down by Gillespie Dam on the Gila River and he had used it many times since. It was in perfect condition, but Sean took it apart and cleaned and oiled the metal parts. Its action worked smoothly and flawlessly. His K-Bar knife hadn't been used since he last cleaned and sharpened it, but he went through the process again, anyway. He smiled at the memory of one of his teammates in the Screaming Eagles who called the knives Arkansas toothpicks. Then he put a drop of oil in the hinge on his paratrooper's switchblade knife, wiped it clean, and laid it out with the rest of his gear. His monocular completed the collection—you never knew when you needed a closer look. Finally, he set out a box of .45 caliber ammunition and a box of shotgun shells. These would fit nicely under the seat of the truck, well out of sight.

He was satisfied he was as well-equipped as he could be for what lay ahead. *If Kiefer wants a war I'll give him one,* he told himself.

Ricky had warned him about Mexican border agents checking what they were carrying into the country. He said it was illegal to take firearms across the border and they would likely confiscate their firearms and arrest both of them if they find weapons. Sean came up with what he considered a novel way to avoid that.

His father had been an avid fisherman, and Sean had kept all his fishing gear stored in the garage. They would pretend to be going fishing at *Puerto Peñasco* on the Sea of Cortez. Their route would take them on the highway into Mexico where there was always traffic headed for the port, which most non-Mexicans called Rocky Point. He emptied the miscellaneous gear from the bottom of the large tackle box, then wrapped his pistol in a cloth and placed it in the bottom. Then he did the same with the K-Bar Knife, arranged assorted pieces of fishing gear over and around it, and closed the box. Next, he took off the shotgun's barrel and slipped it into the fabric sleeve of a deep-sea fishing rod. The rod was in three pieces, with the reel attached to the handle. He took one of the sections out to make room for the barrel. Lastly, he laid out the shotgun's stock on a piece of canvas, placed two more fishing rods on either side, then rolled and tied it into a bundle. All that was visible were the handles and reels of the two rods. The switchblade knife would go into his pocket.

He was satisfied with the weapons' camouflage and turned his attention to clothing and essentials he would need for the trip: a change of clothes, a toothbrush and toothpaste, a comb, extra socks, and a pair of boots. He put all of it in his old Army duffel bag, along with the monocular and his flashlight. Jeans, a T-shirt, and a pair of tennis shoes were all he needed for the drive to Guaymas.

The day passed in a blur of phone calls from sympathizers and making final plans for the trip to Mexico. It was dinner time, and he was hungry. He opened a can of pork and beans, made himself two fried bologna and tomato sandwiches, and opened a can of beer. He figured a full belly and two or three more cans of beer should help him get a decent night's sleep.

***

Once again, a warm tongue sliding down his cheek woke Sean from a horrible dream. He roused enough to tell Sarge he was a good dog and scratch his ears. But the echoes of the dream persisted, and he had a splitting headache. *Too much beer*, he thought. He tried to shake the images of the dream: preparing to jump from the transport over Normandy, flack shells bursting all around the airplane, constant thunder from the shells' explosions, and finally, the direct hit on the plane. The plane was going down when he jumped out. His chute opened, and as he looked up at the doomed aircraft, he saw Annaleigh standing in the doorway, beckoning to him. Then the big transport burst into flames, and she was lost in the inferno.

Sean felt terrible and swore to himself to lay off the beer. Besides, it made no difference in preventing the dreams. He got up and ate some breakfast, took care of Sarge for the day, and headed out. It was Monday, and his plan for the day was to buy something to drive. He drove to the Chevrolet dealer's lot in Buckeye in Annaleigh's truck and asked to see the owner. The man came into the showroom and shook Sean's hand, offering deep condolences for his losses. "I knew your father, Sean. He was a great man. And I never met a finer lady than your mother. Now this business with Miss Childs. I'm deeply sorry for all you've been through."

"Thank you, sir. I'm sure you heard my dad's pickup was destroyed in the blast that killed my fiancé. I need a replacement, but I don't have a lot of money. What do you have available?"

The man considered his inventory for a minute and said, " I have a 3-month-old, like new Chevy pickup truck you might be interested in. The gentleman who bought it fell into financial hardship and had to return it. It's the best deal on my lot. Come with me, and I'll show it to you."

Sean looked the vehicle over. It did indeed look brand new. The odometer only showed a little over three thousand miles. The dealer told him it was one of the first 1945 production models Chevrolet had offered for sale to the public. They were previously only available for military use, and the company now wanted them to stand out from the competition. Sean thought it was a real beauty; a step-side model in the AK series with a vertical chrome grill that set it apart from other models, and a side mirror on both sides. It had a very distinctive look: light metallic blue paint, a contrasting white belt around the cab, and a covered spare tire mounted on the driver's side runner. The interior featured a radio, a standard four-speed transmission, and blue and grey upholstery with custom stitching. It even had dark grey floor mats, which matched the upholstery.

The dealer told him to take it for a test drive. He hit the starter, and the V-8 engine purred like a jungle cat with underlying power. He drove around town for a few minutes and decided it was perfect for him—if he could afford it.

He drove back to the lot. "How much," he asked.

"I checked the sales records, Sean, and the truck was twelve hundred and forty-five dollars new. I can sell it to you for eight hundred."

Sean figured he'd never find a better deal, and it was within his budget. "Sold!" he said.

They went into the office while the dealer drew up the paperwork. While he waited, Sean asked if he could use a phone. A secretary showed him to an unused desk. He dialed the Childs' number, and Annaleigh's father answered.

"Mr. Childs, I'm at the Chevy dealership in Buckeye. I just bought a new pickup. Can I come pick you up and bring you back here to take Annaleigh's truck back with you?"

"Of course, Sean. Be happy to do that. I'll be looking for you!"

The paperwork finished, Sean wrote the dealer a check for his purchase and headed for the Childs' place in the new truck.

"Nice truck, Sean," Mr. Childs said.

Sean gave him a rundown on all the truck's features as they drove back to Buckeye. He dropped Childs off at the Chevy dealership and then headed back towards Goodyear.

He stopped at Martinez's store on his way home. Ricky was working in the back, stacking boxes of new stock. "Hey, Ricky! Come outside. Got something to show you!"

Ricky took off his apron, draped it over some boxes, and followed Sean out the front door. Sean struck a nonchalant pose leaning against his truck, pretending to examine his fingernails.

"*Dios mio! Que es esto*? What is this? Did you rob a bank?"

"Nah," Sean said matter-of-factly. "I used some of my folks' life insurance money."

"This is a great-looking truck, *hombre*! Tell me about it!"

Sean gave him the details of his purchase.

"Sounds like a great deal! The thing looks brand new!"

"Yep."

Ricky studied the truck. "You sure you want to take this to Mexico, Sean? Things can get dicey in a hurry down there. This rig is gonna stand out like a big neon sign when we cross the border."

"You think something might happen to it?"

"To it, to us. *Quien sabe*? Who knows? It's Mexico, *amigo*. In some places, there's no law. I hear there are gangs doin' pretty much whatever they want. This truck would make a juicy prize for them."

"You got a better idea, Ricky? This is all I have."

"I got nothin'. But we better be prepared for anything once we cross that border."

"I have my .45 and a shotgun stashed in my gear. You bringing anything?"

Ricky smiled and said, "I'll bring my Dad's .357 revolver. He keeps it behind the store counter, but he shouldn't need it before we get back. Like we talked about before, any firearms we take with us gotta be well hidden. They catch us with them at the border, they'll take 'em and throw our young asses in a Mexican jail till they're old and wrinkled! It won't matter that you're a cop here. In fact, it could make things worse.

Both men laughed, but they knew how dangerous it would be. Sean said, "I'm ready as I can get. If they find my guns, it won't be because I didn't do my best to hide them."

Ricky nodded. "That's all we can do. I'll be ready. If the border guards think we're going fishing, they probably won't look us over too closely. Lots of gringos go down there to fish and party… Mostly party!"

***

Sean awoke to early morning light shining through his bedroom window Tuesday morning. The first of the days he had dreaded had arrived. He had lain awake most of the night, thinking about what was to come. It took an effort to drag himself out of bed and prepare for the day.

He had seen all kinds of bloodshed and horror during the war, had grieved for lost comrades, and endured the loss of his parents. But this was different. Rachel and Annaleigh had died because of him. Rachel was simply sitting at her desk, doing her job. Annaleigh was going shopping for a wedding dress. Sean couldn't help thinking about all the what-if scenarios: *what if Annaleigh had chosen another day for shopping, what if he had stayed around the office later that morning, what if he'd caught Kiefer sooner……*on and on. He knew on a conscious level it was simply a hazard of the work he chose, a hazard to himself and those around him. But, deep in his gut, a gnawing feeling persisted that he should have somehow seen it coming and stopped it.

Sean hadn't been to a funeral since he was young when he attended the services for an aunt. All he knew was he should dress in black. He had gone to pains to do that; it had taken a big bite from his savings.

Parking for Rachel's funeral was already tight. Sean pulled into the Methodist church's parking lot and parked in one of the few vacant spaces. He went inside and took a seat beside two of his fellow deputies toward the back of the chapel. The pastor talked about Rachel's life, her devotion to her family, and her love of her job. He droned on about how it was God's will that she was taken while innocently doing her job. Sean knew he was right, but it made him uneasy to hear it in public.

The service concluded, and the attendees began filing up to the casket and offering condolences to the line of family members beside it. Sean saw the commander and his wife in the second group of people who lined up. He and the other deputies were nearly the last ones in the line. As he approached Rachel's husband and extended his hand, the man blew up. "O'Conner!" he shouted. "How dare you show your face here! My wife is dead because of you! YOU!" Sean took a step back. A couple of his family members were restraining the man, but he yelled, "You have some nerve coming here. Get out! Get out of my sight!"

Sean was completely unprepared for such an outburst. He didn't know what to do. He certainly wasn't going to argue with the man. He simply said, "I am so sorry," and walked out of the church. The other deputies waited for him along with the commander, who said, "Forgive him, Sean. He blames you because there's no one else. He can't blame God. Maybe he'll come to his senses one day. There's nothing for you to do until then."

"Thank you, sir. I understand."

The other deputies voiced similar beliefs, but it didn't take away the pain of what the man had said. *Kiefer was responsible for this*, Sean thought as he made his way to his pickup. *Another death I must avenge.* He waited as the people were leaving for the funeral procession to the graveyard. He needed Annaleigh's touch and comfort now more than ever. He didn't know how he was going to get through her service on Thursday.

He stopped at a diner on Van Buren Street as he headed for home. He ordered a plate of comfort food: meatloaf, mashed potatoes with gravy, cream corn, and sourdough bread. A piece of cherry pie with ice cream for dessert. It was a poor substitute for human companionship, but it was better than drowning his feelings in beer.

The phone rang as Sean walked in the door of his house. It was the representative of the insurance company for his father's truck. "I'm dreadfully sorry, Mr. O'Conner, but the company is not able to pay any benefits for the loss of your truck. It was an unfortunate oversight not to convert the policy to your name when you changed the vehicle's registration. There is a specific clause in the policy that states the policy terminates when the ownership of the vehicle changes. You changed the ownership to yourself after your father's death, so there was no coverage. Therefore, the company has no liability." There was a pause. "Mr. O'Conner? Are you still there?"

"I'm here," Sean growled. "You might have advised me of that oversight sooner. I understood the coverage was paid through March of this year."

The representative said, "Again, we are very sorry for your loss, sir. The company has agreed to refund the balance remaining on the policy since your time of loss. Perhaps we can do business on your next vehicle? I'll be happy to assist you with a new policy."

"I just bought another vehicle and insured it with another company because you were so slow getting back to me. I can't believe this is the way you do business. I'll be damned if I will ever do business with your company again."

Sean slammed the phone down and cursed to himself. *How could I have overlooked that detail?* An old saying from his father came back to him— 'If you assume something, you make an ass of you and me.' This was a cruel reminder.

That evening the commander and his wife came to his house. He only had one bandage remaining on the side of his head and seemed otherwise okay. They wanted to sit and talk; offer some comfort to Sean after what had happened earlier that day. They also hoped to help prepare him for the more difficult task he had to face with Annaleigh's service. Sean was glad for the company.

***

Sean sat on his couch with an unopened beer. It was the night before Annaleigh's funeral; it felt like it was the worst night of his life. Sarge laid his muzzle on his lap and looked at him with concerned eyes. He could sense the sadness in his master. Sean stroked the dog's head and talked to him, telling him what a good dog he was. He asked him if he missed Annaleigh, too. The dog only continued to watch him, and his tail beat the cushion on the chair a couple of times. Sean said, "Thanks, old buddy. You're a good friend." The dog thumped his tail several more times on the cushion.

315

Sean put the unopened beer back in his refrigerator and went to bed, hoping his night would be free of any nightmares.

He managed to get some dreamless sleep and woke up to Sarge snoring peacefully beside him. The dog jumped off the bed as soon as Sean started stirring, looking hopefully toward the kitchen and some breakfast for him. Sean put on his coffee, opened a can of food for Sarge and put it in his bowl, made sure his water bowl was full, then made his way to the bathroom.

His eyes were not as bloodshot as the day before, but he still looked like hell. Worry wrinkles lined his forehead where there had been none until recently. There were even frown wrinkles around the corners of his mouth. He took his first cup of coffee into the shower with him. The flow of hot water over his head and body was relaxing. He stood with the shower head pointed at his back and let the water run while he drank his coffee and considered the day ahead.

He had been trying to organize his thoughts about what he would say at the funeral; he was still trying as he drove to Annaleigh's parent's home. It was difficult to look past the horror of what had happened. Her parents had invited him for a late breakfast before the funeral. Several of their relatives were there, and Annaleigh's father introduced Sean all around. There were many hugs from the people he had only just met. Mrs. Childs served up a large egg casserole and toast on the side.

Sean told them what had happened at Rachel's funeral on Monday. They were aghast that something like that could spoil the solemnity of a service. Most of the other family members just shook their heads and said nothing.

Sean said, "I understand her husband's grief and why he is angry with me. Her death was an entirely senseless act and would not have happened without my involvement in the Orange Palace case. Maybe in time, he will come around to more clear thinking."

"It's good you can look at it that way, Sean," Mr. Childs said. "You are a good man, and Rachel's husband will see that one day. All you can do is go on with your life."

It was nearing time to leave for Annaleigh's service in Buckeye. Her parents invited Sean to ride with them, but he said he had business to attend to after the graveside service and needed to leave from there. Mrs. Childs made him a covered plate of leftovers from breakfast's egg and cheese casserole with bacon for later. He followed them into the town where there was already a large gathering at the church. A few parking spaces near the entrance had been reserved for them.

Sean sat with Annaleigh's parents and their relatives in the front pew. He did his best to keep his emotions under control but couldn't help tears as the preacher talked about her life. Mrs. Childs put her arm around him when the preacher described their relationship and planned marriage. Then he asked Sean to come up and say a few words.

He reached the pulpit and stood looking over the mourners. It took him a minute to compose himself. "It's an honor for me to talk about Annaleigh," he began. "She was the light of my life, the greatest thing that ever happened to me, and the most loving, caring, and giving person I ever met. I know she touched the lives of many of you here today." He paused to regain his composure. "Knowing she was here waiting for me was an inspiration during my time overseas in the war. She was my motivation to make it through whatever challenges I faced. I'll be forever grateful to her for that." He struggled to hold back tears, and continued, "What happened to her was beyond imagination. Her death was because of me; I will have to live with that for the rest of my life. Thank you all for being here to grieve with her family and me. Please keep Annaleigh in your prayers and memories."

Sean sat back down with Annaleigh's parents. They cried together through the remainder of the service. Then he stood with the family in the reception line as the mourners filed past. It was a blur of people, a few he knew, but most he didn't, shaking his hand and offering their condolences. Sean felt like it was one of the most difficult things he had ever done. Afterward, he followed the hearse and the Childs' car to the Buckeye Cemetery. He stood with the family and threw a handful of soil onto the casket after Annaleigh's parents did the same. The mourners filed away in small groups, finally leaving Sean alone. He stood by the grave for long minutes, thinking about Annaleigh. He promised her he would avenge her death. He doubted that would have been what she wanted, but his rage was too great to let it pass.

He drove back to his home—the place felt empty and foreboding with Annaleigh gone from his life.

Sean loaded up his gear and went over his list one last time to make sure he had everything. He ate the leftovers Mrs. Childs sent with him for dinner, fed Sarge, checked the dog's in/out door and water bowl, and got ready for bed. He had made arrangements with his next-door neighbors to feed and water the dog each day until his return. Sarge followed him closely through the house. Somehow, he knew his master was doing something dangerous, and he might never see him again.

He left his house at daylight. Ricky was waiting for him on the front porch of his parent's house, and he quickly stowed his gear in the pickup's bed. He hopped in the truck's cab, took a look at Sean's new cap, and burst out laughing. "Yeah, that'll fool the border guards, all right. Fishing is Life, huh?"

Sean tipped the cap and laughed. "It's my secret disguise. You'll see."

They hit the road and Ricky said, "Hope you got good insurance on this truck. But it won't be worth a damn in Mexico— U.S. insurance is no good there. You will need to buy Mexican insurance before we cross the border. I know a good place to do that in Ajo."

"Yeah, I've heard lots of stories about that. We'll gas up in Ajo and take care of it."

He told Ricky about how the car insurance people refused to pay up for his dad's truck.

"No! You gotta be kidding!"

"Yep. I hadn't changed it from Dad's name. So, they said the policy was no good."

"Greedy bastards! Maybe you need a lawyer."

"Nah. I read the fine print in the policy, and it's pretty clear. Not a damn thing I can do."

The new truck drove like a dream compared to Sean's father's old truck. Ricky said, "Man, this thing rides like a car." He wiggled around a little and said, "Comfortable seats, too. Wake me up when we get to Guaymas!"

Sean laughed and said, "You're gonna have to drive after a while so I can take a nap!" Both men chuckled.

They passed through Buckeye, then on to Gila Bend, and south to Ajo. They stopped at the small store Ricky recommended. It was a combination gas station and a market. Sean bought gas, then went inside to purchase insurance, the real reason he had stopped there. The owner took a look at Sean's new truck and whistled. "You sure you want to take this rig into Mexico? Lots of things can happen down there. Crazy drivers, bad roads, bandits, you name it."

Sean said, "Sell me the best insurance you have, and I'll take my chances."

The owner shook his head, filled out the paperwork, had Sean sign it, and pay the premium. He gave him his copy and wished him luck. He was still shaking his head when Sean walked out.

It was a little over forty miles south on Highway 85 to the border with Mexico. Sean silently hoped their preparations would pay off and they would pass through with no problems.

Ricky said, "Remember what I told you about *la mordida* in Mexico? It means the bite or the bribe. It's a way of life; people expect it. Offer the border guard five bucks when he starts to ask questions. We should be good."

Sean put his fishing cap back on as they passed through the little border town of Lukeville. They pulled up to the gate at the border and a guard came out and looked Sean's truck over with an admiring gaze. *"Buenos dias, señor,"* he said. "This is a very nice truck".

"Gracias, señor," Sean replied.

"What is your business in Mexico?"

"We're going to *Puerto Peñasco* for some deep-sea fishing. Maybe a little good food and tequila," Sean said with a smile. He offered the man a five-dollar bill which he accepted and smoothly pocketed.

The guard smiled back. *"Si. Puerto Peñasco* is good for all those things. I see by your cap you are a big fisherman." He laughed, then gave a cursory inspection of the gear in the bed of the truck. He stepped back to Sean's window and said, "Good luck. Have a good time," and waved them through the gate.

Both men let out big sighs. Sean said, "That was easy."

Ricky laughed and said, "Yeah, that cap of yours did the trick!"

They stopped after crossing the border, a short way past the turn off for *Puerto Peñasco* outside the little Mexican border town of Sonoyta. Sean got his pistol and knife from the fishing gear box, then reassembled the shotgun and put it in easy reach behind the seat. He checked that both weapons were loaded. Ricky had also stowed his pistol in his Dad's big tackle box. He retrieved it with a box of ammunition. They put the pistols on the seat between them and agreed that they hoped they wouldn't have to use them. At least not yet. Then they headed south on the main highway. Their next stop would be the town of Caborca. They would get gas and something to eat there before going on to Guaymas.

***

Other eyes had watched them cross the border. Two men in an old Ford sedan were parked at the side of the road, where they could watch incoming traffic. One of them whistled as Sean's new truck passed by. He went to a pay phone and called some associates in Caborca. They agreed on a plan, and the two men took off in pursuit of the new Chevy truck. They followed Sean and Ricky at a respectable distance, biding their time.

Sean pointed to a car parked on the side of the road ahead about halfway to Caborca. It was an ancient Model A Ford with its hood open. As they got closer, they could see a young Mexican woman standing beside it, waving for them to stop.

"What do you think, Ricky?" Sean asked.

Ricky said, "Slow down and drive past. I'll look it over."

Sean eased past the beat-up old car. It was stopped beside a low bridge over a desert wash.

Sean said, "I don't like the looks of this. It's parked conveniently close to that bridge."

"I don't see anyone but the girl," Ricky said.

Sean pulled over about fifty yards past the car, just before the bridge, and said, "Maybe that's what we're supposed to see. You go back and have a closer look. Have your pistol ready. I'll keep watch from here."

Ricky started toward the car, but before he could get there, a beat-up old Ford came racing up and squealed to a stop between him and the girl's car. Two men jumped out of the car with guns drawn. Sean caught movement out of the corner of his eye as two more men with guns came up on the road. They had been hiding under the bridge.

"Get down, Ricky!" Sean yelled. "Hit the dirt." Ricky's Marine training kicked in, and he dropped into the prone position, drawing a bead on the two men in front of him.

Sean pulled the shotgun from the truck cab and crouched at the corner of his truck, covering the other two men. "Drop your guns!" he shouted. One of the men fired wildly at Sean; the bullet ricocheted harmlessly off the pavement. He returned the fire, hitting the man squarely in the chest. He toppled off the side of the road. The other man dove for cover back under the bridge, firing over his shoulder into the air. Sean fired another round from the shotgun, and the #00 buckshot hit the man in the leg before he dropped out of sight. Sean could hear him screaming in pain.

Ricky was exchanging shots with the other two men. Their shots were hitting wildly around him on the ground. He aimed carefully, hit one man in the leg, and he went down. The other man ran for the cover of their vehicle, but Ricky clipped him in the shoulder, and he dropped his gun before diving into the car.

It was over in seconds. The girl slammed the hood down and dove into her supposedly disabled car. Its engine roared to life. She fishtailed onto the pavement and sped past Sean and Ricky, and her wounded partners. The first man who took the blast from Sean's shotgun lay where he had fallen, his chest a mass of blood. He had not moved. The man under the bridge stayed out of sight. The wounded man in the second car peeked cautiously ahead through the steering wheel. His pistol still lay on the asphalt where he dropped it.

Sean got in the truck and backed up to Ricky. "Get in!" he shouted. "Let's get the hell out of here!" Ricky jumped in the cab, and they sped away.

"Man, that was close!" Ricky said. "I was sure those guys had me when I was on the ground. Good thing they couldn't shoot for crap. They were shaking too bad to aim!"

"Yeah," Sean said. "Those two didn't seem prepared for someone to shoot back at them. But their wild shots managed to put two bullet holes in the tailgate of my new truck! The other two under the bridge seemed a bit more experienced. But when one went down, it convinced the other he didn't want to fight. He probably wet his pants diving for cover, but he managed to fire a shot into space before I winged him. I bet he's still hiding under that bridge crying like a baby. I saw the other guy you wounded in my rearview mirror. He got back in their car— I doubt that pair's up for any more action!"

"Welcome to Mexico, *amigo*! I hope the rest of our time here is less exciting!"

Sean nodded. "I never did get a good look at that girl. Did you?"

"She wasn't anything to get excited about," Ricky laughed. "And she sure didn't look worth dying for. That whole setup looked like something they've pulled off before. They rob people and steal their car, then leave 'em standin' there on the roadside. Or worse…"

They were silent for a few miles. Sean said, "You know, I hope this doesn't somehow bring the Mexican cops down on us. There's no telling what kind of wild story that girl or the other guys might tell." He paused, watching the highway's centerline marks go by, and continued, "That first guy I shot might be dead or dying. I hit him center mass in the chest. It's tough to survive a wound like that from a twelve-gauge loaded with #00 buckshot."

"You're right, *amigo*. We can find some side roads and skirt around the town. They'll likely be looking for us on the main road—that is if they're looking for us." He took a Mexico map out of his pocket and unfolded it. "I can't tell much about the streets in Caborca. But if we can avoid the main part of town, we can pick up Highway 2 on the other side. That will take us to Santa Ana. We can get gas and food there, then it's a straight shot to Hermosillo. If the police are looking for us, we might be able to outrun the news. Hermosillo's a fair size town, and we should be able to avoid the main streets. Then it's another straight shot to Guaymas."

They felt their way through the dusty side streets of Caborca. The locals stared unabashedly at the shiny new Chevrolet pickup. It was an uncommon sight anywhere in Mexico—even more so on the streets in the poorest part of town. They eventually found their way to the main highway. The drive was uneventful to Santa Ana. They gassed up, found a roadside taqueria, bought tacos and burritos, and kept driving south.

It was late afternoon when they rolled into Hermosillo. They stopped at a gas station, and Ricky used a payphone to call his cousin Ramon in Guaymas while Sean filled the truck's tank. His cousin said he was anxious to see him, and they would have dinner waiting when they arrived. They again found their way through side streets in the town. It took about a few minutes wandering before they came upon Highway 15. One more leg to go—about ninety miles to Guaymas.

They were dog-tired when they arrived. There was a big fiesta going on in the streets when they arrived, and they were barely able to thread their way through the crowds to Ricky's cousin's home. Ramon didn't speak much English and Ricky had to translate. He explained that the *Carnaval* was the oldest in Mexico, dating to 1888. Guaymas had always been an important and desirable port, and over the years, the French, English, and Americans had all tried to claim it. But they had been repelled by loyal Mexican forces. The formal name of the place was *Heroica Ciudad de Guaymas* or the Heroic City of Guaymas. The *Carnaval* was a celebration of the independence and heroism of the city. It had started on Thursday and would go on through the next Tuesday night. Ramon said it was a big street party, and not much business happened over the four days.

The family treated them like long-lost relatives, and they enjoyed a dinner of fresh grilled fish with potatoes and black beans.

Ricky's cousin had a spare bedroom the men could use. They apologized for being poor guests, but they were asleep on their feet after a long and stressful day. They hit the two twin beds and were instantly out.

CHAPTER 29

Ramón lived in a small house with his wife and two young boys. He was a couple of years older than Ricky. His boys were fascinated by having a couple of *norteamericanos* stay in their home. None of the family spoke much English, so Ricky had to do all the talking. He thanked them for their graciousness to let them stay there, and for the delicious food Ramón's wife Lupe had prepared for them.

The three men stepped outside the house early the next morning after a breakfast of fresh fish and fruit. They drank rich, black coffee on a small veranda. Ricky explained that they were looking for an extremely dangerous man who had committed many crimes in Arizona. He said they didn't want to put him or his family in any danger, but they needed some help to find him. They would do the rest.

Ramón said he knew of the man they were seeking. He owned a beach house a couple of miles out of town— Ramon said it was easy to find because it was painted a bright purple color that almost glowed in daylight. It was the only one of that color. The man was only there part-time, Ramon said. He also knew the boat the man and his partner owned and was acquainted with the local partner. Ricky asked him to show them the boat; it would likely be all they would need. They took Ramón's car to the pier because Sean's truck would have been too conspicuous. Ramon pointed out toward the dock and said it was the fourth boat from the end; the partner's name was Hector. Then he took them back to his house and told them they were welcome to stay as long as they needed. He apologized and said he had to get busy with his fishing boat.

***

Sean parked his truck on a side street a little way from the dock, and he and Ricky walked out to the fourth boat. A man was busy scrubbing down the boat's deck. It looked to be about a thirty-foot sport fishing set up with a small cabin. It was old but appeared to be well-maintained.

Ricky said, "*Buenos dias, señor.* Can we come aboard?"

The man put his cleaning tools aside and waved them to come on. He said, "*Buenos dias*! My name is Hector. Are you looking to go out today? I know the best spots! But we must hurry because a storm is coming, maybe be here tonight."

Sean said, "Maybe another time. Right now, we're just looking for information."

Hector looked at him with a little suspicion and said, "Certainly, *señor*. I'm glad to help in any way I can. What do you wish to know?"

"I'd like to talk to your partner," Sean said. "I need to see him today about some urgent business. Where can I find him?"

Hector's eyebrows shot up in surprise, and he said, "My partner? Oh, he's in Arizona picking cotton. He won't be here until summer. But I could send him a message if you want."

Hector was a small, wiry man with muscles standing out on his arms from years of working on fishing boats. His chest was bare, and his sun-scorched skin was burnt very dark brown, like old leather. It made it hard to guess his age. He had quick brown eyes and black curly hair flecked with grey showing under a sweat-stained long-billed cap. He also had a fishing knife with a long blade in a belt scabbard on his short pants.

Sean said, "I know that's not true because he sold his house and left Arizona. I also know he has a house here. So, please don't lie to me. I need to find him. Now."

Hector took a step back. "*Señor*, I do not lie. Please get off my boat, or I will be forced to call for the police."

Sean reached out in a lightning-quick move, pulled the fishing knife from the scabbard on Hector's belt, and tossed it over the side. The man was too stunned to speak. Sean got up close to his face and said, "Your partner is a criminal wanted for many serious crimes in Arizona, including kidnapping, sex trafficking, and murder. I'm here to take him back if I can. If you hide him or refuse to help me, the Mexican government will consider you an accomplice in those crimes. You will likely spend the rest of your life in jail. It's your choice. But make it now!"

Sean could see the uncertainty in the man's eyes, thinking about his options. He wasn't sure if his gambit about the Mexican government arresting him would work, but it was worth a try.

Finally, Hector sagged, and Sean knew he had won. The boatman said, "*Señor*, I know nothing of these crimes you speak of. I am a simple fisherman. *Señor* Kiefer came to me many years ago with enough cash to help buy this boat, and we became partners. He would sometimes use the boat, but I ran the business. I have a family, and I don't want trouble. What do you want to know?"

"Where is his house?" Sean demanded. Hector explained it was a couple of miles south on a beach. He described the house as the only one in that area painted purple. It was easy to see from the road.

"When will he be here, on the boat?"

"He should have been here a while ago. We were going to talk about some business. But he may have partied too much last night and drank too much tequila, eh? He is probably still sleeping."

"If he comes here, you tell him nothing," Sean glowered at the man and said again, "Nothing! Do you understand? If you do, I will report you to the Mexican police!"

"*Si, señor*. I will do as you say."

Sean and Ricky went back to their truck. Sean said, "Keep your pistol nearby, Ricky. There's no telling how this will go." They had reloaded after the aborted truck theft on the highway, but both men checked their weapons again. They headed in the direction of Kiefer's beach house.

Hector watched the men walk back up the dock. He considered his options: He could go to a pay phone and try

to warn Kiefer, he could wait and see if he comes to the
boat, or he could just pretend he knew nothing and go into
town and join the party. He considered what the *gringo* had
said. If Kiefer is as bad a man as he said, it could cause big
trouble for him. He might even lose the boat. He had
always suspected the man might have been up to no good
and found it hard to trust him. *Yes,* he thought, *doing
nothing is the best way. Let the gringos find him and see
what happens. Maybe I will soon be the only owner of this
boat, my sweet Esmeralda.* He closed the boat's cabin door
and headed for his favorite cantina in town. He would party
with the rest of the *Carnaval's* revelers until this business
blew over.

***

Kiefer was on his way to the dock to deliver some supplies
for the boat and go over schedules with his partner. He was
stopped at an intersection when a shiny new Chevy pickup
passed by in front of him, headed back in the direction of
his beach house. He just had a glimpse of the driver, but
there was something familiar about him. He could see it
had an Arizona license plate, too, and that raised his
suspicions further. He waited until the strange truck had
passed and followed at a respectable distance. The truck
had slowed, obviously looking for something. Then it
pulled into the driveway of his house. He pulled to the side
of the road and watched two men get out of the Chevy and
cautiously approach the front door.

It's that damned deputy, he thought. *How the hell did he
find me here?* He didn't recognize the man with him; he

looked Mexican from a distance. His mind churned with a jumble of possibilities. He decided he would have to run. There was no way he was going to face a trained commando by himself, especially if he had help.

The weighmaster had long ago planned for such a problem. He made a U-turn and drove a short way toward town. Then he backed into a driveway out of sight where he could watch the road. About an hour later, the gleaming new pickup passed by his hiding place and headed back toward town. He watched until he was sure they were gone, then sped back to his house.

He rushed inside and first grabbed his .38 police special revolver and his .30-.30 rifle. He stowed them in the cab of his truck and then loaded two large duffel bags into the pickup's bed. He had previously loaded the bags for just such an event as this. One was loaded with canned food and supplies for a couple of weeks' stay, the other with camping gear, a small tarp, and rope.

He kept his suitcase full of cash tucked into a hollowed-out space beneath the floor of the bedroom. It went into the cab of the truck. He surveyed his comfortable little house. This was to be his permanent home. Now that damn deputy was back, his plans may again be ruined. *I'll somehow find a way to get even*, he thought—*no matter what it takes*!

It was late in the afternoon when he had loaded all his gear into the truck and left his house. He drove to town and parked behind an empty office building to conceal his truck. He waited until the sun was down to leave; darkness would provide him with needed cover.

CHAPTER 30

Sean didn't think for an instant that Kiefer's partner would not warn him of their presence. They had made a second trip to his house and, again, found it empty. He pondered what he might do if he were in Kiefer's shoes. It seemed logical that if he knew they were looking for him on land, it would be safer to hide out on the water. He had access to a boat with seagoing ability and could go anywhere along the coast.

Sean couldn't let him escape again. He decided to go back to the dock, park his truck out of sight, and wait. He instantly recognized the older Dodge truck Kiefer drove in Arizona, parked haphazardly by the entrance to the dock. Kiefer had beaten him there. He stopped beside the Dodge and saw it was empty.

"I'm going down to Kiefer's boat, Ricky. Stay here and keep an eye out in case he shows up. Fire a warning shot in the air if you see him."

"Cuidado, hombre!"

Sean grabbed his pistol and knife, then took off at a hard run down the dock. He heard a boat's engine fire up as he ran toward where the Esmeralda was tied up. He got there just as Kiefer had cast off the lines and started to move away from the dock. Sean gave it all the strength he had and made a flying jump. He hit the side of the boat, knocking the wind out of his lungs. He grabbed onto the rail and pulled himself onto the deck. Kiefer felt the impact of his landing on the boat and spun around on the captain's chair.

His face was a mask of pure hate when he recognized Sean in the dim glow from the dock's lights. "You!" Kiefer screamed over the engine's noise. "Die, you bastard," he yelled, reaching for his pistol lying on the dash in front of him. Sean caught his breath, found his feet, and launched himself at Kiefer, knocking him back into the chair before he could bring the pistol to bear. Kiefer's arm flew out and hit the throttle, shoving it to full power, and the boat surged forward. The pistol skittered across the deck to the stern of the boat.

Sean grabbed Kiefer by one arm and pulled him off the captain's chair and they fell to the floor struggling as the boat lurched ahead. The wheel was spinning wildly, causing the boat to careen from the dock out into the bay. Large swells were entering the bay from an approaching storm in the Gulf. The boat's rudder pushed the out-of-control boat directly into the swells as it sped ahead. The wide-open throttle had the boat at its top speed, slamming over the waves at a bone-jarring speed. The swells had begun to push the boat to starboard in the direction of a large island at the entrance to the bay. It slapped hard as it sailed over each incoming swell, and its bow sprayed water over the cabin as it plowed into the next one. Sean briefly caught a glance of the huge rocks at edge of an island they were approaching in the bay. They were headed directly for them, but he was too busy to do anything about it.

Kiefer produced a knife from a scabbard at his waist and made a slashing stab at Sean. The blade bit into his chest just below his left shoulder. Sean knocked it out of his opponent's hand, and it clattered against the opposite rail. He managed to pull out his own knife and stabbed deep into Kiefer's leg. Blood instantly spurted from the wound, and the water on the deck ran red. Sean guessed he may have severed an artery— if so, the man would soon be dead. But Kiefer rolled back onto him, punching him in the back, trying for Sean's kidneys. Sean thought the man had to be growing weaker from his blood loss, but he continued to fight like a demon.

The boat hit the jagged rocks of the point at edge of the island. There was a sickening grinding crunch of wood, then the boat's starboard side scraped past the rocks and sped out toward the open ocean. The Gulf was roaring with a gale-force wind blowing the tops off huge waves and the incoming swells grew larger as the boat neared the bay's entrance. Neither man was able to gain a footing due to the deck being awash in seawater from breaking swells and the constant erratic movements of the boat. Esmeralda was taking on water from the collision with the rocks and water surging over the deck, and the boat listed dangerously to starboard. The swells were much larger as they passed through the opening to the bay, breaking into eight to ten-foot waves. The boat rocked violently at the mercy of the waves. Neither man noticed nor cared. It was a struggle to the end, and it would end now.

They had rolled across the deck when another huge wave struck the boat, and the violent motion threw them back against the starboard side of the deck. They were locked in a struggle for one or the other to get free and try to deal a death blow. Kiefer's knife had slid into reach. He grabbed it and slashed at Sean's side, opening another deep wound. Another big wave struck the port side. The boat topped the wave and then leaned to port, sliding down the backside of the swell, and causing the men to skid across the slippery deck and slam into its opposite side. Kiefer was partially on top; then Sean was able to get both his legs under the man's body and position his feet against his chest. He gave a tremendous push with both legs, lifting Kiefer into the air and thrusting him backward. He hit the port side rail, and the inertia of the boat's movement tossed him overboard in a flailing backflip. He hit the water and was pushed under the boat by the force of the next incoming swell.

 Sean heard and felt a loud thumping noise as the boat's engine growled against an obstruction in the propellers, then smoothed out. He knew it was Kiefer, and the blades would have done serious damage to his body. He scrambled to the controls and managed to turn the boat into the next wave. The list to starboard was noticeably increasing, but he had to know what had happened with Kiefer. He turned the boat back in the direction they had come, turned on the searchlight mounted on top of the boat's cabin, and surfed down the face of the next wave. He urged the boat up the next swell. As it topped out, the searchlight's beam briefly caught a flash of Kiefer's white t-shirt about halfway up the next swell. A large fin surfaced beside him, there was a violent disturbance in the water, and Kiefer disappeared under the surface. Sean figured that blood surging from the

wound in Kiefer's leg, plus whatever damage had been
done by the propeller's blades, had been like a beacon to
the numerous sharks in the area. He continued searching for
a couple of minutes, but there was no more sign of Kiefer.
It was a fitting end to a thoroughly evil man, he thought
briefly. But there was no time to dwell on that; he turned
his attention to his own survival.

He judged from lights on shore that he was about a mile
from the harbor's entrance. The boat was under control
now but continued to take on water through the damage on
the starboard side. The ocean swells were running at an
angle to the harbor's entrance from southwest to northeast,
putting additional pressure on the boat's damaged side. The
wind howled like an army of banshees, blowing water off
the tops of the waves into Sean's face and making it
difficult to see. He tried to keep his bearings and carefully
maneuver the boat as best he could in the general direction
he needed to go. Esmeralda was cutting across the swells,
and he prayed he would at least make it into the harbor
before the boat sank out from under him. He figured he
could swim that distance, especially with the incoming
swells giving him more momentum. But the blood loss
from his knife wounds was making him weaker, and his
survival in the water would be a race against time before
the sharks found him.

He kept the throttles about half open to maintain
maneuverability in the growing seas. The silhouettes of the
rocky peninsulas on either side of the bay were visible in
the starlight as he passed them and the island they had

struck loomed just ahead. He skirted past it and put the boat on a direct line for the docks.

At least the size of the swells are decreasing, he thought, *but it's going to be a nip-and-tuck race to keep this boat afloat.* The Esmeralda's list to starboard was increasing by the minute. He took small comfort in knowing every foot of forward motion now meant that much less distance he would have to swim. He tried not to think about the sharks that had found Kiefer.

Dazzling flashes of lightning in the distance showed the outline of a dark mass of clouds approaching from the southwest behind him. The wind was rapidly growing stronger, the waves in the bay were growing higher, and the wind was blowing spumes off their crests into the boat. The full brunt of the storm might soon overtake the boat before Sean reached safety.

The Esmeralda was listing precariously as the dock came in sight. Lightning flashes were much closer and more frequent, and the waters were churning violently in the near hurricane-force winds. Sean didn't care where he made contact with the dock so long as he could avoid having to swim with the sharks. He cut the throttle and maneuvered the boat's port side toward the dock and let the incoming swells slam the boat against it. The wood scraping on wood was one of the sweetest sounds he had ever heard. He backed the engine to stop the boat's motion and it was held against the dock by the movement of the water. Sean climbed up onto the port rail—it was now sticking up at a dizzying forty-five-degree angle as the boat listed to starboard. He found his balance, gathered what was left of his waning strength, then leaped for the dock. He barely got over the side with one leg and arm, then scrabbled desperately to pull himself the rest of the way to safety. The Esmeralda was now rolling faster to starboard, and most of the deck was underwater. It would sink completely in another minute or two. *Good riddance*, Sean said to himself. *The damn thing had been paid for by the tears of who knew how many innocent girls Kiefer had kidnapped.*

His wounds were bleeding profusely, and he needed to get them dressed before he passed out. He staggered along as quickly as he could to the end of the dock, where Ricky waited anxiously. He took a look at Sean's blood-soaked clothes and exclaimed, "*Dios mio!*" He held Sean under his undamaged shoulder and helped him to their truck. "Hang in there, *amigo*! My cousin will be able to help. We'll be there soon."

He raced away from the dock and cursed the crowds in the street. The *Carnaval* had been in full swing, but the fierce incoming storm had caused pandemonium with the marchers, mariachi bands, floats, and people in a bewildering array of elaborate costumes trying to get off the streets into shelter. Ricky had to thread his way through the crazy maze of people going in all directions. Sean was dizzy and barely able to stay upright; everything was a blur to him. He hardly noticed all the commotion as Ricky crept through the crowd.

It seemed like an eternity to Ricky until they reached his cousin's house. Thankfully, the family was home instead of celebrating in the street with the rest of the town. The storm had roared onshore and now lashed them with blinding wind-driven rain as they pulled into the driveway. Nearly constant lightning gave the scene a surreal look as Ricky helped Sean out of the truck. The thunder was a constant roar over the wind. Sean was aware enough to feel the weight of his pistol against his hip. He was amazed that its clasp had held it in the holster, and it wasn't at the bottom of the ocean with his K-Bar knife.

Ricky and Ramon helped Sean into the house. They had to struggle to keep their balance in the buffeting wind and were instantly soaked by the torrential rain before they could get inside. They got Sean onto a bed and stripped off his t-shirt to examine his wounds.

"Aieee," Ramon exclaimed. "*Mucho sangre*!" Blood flowed freely from both wounds. Ramon's wife brought towels and a bucket of water. She helped clean the wounds while Ramon tore up a clean sheet for bandages. He told Ricky the wounds needed to be stitched closed to stop the bleeding. "Finding the doctor here tonight will be impossible. But I have closed such wounds before, using fishhooks and light fishing line. It will do until you can get to a doctor."

Ricky agreed. Ramon got the supplies he needed and brought a bottle of tequila. Ricky had Sean take two big swallows of the liquor, then held him down as Ramon cleaned the wound with the liquor. Sean groaned but tried to hold still. Ramon dipped a fishhook in the tequila, then poured some of it onto a spool of fishing line. He told

Ricky, "This will be much more painful— hold him tight." He motioned for his wife to help hold his patient still while he passed the fishhook and thread through the skin of the wounds. Sean passed out before it was done.

Ricky, Ramon, and his wife all had stiff shots of the tequila when it was over. They were soaked in sweat and Sean's blood. They covered him with a blanket to keep him warm. Ricky said, "Let him sleep. He's going to need all the rest he can get. I suspect we're going to be very busy tomorrow."

He thanked Ramon and his wife for their help and for allowing them to be there. "Do you know what happened, Ricky?" Ramon asked.

"He was too far gone to tell me anything. All I know is that he somehow caught Kiefer as he pulled away from the dock on his boat and jumped onto the deck. They took off into the darkness, and I didn't see Sean again until he stumbled off the dock covered in blood about an hour later. We'll hear the story when he wakes up."

They left Sean to sleep, had some dinner, and talked far into the night about their families. The tropical storm hammered on the house with pouring rain, strong winds, and thunder rattling the window panes—the *Carnaval* in the streets had come to an abrupt end.

CHAPTER 31

Sean woke up sometime in the darkness of the early morning. He was disoriented, unsure of where he was. The mental fog began to clear, and the previous day and night's adventures came back to him. Warning bells started ringing in his mind. He got up and found the light switch on the wall, then shook Ricky awake.

Ricky shook off sleep. "What? What's happened?"

Sean said, "Get up, Ricky. We have to leave. Right now. Grab your stuff!"

Ricky was fully awake now. "Why? What's up?"

"I'll explain more on the road. We've gotta get out before the Mexican police find us, or we'll be stuck in Mexico for the rest of our lives. We need to leave. Right now!"

Ricky didn't fully understand what was driving Sean's worry and excitement. But he trusted his judgment with his life. If he said they were in danger, that was good enough for him.

Their noise had awakened Ricky's cousin and he came into the room. "What's up, Ricky? Why are you leaving at this hour?" he asked in Spanish. Ricky explained Sean's worry and apologized for the early hour and for waking the household.

Sean explained briefly what had happened on Kiefer's boat, and Ricky translated it for his cousin. Ramon listened in wide-eyed amazement. "You are very lucky to be alive!" he exclaimed in Spanish.

Sean explained his concern that the police would be searching for him when the boat is discovered, and it was better not to involve Ramon and his family. It was better that Ramon and his family had never seen them.

Ricky translated for Ramon and his eyes grew even larger as he digested what Ricky said. His head bobbed in agreement, and he said he understood.

Sean said, "Please offer my sincerest apologies and thanks to your cousin for all his help. Tell him if there is ever anything I can do for him or his family, I will do it if I can." Ricky translated.

"*De nada*," Ramon said. "*Mi casa es su casa. Viajes seguros!*"

Ricky translated, "It was nothing. My house is your house. Travel safe!"

Sean said, "*Muchas gracias, amigo. Muchas gracias!*"

With that, the two men tossed their gear in the pickup, and Ricky headed them out of town. The streets were deserted at that hour. The rain had stopped and there was debris scattered everywhere: limbs off palm trees, shingles from houses, and even a couple of small fishing boats that had been blown inland. Some streets had flowing water up to the pickup's running boards; sometimes it felt like the truck was floating. They moved slowly out of the city, dodging obstacles in the streets.

Sean said, "I hope conditions will get better as we move inland from the coast. That was some storm…at least what I remember of it!"

"Yeah, it was a bad one. Now, *amigo*—tell me the rest of what happened on that boat!" Ricky said.

Sean explained what happened on the boat in as much detail as he could remember. "It was all a blur. The last thing I saw in the boat's spotlight was a big shark fin just before Kiefer went under. All I could think of was, God, please don't let that happen to me! It was a close call—that boat barely made it back to the dock! I doubt I would be here now if I'd had to swim for it."

Ricky made a low whistle "Whewww, you are lucky to be alive, *amigo*! What happened to the boat?"

"The swells slammed it into the dock, and it was sinking fast. I jumped from the port side rail onto the dock, just before it went under." Sean paused and looked off into the distance. "That's why I was in a hurry to leave. That boat will be discovered when the weather clears, and a lot of people are going to be asking many questions. I hoped the *Carnaval* might delay that, but it will happen soon. Kiefer's partner will point the finger at me—a *gringo* in a new Chevy truck shouldn't be too hard to find in these parts. We don't want to be anywhere around here when that happens!"

Both men were silent for a few miles. Ricky said, "They may still be on the lookout for us between Hermosillo and

Caborca, too. As soon as this news gets out, there will be a lot of police trying to find us.”

"I've been thinking about that," Sean said. "We need to study the map again. I remember a road that cuts east just before we get to Hermosillo. If we can do that, we should be able to find a back way to Nogales. They might not be looking for us there yet." Sean unfolded the map on his lap and shined the beam of his flashlight on it. He found the road he remembered, then traced its connections with other roads until one finally intersected the highway to Nogales, many miles northeast of Hermosillo. "Yep," he said. "We can do that. With luck, If we drive hard all day, and the roads aren't washed out, we might be able to cross the border before the news reaches Nogales."

Sean shifted on the seat to take some pressure off the wound in his side. "I'm sorry, buddy, but I don't know how much driving I can do."

"No worries, *hermano*. I got this!"

Sean dozed until they found a little place open early to get gas before they came to the road they wanted. The ancient store owner sold them some potato chips and candy bars along with a couple of cups of weak coffee. Then the men headed off into the backcountry of Sonora. The storm damage was much less as they traveled inland; the roads were muddy but there was less water on the road to slow them down. They took a couple of wrong turns and had to ask for directions, but eventually connected with the Nogales highway. They stopped and camouflaged their weapons again before they came to the town of Nogales.

Sean sat upright in the seat and put on his FISHING IS LIFE cap again as they were coming to the port of entry. He said, "Well, this is it, *amigo*. If we get through here, we're home free." Both men took deep breaths and exhaled as the guard waved them forward.

"Identification, please. Anything to report?" the guard asked.

"No, sir," both men said as they handed over their passports.

The guard studied the documents briefly, looked at both men and noticed Sean's cap. He grinned and said, "Nice cap. What was your purpose in Mexico?"

"Visiting some relatives and a little fishing on the coast," Ricky replied.

"I couldn't tell", the guard chuckled. "Catch anything?" the guard asked.

Sean laughed, pointed at Ricky, and said, "Yeah, but his relatives ate 'em up as quick as we could catch 'em!"

The guard laughed and motioned them on through the gate.

Both men exhaled and looked at each other, then started laughing. Sean said, "I told you this cap would be a good disguise! Let's find someplace to eat. I'm starving!"

They ate an early dinner and decided to push on to Tucson and Phoenix. They could be home by midnight. Sean slept most of the way.

***

Sarge started barking as soon as Sean pulled into his driveway and killed the engine. The dog nearly knocked him down when he opened the front door. He bestowed some slobbery licks on Sean's face then cavorted around like a puppy. Sean gave him a big hug and told him what a good boy he was. He smiled at something he had heard— your absence seems an eternity to a dog no matter how long you've been gone.

He was exhausted and crawled into bed. Sarge lay down beside him, and they were both instantly asleep. A burning pain in his side woke Sean before sunrise. His knife wounds had been crudely sewn closed and now throbbed with intense pain. He made coffee and ate some breakfast while he turned over the recent events in his mind. How could he have been so reckless? How could he have jeopardized his career? How could he have endangered his best friend? He could have been shark bait like Kiefer, gotten Ricky killed or injured, and wound up in a Mexican jail. What was he thinking?

Another saying from his father came back to him— revenge is often blind. He had learned that lesson painfully in grade school when he went after the school bully for giving him his first black eye. He hadn't considered the fact that the bully usually had several of his toadies nearby.

That mistake cost him another black eye and a lot of bruises.

His father's words echoed again in his mind. He had indeed allowed himself to be blinded by a consuming hatred and lust for revenge. He was lucky. Incredibly lucky. He could see now that his plan had been ill-conceived, and only sheer dumb luck had gotten him through. But he had avenged Annaleigh's death, and that gave him some comfort.

He called Dr. Morgan as soon as his office opened. The doctor had been his family's doctor for as long as Sean could remember. He explained his problem, and the nurse told him to come right in.

The doctor said, "Sean, I'm glad to see you made it home from the war in one piece. And I'm deeply sorry about your parents. We did all we could to save your mother."

"I know you did, Doc, and I appreciate it. I wish I could have gotten home sooner."

"You look like hell, son. What have you gotten yourself into?"

Sean briefly explained he had been in a fishing accident in Mexico and was having trouble with the wounds. The doctor had him undress and examined both wounds.

Dr. Morgan said, "That must have been some fishing accident! Let's have a look." He suspected the wounds were more than a mere fishing accident. It was obvious both of them had been sliced cleanly by a sharp blade, but he kept his suspicions to himself. He poked and probed the wounds, causing Sean to wince. "You've got yourself a nasty infection here, Sean. What did you treat them with?"

Sean looked at his feet and said, "Tequila, doc. It was the only thing available. My friend sewed them up with a fishhook and fishing line."

The doctor clucked and shook his head. "Well, we're going to start over."

He called his nurse to assist him. "This is going to be very painful, Sean. I'm sorry." Each fishing line stitch he removed was agony for Sean, but he gritted his teeth and endured it. The nurse sponged out the wounds and applied an antiseptic rinse. It felt like it burned through to the other side of his body. Then the doctor methodically stitched the gashes together again. He felt dizzy when it was done but tried not to show it. The nurse bound both wounds tightly with bandages.

The doctor gave him a tetanus shot and said, "I'm prescribing an antibiotic to clear up the infection. Be sure to take all of it, even if you feel better. I want you to go home and rest; try not to do anything that might open those wounds again. Take aspirin for pain if you need it. Come back and see me in a week."

As Sean dressed and started out of the exam room, the doctor said, "And Sean.... Stay out of Mexico!" Sean grinned and went out to the office to settle his bill.

He was indeed tired and weak from the infection. He returned home, fed, and watered Sarge, then called the sheriff's department main line. The receptionist put him through to the acting district commander, Sergeant Walters. "It's good to hear from you, Sean," Walters said. "How are you doing?"

"I'm okay," Sean replied. "I had a little accident over the weekend and got a nasty gash in my side. Doc says I need to give it a few days to heal."

"What did you do?"

"Aw, I had a clumsy accident on a fishing boat and fell onto a pike. It's a minor thing, and I expect to be back on duty next week."

Walters said, "Take your time and be sure you're healed before you return to work. We'll be glad to have you back."

"Thanks, Sergeant. I will." He took two aspirins and went to bed.

***

The Buckeye cemetery sat off to itself on a stretch of farm road north of the town. It was bordered by cropland and a few distant houses.

Sean was completely alone this Sunday morning when he parked his pickup and walked to Annaleigh's grave site. He carefully placed a large bouquet of fresh flowers on the grave. He stood for some minutes with his head bowed, remembering their time together.

"Good morning, sweetheart," he said to the grave. "I miss you more than I have words to speak. Miss you every day, every night. I still can't believe you are gone from my life forever."

He paused and watched a passing cloud. "A lot has happened I need to tell you about. The man responsible for your death is no more. I killed him. I wish I could say I regret it. But I don't. I'm glad he will never hurt anyone again. I know it was not your way. You were too good a person to let revenge find a place in your heart, but I am not as strong as you were. I followed my heart down a very dark path, and it's done now. I hope you can forgive me for avenging your death with more death. I didn't know any other way."

Sean stood in silence for a few more minutes. Then he turned and walked back to his truck and drove to Annaleigh's parents' house.

Mr. Childs met him at the door. "You look like hell, son. Come in."

He gingerly hugged Mrs. Childs, explaining he had an injury on his side.

She said, "Are you all right, Sean? What happened?"

Sean said, "Aww, it was just a minor boating accident. A little sore is all. The doc fixed me up this morning."

Mrs. Childs clucked and told him to take better care of himself.

"I will," he said. He sat for a moment and looked at each of them before continuing, "I want you to know that the man responsible for Annaleigh's death is dead. I thought it was important for you to know. What I am going to tell you now must stay between us. I would be in serious trouble if it ever got out." He recounted the events of the last few days in detail and explained that the police were still looking for the man Kiefer hired to plant the bomb. They were close to finding him. Annaleigh's parents listened in stunned silence.

When he finished, Mr. Childs said, "We're thankful you are all right, Sean. It was a huge risk you took. I know you would have captured the man if you could, but it sounds like he gave you no choice. I hate to say it, but I'm glad he will do no more evil on this earth. You shouldn't regret it, and neither will we. I know I will sleep better knowing he is gone." He paused and looked out the window, then continued, "Please let us know when the bomber is caught. There will be bitter comfort in knowing he won't cause harm to anyone else.

Mrs. Childs nodded her agreement and said, "Thank you for letting us know, Sean. It means a lot. Your secret is safe with us. We love you like a son, and we will always be here for you. You are welcome in our home anytime."

Sean felt a huge weight lift from his chest. Now he could get on with his life.

CHAPTER 32

Sean's first day back at work coincided with the district commander's first day back. The office was operating out of temporary rented space. It had no jail space, so any miscreants had to be taken to the county jail in Phoenix. It was cramped, but it would do until their old office was repaired. Sean met with the commander and the other deputies for a briefing on what had transpired with the Orange Palace investigations.

Sergeant Walters explained what they knew from the previous few days. He said, "A joint task force with the Phoenix Police and our investigators established a link to the bomber. The bomb specialists identified a couple of likely candidates from what they learned from the bomb itself. The most likely one is a man named Bobby Riggs from Los Angeles. Investigators in L.A. have found a connection between him and Kiefer that dates back to a bank robbery in San Diego. The pair were never formally charged, but investigators eventually uncovered circumstantial evidence pointing to them. We are looking for evidence that would place him in this area when the bombing occurred."

Sean said, "You know, I remember seeing a strange car around about then. It was a new black Chrysler with California plates. It looked out of place in the neighborhood."

"That's great information, Sean," the Commander said. Maybe we can tie the bomber to that type of car. It could be the break we need. He might even be a link to finding

Kiefer in California. They have a history, and Kiefer once lived there."

Sean nodded and stayed quiet.

Sergeant Walker continued his briefing. "The woman known as Madam Trudy, or Gertrude Coburn, was found dead in a Detroit apartment a couple of weeks after we raided the Orange Palace. Detroit police say it was a pro mob hit with a small caliber pistol at short range."

The commander asked, "Were they able to establish any direct connections to her and the mob?"

"Nothing," Walker replied. "But there is some good news. The Detroit Police busted a prostitution ring there and found several young women who said they had been kidnapped in Arizona and forced to do sex acts. Their information led to breaking down several other local operations and more women who had been kidnapped in Arizona. The last we heard they had identified a dozen girls. There could be more. We are coordinating with the Detroit police and the FBI on arrangements to bring the girls back here."

Sean asked, "What's going to happen to them?"

The commander said, "It's probably going to fall to us and Social Services to try and track down their families. We will have to set up a task force to coordinate with California and other states to find them. It will take a lot of time."

They talked about how to do that, and the commander said, "Sean, I'm going to assign you as our lead for tracking down families locally. We'll get someone in headquarters to coordinate with you and the other state investigators. That's your primary job for now."

There was no more information about the Detroit mob's activities in the area. The Orange Palace property was in limbo, and investigators were still combing the premises for evidence. The department's investigators were continuing to work with counterparts in the Phoenix Police Department to identify properties under the mob's control.

There was no more new information. Sean started making a list of people and places he could contact to try to find the rescued girls' parents. It would be a long and difficult task. Kiefer the weighmaster's legacy would haunt him for a long time to come.

***

Jose Alvarez lived with his mother, two younger brothers, and an older sister. His father had died in a fishing accident five years earlier. His death left the family destitute; their home was a run-down shack near the beach on the outskirts of Guaymas. They subsisted on handouts and whatever Jose and his siblings could scrounge from stores and restaurants in town. Jose was barefoot and wore only a ragged pair of pants. He frequently combed the beach near their home, looking for anything useful the sea might have offered up overnight.

The ocean had been restless with the previous storm. Sometimes the big waves provided surprises. On this morning, he spotted an unusual shape a little way ahead, flopping back and forth in the surf. The sea had indeed provided something interesting—a medium-sized, brown suitcase. It appeared to be intact, with both latches closed. Jose waded into the surf and brought his prize up onto dry sand. He was almost afraid to open it, afraid it would be just another empty disappointment. But he might get a few pesos for the suitcase.

He squatted beside his find, then reached down and opened the two latches. Water dripped off the top as he carefully raised it. For a few seconds, he squatted there rubbing his eyes as if he were seeing a mirage. Then he caught his breath and fell back on his butt in the wet sand. It was something he never dreamed he would see—a suitcase full of money.

"*Dios mio!*" he exclaimed aloud. There was no name tag on the case, and he didn't see anything to identify its owner inside. He squatted beside his treasure and gingerly touched some of the U.S. currency. It was the first time he had actually touched *norteamericanos'* money. Amazingly, the suitcase was sealed well enough that the bills were only slightly wet. He stayed there for about five minutes, lightly fingering the bills, and thinking about what to do next. Finally, he reclosed the suitcase, picked it up, and took off at a dead run for his house, yelling, "*Mama! Mira! Mama! Mira! Nosotros somos ricos!* — Mama! Look! We're rich!"

This is a work of historical fiction. All characters are fictional except:

-    Sheriff Jewel Jordan, the first female sheriff of the Maricopa County Sheriff's Department.

-    Sheriff Ernie "Goldie" Roach, who succeeded Jewel Jordan as sheriff when her term expired.

-    Captain Jürgen Wattenberg, the leader of the German POW camp escape near Phoenix.

The places and settings in Maricopa County, Arizona, are real, and as they were in 1944/1945, with the following exceptions of fictional locations:

-       The Orange Palace. However, there were large acreages of citrus present in the area.

-       The sheriff's department district office in Avondale.
-       The weighmaster's home.
-       The office of the weighmaster's attorney.
-       Sean's and Annaleigh's parents' homes.
-       The home of Pastor Billings.
-       The settings and places in Guaymas, Mexico, are fictional but typical of the area at the time. However, the dock and harbor layout was as described.

Other items of interest:

-       The village of Perryville figures prominently in this story and was as described. It began a gradual decline as farm hand labor was replaced by mechanization, and the merchants closed up. All that remains as of this writing are two buildings that used to house the bar and a garage. Notably, the state of Arizona built a prison a few miles northeast of the old town site and named it the Perryville Prison, or more formally, the Arizona Department of Corrections Perryville.

-	Combat fatigue was the term used at the time for what we now call Post-traumatic stress disorder (PTSD). Thousands of soldiers in World War II suffered from its effects. Then, as now, it was a difficult condition to treat.

-	The German POW camp escape occurred as described. The camp was located near present-day Papago Park and the Phoenix Zoo. On January 27, 1945, Captain Wattenberg, the leader of the German POW escape, cleaned up and hiked into Phoenix. With 75¢ in his pocket, he enjoyed a meal at a restaurant and then slept in a chair in a hotel lobby for a few hours. While walking around at night, he asked for directions from a member of a street cleaning crew. Wattenberg's thick German accent and ragged clothing seemed suspicious to the worker, and he called the police. Phoenix police arrested him the following morning. He was the last of the escapees to be caught—he had holed up in a cave in the mountains north of Phoenix.

-	The Papago Indians referenced as trackers during the German POW's escape were part of the Indian tribe known today by its true name of Tohono O'Odham.

-	The Hellzapoppin Rodeo has been a Pro Rodeo Cowboys Association (PRCA) event in Buckeye, Arizona, since 1929 and continues to this day.

\-   The irrigation canals of the Salt and Gila river valleys are still significant features. Road names gradually were changed from lateral ditch numbers to their present-day names. Road names used in the story are accurate as of the dates.

\-   Gillespie Dam was constructed in the early 1920s by W.S. Gillespie of Tulsa, Oklahoma for irrigation purposes. He owned a large parcel of land west of Gila Bend. The dam initially allowed for the irrigation of 10,000 acres. It was supplemented by a series of wells drilled along the canal which carried water from the dam. A portion of the dam failed in 1993 during heavy flooding, mainly from the Salt River watershed into the Gila River. It was never repaired. The dam's remnants still exist, but a small earthen structure now diverts what is mostly upstream irrigation runoff water to the canal.

\-   The bridge across the Gila River below Gillespie Dam was completed in 1927 and is still in use as part of Historic Highway 80 in Arizona. It is on the National Register of Historic Places.

\-   Organized crime interests in Detroit are a fictional vehicle for much of the action in the time period of this story. There were rumors in the 1960s and 1970s that such organizations acquired substantial real estate holdings in Maricopa County, including large acreages of citrus. However, the rumors are only that. I took the liberty of moving the dates back in time for the purposes of this story.

\-   Human trafficking for sex was a serious problem at the time of this story and continues in the present. Migrant and homeless women from many countries in Latin America, Asia, Africa, and Europe, as well as the United States, are sold into the sex trade today. It's a long-standing and difficult problem worldwide.

-        The *Carnaval* in Guaymas has occurred each year from 1888 to the present.

Tucson, Arizona

2023

www.ingramcontent.com/pod-product-compliance
Lightning Source LLC
Chambersburg PA
CBHW070602300726

48975CB00006B/1690